TEACHER'S MANUAL

IMPACT

FIFTY SHORT SHORT STORIES

SECOND EDITION

HOLT, RINEHART AND WINSTON
Harcourt Brace & Company
Austin • New York • Orlando • Atlanta •
San Francisco • Boston • Dallas • Toronto • London

Acknowledgments appear on page iii, which is an extension of the copyright page.

Printed in the United States of America

ISBN 0-03-008624-8

1 2 3 4 5 085 97 96 95

Acknowledgments

For permission to reprint copyrighted material, grateful acknowledgment is made to the following sources:

Agenzia Letteraria Internazionale: Quotation by Dino Buzzati from Introduction and "The Colomber" ("Il Colombre") from *Restless Nights: Selected Stories of Dino Buzzati,* translated by Lawrence Venuti. Copyright © 1966 by Arnoldo Mondadori Editore.

Associated Press: "Dogs Bark, Beasts Blessed at Unusual Church" by George W. Cornell from *Huntsville News,* October 12, 1985 (an Associated Press article).

Toby Cole, agent for The Pirandello Estate: From a quotation by Luigi Pirandello from the *New Encyclopaedia Britannica,* Vol. 14, 1981.

Joan Daves Agency as agent for the proprietor of the Estate of Frank O'Connor: From "The Slave's Son" from *The Lonely Voice* by Frank O'Connor. Copyright © 1964 by Frank O'Connor.

Doubleday, a division of Bantam Doubleday Dell Publishing Group, Inc.: From "The Panther: A Bedtime Story" from *The Wrecking Yard* by Pinckney Benedict. Copyright © 1992 by Pinckney Benedict.

Dutton Signet, a division of Penguin Books USA Inc.: From "A Nincompoop" from *Selected Stories of Anton Chekhov* by Anton Chekhov, translated by Ann Dunnigan. Translation copyright © 1960 by Ann Dunnigan.

Farrar, Straus & Giroux, Inc.: From the Preface from *The Magic of Shirley Jackson,* edited by Stanley Edgar Hyman. Copyright © 1965, 1966 by Stanley Edgar Hyman.

Gale Research Inc.: From "Sandra Cisneros" from *Contemporary Literary Criticism,* Vol. 69, Roger Matuz, Editor. Copyright © 1992 by Gale Research Inc.

GMI: From "The Dinner Party" by Mona Gardner from *Saturday Review of Literature,* 25:15-16, January 31, 1942. Copyright 1942 and renewed © 1969 by Saturday Review, Inc.

Harcourt Brace & Company: From "Success Story" by James Gould Cozzens. Copyright 1935 and renewed © 1962 by James Gould Cozzens. From "The Piece of Yarn" by Guy de Maupassant, translated by Newbury LeB. Morse from *Adventures in Appreciation,* Classic Edition by Laurence Perrine and G. B. Harrison. Copyright © 1968 by Harcourt Brace & Company.

HarperCollins Publishers, Inc.: From p. 270 from *The Autobiography of Mark Twain,* edited by Charles Neider. Copyright © 1917, 1940, 1958, 1959 by the Mark Twain Company; copyright © 1924, 1945, 1952 by Clara Clemens Samossoud; copyright © 1959 by Charles Neider. From "Zlateh the Goat" from *Zlateh the Goat and Other Stories* by Isaac Bashevis Singer. Text copyright © 1966 by Isaac Bashevis Singer.

Francisco Jiménez: From "The Circuit" by Francisco Jiménez from *The Arizona Quarterly,* Autumn 1973. Copyright © 1973 by Francisco Jiménez.

William Kaufmann, Inc.: From p. 171 and p. 276 from *The Almanac of American Letters* by Randy F. Nelson. Copyright © 1981 by William Kaufmann, Inc.

Los Angeles Times: From "Bradbury Hears Voices in the Night" by Marshall Berges from *Los Angeles Times,* April 17, 1985. Copyright © 1985 by Los Angeles Times.

The New York Times Company: From review by Lorrie Moore of "No One's Willing to Die for Love" from *The New York Times Book Review,* May 8, 1994. Copyright © 1994 The New York Times Company.

Peters Fraser & Dunlop Group Ltd.: From *Literature and Western Man* by J.B. Priestley, 1960.

The Estate of Quentin Reynolds: From "A Secret for Two" by Quentin Reynolds. Copyright 1936 by Crowell-Collier Publishing Co.

Scovil Chichak Galen Literary Agency, Inc.: From "Who's There?" by Arthur C. Clarke. Copyright © 1958 by Arthur C. Clarke. From *2010: Odyssey Two* by Arthur C. Clarke. Copyright © 1982 by Arthur C. Clarke.

Charles Scribner's Sons: From "A Day's Wait" from *Winner Take Nothing* by Ernest Hemingway. Copyright 1933 by Charles Scribner's Sons; copyright renewed © 1961 by Mary Hemingway.

James Robert Squire: From "The Responses of Adolescents to Literature Involving Selected Experiences of Personal Development," an unpublished Ph.D. thesis by James Robert Squire, University of California, Berkeley, 1956.

Time, Inc.: From "Missing in Contemplation" by Pico Iyer (a book review of *In the Lake of the Woods* by Tim O'Brien) from *Time* Magazine, October 24, 1994. Copyright © 1994 by Time, Inc.

University of Washington Press: From *Desert Exile* by Yoshiko Uchida. Copyright © 1982 by Yoshiko Uchida.

Donald A. Yates and Hernando Téllez, Jr.: From "Just Lather, That's All" by Hernando Téllez, translated by Donald A. Yates.

Contents

TEACHING WITH IMPACT

The second edition of *Impact* includes many well-known classroom favorites as well as a number of new stories chosen for their appeal, narrative skill, and cultural breadth. You will find the variety of selections suitable for a range of student interests and abilities. Because of the brevity of each story, students will be able to read and respond to a selection within one or two class periods. The exercises in the anthology and the information in this manual have been carefully prepared to help you integrate reading, vocabulary, and writing skills. By using these resources freely, you will gain time to teach creatively and to meet students' individual needs.

STUDENTS' OBJECTIVES

When you introduce *Impact* to the students in your classes, propose objectives such as the following. Invite suggestions for additional objectives, and discuss the methods and materials to be used. Several times during the term of study, you and your students should determine how well the objectives are being accomplished.

To extend awareness and appreciation of literature by reading a variety of good stories by outstanding authors.

To involve the mind and feelings in the active experience of reading each story, visualizing characters, settings, and actions.

To increase understanding of human nature by relating the experiences of fictional people to individual experiences.

To recognize the elements of short stories, such as plot, character, setting, point of view, tone, theme, and total effect, and to examine each author's handling of these elements.

To participate in honest and thoughtful discussion of stories, using personal experience and insight.

To achieve personal growth in vocabulary knowledge, language and usage, and reading competence.

CONTENTS

The first three units in *Impact* are thematic: *Tales with a Twist, Turning Points,* and *The Heart of the Matter.* The remaining units focus on literary elements: *Plot, Character, Setting, Point of View, Tone, Theme,* and *Total Effect.* The opening units deal with general strategies of storytelling; the later units sharpen students' understanding and appreciation of narrative techniques.

Story elements are fully explained and illustrated in text exercises. Students' knowledge of each story component is reinforced in discussion and writing assignments. Students also have the use of a convenient *Glossary of Literary Terms,* starting on page 421 of *Impact.* Other useful reference sections are the *Glossary,* beginning on page 429, which contains definitions and pronunciations of words that appear in the stories; and the *Index of Authors and Titles,* on page 447. You will want to familiarize students with these aids to their study.

For your convenience, this manual provides suggested answers for all the study questions in the anthology.

PREREADING

Each selection is prefaced by a question or brief activity that makes use of students' prior knowledge or experience to build context and to arouse interest in the story. Students are encouraged to share their responses in small groups or with the class as a whole. A number of these activities are suitable for journal entries and can be later used as springboards for writing and speaking assignments.

FIRST RESPONSE

Following each story is a reader-response question inviting general discussion of students' reactions to characters and events. You may use this question as a "warm-up" exercise leading to analysis and interpretation. You may also find this a useful diagnostic tool indicating which aspects of the story require close study.

CHECKING UP

The Checking Up exercise (Multiple-Choice, True/False, Putting Events in Order, or Short Answer) is a quick method of ascertaining whether students have read and comprehended the story. Use it in any way that you think will benefit your students.

Probably the easiest method is to have students

write answers for the Checking Up exercise in their notebooks as soon as they have finished reading. You can read the answers from your own notes or from the key in this manual so that students can check their work. You will want to help students with any points of difficulty indicated by their responses.

Now and then a student may object to the key answer, particularly in a True/False exercise. Use the opportunity to encourage clear thinking. Ask the student to note exactly how the question is worded and then try to substantiate his or her answer by reference to the text.

After students have participated in discussion and accomplished the attendant exercises, you will be ready for a more precise assessment of their progress.

TALKING IT OVER

After each story in *Impact,* discussion questions prompt students to examine salient elements and to respond intellectually and emotionally. This manual provides suggested answers and further lines of inquiry. Choose whatever is helpful from this material, and guide the discussion as you think best.

You probably have favorite methods of involving all students in a lively exchange of ideas. Perhaps you vary the class arrangement for different kinds of discussion: circles, small groups, panels, partners. You no doubt encourage students to find many of their answers in the exact words of the story and to draw other answers from their background of reading and experience. You find ways to promote respect for students' varying viewpoints and to welcome all helpful responses.

Your approach, however, need not be bland. Be frank about the difficulties of interpreting some of the stories. Often good readers have different feelings about the same story. To understand complex characters and complicated human problems, students will need to think on a more advanced level than they have attempted before. Through thoughtful reading and discussion they can achieve deeper understanding and appreciation.

UNDERSTANDING THE WORDS IN THE STORY

Impact makes provision for students to learn hundreds of useful and interesting words.

While you and your students are working with the first stories in the anthology, demonstrate how to use context clues to figure out the meaning of unfamiliar words. Show students how to use the footnotes and the two glossaries in *Impact.* The *Glossary* beginning on page 429 defines words as they are used in the stories and also indicates pronunciation. Help students practice using the pronunciation key at the bottom of each right-hand page in the *Glossary.* The *Glossary of Literary Terms,* beginning on page 421, defines literary terms and also refers to pages where longer explanations and examples are given. When students need more information about words and topics, they should consult dictionaries and other reference books.

Several types of exercises are used for building vocabulary: Multiple-Choice, Matching Columns, Jumbles, Completion, and Analogies. You will want to assign these exercises regularly and to work closely with students until you are sure they have formed good word-study habits. If students habitually note and interpret new words, using context clues, footnotes, glossaries, and dictionaries as necessary, they should have little trouble with the exercises.

Answers to the vocabulary exercises are given in this manual. As you help students check the exercises, you can clear up any misunderstanding about the words. Occasionally you may want to grade a set of the exercises yourself or to note the quality of vocabulary work in students' notebooks. Let students practice using their new words in original sentences and in their compositions. Encourage and reward students who use new words appropriately. Reinforce students' knowledge of new words with reviews and tests.

WRITING IT DOWN

The lesson material for each story in *Impact* includes suggested writing assignments. Early in the semester you may wish to teach or review the stages of the writing process so that students understand the concept of writing as a recursive process.

Many assignments use the individual stories as springboards to original narratives. A number of exercises provide graphic organizers to help students plan and develop their own writing. A frequent type of assignment is a paragraph or a brief essay analyzing or interpreting a specific element in the story just read. Some other types of assignments are writing an essay of opinion on a question from the story, comparing and contrasting certain aspects of two or more selections, retelling a story from a different point of view, turning a story into a play, and writing a dialogue between characters from different stories. This manual offers a comment on each writing assignment in the anthology and presents additional topics for your consideration.

Ideally, students should write at least one of these assignments after each story. You might ask students to bring a special notebook or journal to class each day and to record their written assignments in it. Some of the assignments are brief enough to write in class; other assignments will need to be completed as homework. If students keep portfolios, you can ask them to select the work they wish to include in their portfolios.

Devote as much time as possible to preparing students for each writing exercise. An enlightening discussion of a story will give students ideas for writing. Choose a suitable assignment, and give clear directions for it. Try to anticipate any particular problem that might arise, such as how to punctuate a dialogue or how to use the library catalog to locate information for a report.

When students are writing in class, be available to help them individually or in small groups. Try to share some of the written responses to every story. Encourage students to listen thoughtfully and to respond respectfully to one another's writing. Students can profit from the favorable attention and constructive criticism of peers. Some of the writing assignments are well suited to collaborative writing and evaluation by partners and small groups.

For reading and evaluating students' writing, see the suggestions for evaluation that appear on this page.

SPEAKING AND LISTENING

A number of exercises help to develop students' speaking and listening skills. These exercises include such assignments as reading original stories aloud, organizing round-table discussions for the purpose of exchanging opinions, conducting interviews, taking part in panel discussions, improvising a scene, and relating an incident. Students should be encouraged to participate in every class discussion.

EVALUATION OF STUDENTS' PROGRESS AND ACHIEVEMENTS

Your teaching will have much to do with students' rates of progress, but so will their own attitudes and efforts. Tell students honestly that although new reading and language skills sometimes develop as a by-product of reading, more often special study is required. Students need to invest study time regularly on the literary questions, vocabulary exercises, and compositions in the *Impact* lessons.

Inform students of minimum requirements for a passing grade as well as the grade proportion or point value of each kind of work: participation in class discussion, exercises, reports, compositions, tests, supplementary reading, and projects. Correlate your grading system as closely as possible with students' skill development and fulfillment of the learning objectives.

You will probably want a classroom file folder or portfolio for each student. These folders will be useful for evaluation purposes and for conferences with parents. The folders can be used for final revisions of compositions, test papers, samples of exercises, and perhaps special projects. You will need to decide the best way to file papers as they are turned in. Many teachers let students file their own papers; others depend on a student aide or on row monitors.

Give students responsibility for correcting most of their own notebook entries at the time answers are discussed. Occasionally you may want students to exchange notebooks for checking or to turn in an exercise to you for grading.

Whole-class teaching is effective for composition planning and for solving common problems of organization, sentence structure, spelling, mechanics, and diction. Individual conferences are ideal for reviewing students' work and helping them with particular problems. Some teachers manage time for these conferences by scheduling class periods for supplementary reading.

If you are planning to collect notebooks, save yourself some effort by giving the students a check-sheet in advance. They can make up any assignments they may have missed and can mark the check-sheet to show whether their notebook is complete. You can then see how much of the assigned work has been accomplished, spot-check the quality of routine work, and pay attention to creative work. Write a comment or two of commendation and helpful criticism. Mark a few errors in spelling, sentence structure, and the like, but avoid the bleeding-theme syndrome.

Make provision as often as possible for students' compositions to be shared. You may wish to wait until they have written several papers before letting them choose one to read to the class or to a small group of students. You might also please students and save yourself time by letting each student choose from among several of his or her compositions just one to be revised and turned in for special evaluation.

TEACHING GUIDES FOR THE STORIES

This manual contains a teaching guide for each of the short stories in *Impact. Introducing the Selection* provides background information about the author and the story and motivational ideas. *Presentation* suggests ways of approaching the reading and conducting the lesson. Many class activities, special projects, and composition ideas are described in the teaching guides. You will want to choose the best of these for your purposes or to use other methods of your own devising.

For your use in helping students check their work, the guide repeats the questions and supplies suggested answers.

Each story and its accompanying exercises will take at least one class period plus some time for homework.

SCOPE AND SEQUENCE CHART

Page	Selection	Literary Elements	Writing Assignments	Speaking and Listening Activities
1	A Tiger in the House	Tone (irony) Fiction	Story Materials	
9	Rolls for the Czar	Narrative	A Narrative A Response	
14	The Panther	Atmosphere Foreshadowing Oral Tradition	A Well-Known Tale	Retelling the Tale
20	An Astrologer's Day	Exposition Surprise Ending Foreshadowing	A Description	Discussing a Story
28	The Colomber	Fantasy Magical Realism	Notes for a Story	
39	Three Wise Guys	Parable	A Report on an Interview	
48	The Trout		Updating a Fairy Tale A Narrative	
54	The No-Guitar Blues	Internal Conflict Realism Dialogue	A Newspaper Article Writing Dialogue	
64	I Confess		A Personal Essay A Play	
70	War		A Monologue	Evaluating the Impact of War
77	Home	Sketch	A Description	
83	Success Story	Irony The Author and the Narrator	A Persuasive Essay A Personal Essay	A Group Discussion
92	The Man to Send Rainclouds	Setting	An Outline for a Personal Narrative	
101	Dead Men's Path	Irony	A Letter to a Colleague	Improvising a Scene Comparing Stories
108	The Bracelet	Symbol Irony	A Book Review	
117	The Revolt of the Evil Fairies	Climax Plot Suspense Tone (humor) Exposition Internal and External Conflict	A List of Story Conflicts	

Page	Selection	Literary Elements	Writing Assignments	Speaking and Listening Activities
126	The Dinner Party	Irony Climax and Resolution	An Incident for a Story Plot A Dialogue	
132	Stolen Day	Flashback	An Anecdote	
139	Who's There?	Exposition Suspense and Foreshadowing	A Critical Review	Focusing on Suspenseful Details
148	The Interlopers	Exposition Coincidence	A Radio Play	
159	Gentleman of Río en Medio	Direct and Indirect Characterization Protagonist	A Character Sketch	
166	Thank You, M'am	Credibility, Consistency, and Motivation	Notes for a Retelling	Relating an Incident
173	All the Years of Her Life	Static and Dynamic Characters	An Opinion A Conversation A Comparison	
185	The Rifles of the Regiment	Stock Characters Personification	A Character Analysis	
194	Charles	Methods of Characterization	Another Point of View A Comparison A Cartoon	
203	All Summer in a Day	Setting	Notes to Describe a Setting	
213	The Sniper	Verisimilitude	The Setting of a Historic Event	
221	Too Soon a Woman	Setting and Plot Atmosphere and Mood	A Sketch of Time and Place	
230	The Wild Duck's Nest	Setting and Character	A Description Sensory Images	
240	La Puerta	Setting and Mood Atmosphere	A Short Story	
249	A Day's Wait	First-Person Point of View	A Letter	
256	Zlateh the Goat	Third-Person Omniscient Point of View	An Informative Paper	Other Points of View
265	What Happened During the Ice Storm	Objective Point of View Imagery	A Newspaper Article	Discussing Objectivity
270	The Piece of Yarn	Third-Person Limited Point of View Situational Irony	An Advice Column A Literary Analysis	

Page	Selection	Literary Elements	Writing Assignments	Speaking and Listening Activities
280	The Lady, or the Tiger?	Self-Conscious Point of View	Another Point of View	
291	The Circuit	Recognizing Tone Tone (Serious)	An Analysis of Tone	
300	A Secret for Two	Sentimentalism	A Book Report A Personal Account	
307	The Princess and the Tin Box	Genial Satire Incongruity	A Satirical Retelling	
314	Top of the Food Chain	Dramatic Monologue Forceful Satire Irony Jargon and Cliché	Dialogue Another Tone A Research Report	Preparing an Oral Interpretation
325	Just Lather, That's All	Irony (Situational, Verbal, Dramatic)	An Opinion A Defense	Discussing a Comment
333	The Emperor's New Clothes	Understanding Theme	Ideas for a Theme	
342	A Nincompoop	Explicit Theme	A Story Map	
348	Ambush	Implied Theme	A Comparison	Comparing Two Works
355	A Game of Catch	Theme and Conflict	Another Point of View	
363	The Return	Theme and Symbol	A Story	
373	The Tell-Tale Heart	Total Effect	An Account	Discussing an Answer
385	August Heat	Horror and Suspense	A Plan	Comparing Stories
394	Luck	Total Effect Tall Tales	Notes on Literature and History A Comparison	
403	The Gift of the Magi	Total Effect	A Comparison/Contrast Essay	
413	Half a Day	Total Effect Allegory	A Story A Literary Analysis	

Appointment in Samarra

W. Somerset Maugham

Page xi

This brief tale contains in miniature the essential elements of a short story. You may want to read this story aloud so that its dramatic impact is not lost. Ask students to respond. Were they surprised at the ending? Did they anticipate the turn of events? You might then discuss the meaning of the word *impact*.

Before turning to the first unit of stories, you might ask students to recall their favorite short stories and to share their impressions with the class. Do they prefer humorous stories? tales of suspense and adventure? love stories? stories about animals? Make a list of these stories for the bulletin board and refer to individual titles when a similar story is introduced.

A Tiger in the House

Ruskin Bond

Page 1

INTRODUCING THE SELECTION

This story might be read aloud and should take only one class period to cover. Before reading, ask students to contribute stories about unusual pets. Have they ever owned an unusual pet themselves? If so, what were some of its unique attributes? What problems did it pose for its owner? Ask students to imagine what it might be like to have a tiger in the house.

Students will find this story both surprising and amusing. At the end of the story, Grandfather's assumption that the tiger in the zoo is his precious Timothy causes him to act far too boldly. The fact that this tiger does not attack Grandfather builds irony upon irony, as we might have expected it to devour him at the first provocation.

You may want to share some facts with students who are unfamiliar with tigers. Found only in Asia, tigers thrive in a variety of climates. They are common in Bangladesh, India, Nepal, and Southeast Asia, and are found in smaller numbers in several other locations. They are presently on the list of endangered species. A world map on the classroom wall may help students identify the tiger's range. When full-grown, an average male tiger will weigh four hundred and twenty pounds and measure nine feet in length. Tigers usually hunt at night, lurking under cover and lunging after their prey in a series of leaps and bounds. They often hunt large animals such as deer and antelope and, contrary to popular opinion, very rarely approach or attack a human.

Like kittens, tiger cubs are boisterous and playful. They are helpless at birth and weigh only three pounds; about half die before they reach their first year. The tiger cub in the story would not have been able to manage on its own, as cubs cannot kill enough large animals to sustain themselves. At about age two, they are able to provide for themselves. Students who are interested may wish to start a research project on tigers.

This story takes place in India, as do two other stories in this anthology, "An Astrologer's Day" (page 20) and "The Dinner Party" (page 126). The viceroys that the author mentions were rulers over India during the time of the British Raj (1858–1947), when India was a part of the British Empire. The Viceroy of India was the British representative in Colonial India, and at one point ruled over 400 million subjects. As described by the narrator's grandfather, the viceroys led an ostentatious life. The last viceroy was Lord Mountbatten, who engineered India's return to independence in 1947.

India was considered the crown jewel of the British Empire. Not only did it have economic resources, such as its vast mineral deposits, tea crops, and cotton, but it also had the Himalayan Mountains, which provided a strategic military hedge against Russia and China. Britain's hold over India also facilitated trade; it allowed the British safe ports, such as Calcutta, when transporting silk and other goods from Hong Kong. The viceroy's regal status and grand lifestyle were symbolic of Britain's power over the country. Students might want to research aspects of Indian history and culture in connection with some of the stories in *Impact.*

PRESENTATION

Use the questions to guide discussion after reading the selection. Ask students to identify passages in which the author uses humor. Some examples might be that Grandfather was the only person to bag any game on the expedition, and that Grandfather reserved a first-class compartment for himself and the tiger. Much of the humor in the story arises from the understated, polite tone with which the narrator relates some hair-raising incidents. For example, he says that the tiger stalked Mahmoud with a "villainous intent" and licked Grandfather's arm with "increasing relish." We don't expect a potentially dangerous beast to be described in such a formal, polite manner, as one might describe a gentleman. Even the title "A Tiger in the House" is playful and understated.

Although the first unit of *Impact* is thematic, you

might want to start introducing literary elements such as **tone** and **irony. Tone** can be defined as the attitude an author takes toward his or her subject, characters, and readers. In this story, the narrator has a polite, understated, and humorous tone. **Irony,** in this case **dramatic irony,** can be defined as a contrast between what we expect to happen and what actually occurs. We expect the tiger in the zoo to be Timothy, but the scene reveals that it is another tiger altogether. In "A Tiger in the House," irony is used for comic effect. Could any students predict the outcome of the story? When did they suspect that all might not be as it seemed?

Students may be eager to share their own amusing experience with an animal. Direct them to the writing exercise on page 7. Although convincing "tales with a twist" are harder to write than would seem, students might want to try a surprise ending to fool the reader.

CHECKING UP *Page 5*

1. Why was Grandfather asked to join the hunting expedition? He knew the terrain of the Siwalik hills, where the hunt was to take place, better than most people.

2. Who were Timothy's two companions? His companions were a monkey and a mongrel puppy.

3. What was Timothy's favorite spot in the house? Timothy liked to remain in the drawing room, where he would recline on the couch.

4. How old was Timothy when Grandfather took him to the zoo in Lucknow? He was about six months old.

5. Why did Grandfather want to see the Superintendent of the zoo? He wanted the superintendent to move "Timothy" to a different cage, away from the leopard.

TALKING IT OVER *Page 5*

1. A situation is considered *ironic* if its outcome is the opposite of what was expected. Why was it ironic that of all those on the hunting expedition, Grandfather was the only one who "bagged any game"? The expedition consisted of "several Very Important Persons" who brought along fifteen elephants and specially trained hunters *(shikaris)*. Grandfather was not a hunter, but he had more success than all the sportsmen. **What was ironic about the kind of "game" he caught?** He found a helpless tiger cub instead of a huge, vicious beast.

2. What evidence in the story shows that Grandfather was fond of animals and was comfortable with them? He developed a playful, affectionate relationship with Timothy. He also kept a monkey and a small mongrel puppy that he had found on the road.

3. Describe Timothy's behavior during his first few months in the house. Timothy behaved like an overgrown, boisterous cat. He stalked people around the house, took up space on the sofa, and cleaned himself religiously. **What kind of change came over him when he reached six months of age?** He grew less friendly. When he went on walks he would stalk the neighborhood pets, and he raided the henhouse at night. Finally, he began to stalk a member of the household, Mahmoud, with "villainous intent."

4. The author's playful attitude toward the characters and events of the story gives the tale a humorous *tone*. For example, the description of the fancy dinner held in a tent in the jungle is almost comical. What other passages contribute to the story's humorous tone? Answers will vary. Students may cite the prophetic statement Grandmother makes about Mahmoud disappearing, the tiger's train trip in a first-class compartment, and Grandfather's playful, rough treatment of the bad-tempered tiger in the zoo.

5. What is the unexpected "twist" at the end of this tale? Grandfather discovers that the tiger he is stroking is not his old friend Timothy but a strange, dangerous animal. **Did any clues prepare you for the unexpected ending?** Students may cite the first keeper's remark that the tiger in the cage is always very bad-tempered.

FICTION *Page 5*

1. How does the story's opening suggest that the narrator has a knowledge of the places and events he is writing about? The narrator uses the Indian word *shikari* for "hunter," and he speaks in a familiar way of the locale—the Terai jungle near Dehra. The narrator's grandfather has related the story to him, and he is well-acquainted with the precise details of the scene such as the sumptuous jungle feast.

2. Which events and details in the story do you think are true? Answers will vary. Students may suggest that Grandfather really did discover the tiger cub under the circumstances described in the story. Other details may include Timothy's habit of occupying the drawing-room couch and descriptions of him washing himself and roughhousing with the narrator. **Which do you think the author may have exaggerated or made up entirely?** Again, answers will vary. Invented or exaggerated details may have included the stalking incidents, Grandmother's prediction about Mahmoud, and Grandfather's habit of slapping Timothy across the mouth. Some readers may suggest that the final incident at the zoo is also fictitious.

3. The narrator was not present at the hunting expedition he describes in the beginning of the story, and he did not accompany his grandfather to the zoo. How does he explain his knowledge of the hunting expedition and the events that took place at the zoo? In the third paragraph, the narrator uses the phrase "as Grandfather admitted afterwards" to indicate that Grandfather told him the story of the hunting party. The narrator later remarks that he heard about the events in Lucknow after Grandfather returned to Dehra.

UNDERSTANDING THE WORDS IN THE STORY (Multiple-Choice) *Page 6*

1. An expert who advises on the *terrain* knows
   (a.) how the land lies
   b. how to organize a hunt
   c. how the food should be cooked
2. A person has *distinction* if he or she is
   (a.) different or special
   b. well liked
   c. lucky
3. The *intricate* roots of a banyan tree are
   (a.) complex
   b. thick
   c. multicolored
4. When Timothy *stalked* a target, he pursued it
   a. rapidly
   (b.) stealthily
   c. noisily
5. A *crafty* look in the eye is an indication of
   a. good will
   (b.) cunning
   c. humor
6. When Timothy *reclined,* he would
   a. groom himself
   b. lash his tail
   (c.) lie down
7. Grandmother was *prophetic* when she
   a. scolded Timothy
   (b.) made a prediction
   c. instructed the cook
8. A *villainous* intent is
   a. easily interpreted
   (b.) evil
   c. benevolent
9. One place an animal might be *interned* is a
   a. sidewalk
   b. meadow
   (c.) cage
10. The increasing *relish* with which the tiger licked Grandfather's arm was a sign of the animal's
    a. annoyance
    b. playfulness
    (c.) pleasure

WRITING IT DOWN

Story Materials *Page 7*

The suggested writing assignment encourages students to draw on their own lives for fictional material, as Ruskin Bond has done. This assignment will complement the discussion of the literary element **fiction** and help students understand how fiction is shaped from memory, real-life events, and imagination. A Story Materials Chart is provided to help students organize their thoughts.

ROLLS FOR THE CZAR

Robin Kinkead

INTRODUCING THE SELECTION

First published in *The New Yorker,* "Rolls for the Czar" re-creates the glittering splendor of Czarist Russia. The first sentence sounds almost like poetry: "This is a tale of the days of the Czars, of ermine and gold and pure white bread." We follow the Czar from his Winter Palace in Saint Petersburg to a Kremlin banquet room in Moscow. What happens there with the master baker Markov seems a parable of the resourcefulness of human nature under stress.

You might prepare your class for Robin Kinkead's description of the magnificence of these two Russian cities by asking volunteers to bring in pictures or write short reports.

Moscow (Moskva in Russian), is the capital and largest city of Russia. It first developed as a trading center around a wooden kremlin, or citadel, in the twelfth century. The Kremlin was destroyed and rebuilt many times through the centuries—with walls of new oak timbers in the 1330s, with walls and towers of white stone in 1367, and with mile-long brick walls surrounding splendid palaces and cathedrals in the time of Prince Ivan III in the fifteenth century. The Kremlin, which is often shown on television, is still the center of Moscow, now a metropolis of seven million inhabitants.

With his own hands Peter the Great laid the first stones of the Fortress of Peter and Paul on an island on the Neva Delta in 1703. The fortress, which protected Russian access to the Baltic Sea, grew into the beautiful city of St. Petersburg (renamed Petrograd in 1914, Leningrad in 1924, and St. Petersburg again in recent years). As there was little building stone in the river delta, the city obtained building materials in its early days by levying an unusual tax: every wagon coming into St. Petersburg had to bring three stones; every boat, ten; and every ship, at least thirty. With its countless islands, canals, and bridges, the city became known as "the Venice of the North." It also earned the name of "music fixed in stone" because of the marvelous baroque and Russian classical architecture of its palaces, monuments, churches, and museums. A thriving center of commerce and culture and the favorite home of the czars, St. Petersburg was the resplendent capital of Russia before the Bolshevik Revolution.

In "Rolls for the Czar," the royal party travels from St. Petersburg to Moscow by train. Since the railway between the two cities opened in 1851, we can fix the time setting as later than that year. The train arrives on a February morning of "sun and frost." Such a sparkling winter morning would be a welcome sight in Moscow. There, snow lies on the ground from October to early April, winter temperatures average well below freezing, and winter nights are long and gloomy. Summer, on the other hand, is delightful in those northern climes where days are fair and mild, and evening twilight fades into the first glow of dawn.

The Czar of the story is a ruler who inspires awe and fear in his subjects, but the author does not intend for us to identify him as a historical personage. As a matter of interest, however, we might note that the last czars of Russia were Nicholas I, who reigned from 1825 to 1855; Alexander II, who freed the serfs but was killed by a terrorist bomb; Alexander III, who reigned from 1881 to 1894; and Nicholas II, who as executed by the Bolsheviks in 1918.

The tale told by Robin Kinkead is bright and amusing. We can enjoy the richness of the scene and the quick wit of the baker Markov.

PRESENTATION

Ask your students how bread fresh and hot from the oven smells on a crisp winter day. Would even a czar long for such simple goodness? After students have read the story, use the text questions to guide discussion. Review footnoted words with students to see how well they have understood explanations, and continue with the exercises.

CHECKING UP (Short Answer) *Page 11*

1. At what time of year does the story take place? The story takes place during winter.

2. What form of transportation does the Czar use to travel from St. Petersburg to Moscow? He travels in a private railway car.

3. What is in the roll that the Czar breaks open? A dead fly is embedded in the roll.

4. What does Markov say is in the roll? Markov claims that the dead fly is a raisin.

5. How does the Czar reward Markov? The Czar grants Markov a coat of arms with a fly as the motif.

TALKING IT OVER *Page 11*

1. The word *czar* comes from the name *Caesar.* How does the story show that the Russian Czar had unlimited power in his empire? After the Czar finds the fly in his roll and sends for Markov, the baker is frozen for a moment. The courtiers are waiting for doom to strike. They know that the Czar could order Markov exiled to Siberia.

2. Instead of punishing Markov, the Czar rewards him. Why? What does the Czar find admirable in Markov? The Czar is amused. He admires Markov's quick wit and boldness. Also, he admires Markov's skill as a baker.

3. Is this story merely an entertaining anecdote, or does it reveal insight into human nature? It reveals that a resourceful and brave person may save himself or herself from a dire predicament. It also reveals that a powerful person may appreciate an opportunity to laugh and to show respect for courage.

NARRATIVE *Page 12*

1. Look at the passage that describes the Czar eagerly awaiting the rolls. How does the storyteller cause you to feel that things are about to go wrong? The Czar is so anxious to taste the rolls that he barely notices the other delicacies placed before him. He has made a special journey to get the rolls, and we realize how important it is that they please him. The narrator's tone grows more clipped and suspenseful as the rolls are brought out—"He watched the door." When the narrator states "All was well," we get the sense that something is about to happen that will change the situation.

2. How does the author make that scene come to life? The author describes the exotic, gourmet food placed on the table: caviar, smoked sterlets, and pheasant in aspic. The Czar is depicted as an eager, hungry boy who can barely wait for the rolls to arrive. The presence of the royal footman carrying the silver platter reminds us of the Czar's power.

UNDERSTANDING THE WORDS IN THE STORY (Matching Columns) *Page 12*

1. ermine	i. white fur
2. pomp	d. brilliant display
3. dazzled	a. overpowered with brilliance
4. renowned	e. well known
5. moat	j. deep trench
6. distracted	c. diverted; turned aside
7. embedded	h. enclosed
8. bleak	f. severe; empty
9. wrath	g. violent anger
10. imperiled	b. endangered

WRITING IT DOWN

A Narrative *Page 13*

The writing assignment asks students to focus on one specific incident that lends itself to a short-story plot. They are encouraged to draw on their own experience for ideas.

A Response *Page 13*

The exercise asks students to imagine what went on in a character's mind during a story's climax. This will help them to see how much information is left out of a story's final version and how much an author needs to know about his characters' backgrounds, thoughts, and personalities to make them lifelike and believable.

THE PANTHER A BEDTIME STORY

Pinckney Benedict

INTRODUCING THE SELECTION

From the opening lines of "The Panther," Pinckney Benedict creates an atmosphere of unreality. Benedict's details—the spavined horse, the heavy brass cartridges slung over the boy's shoulder—bring us directly into a sensory, physical landscape, yet one in which natural law is suspended. At once we are enchanted, brought deeper into a mythic world that offers no clearly marked trails toward a safe and predictable reality.

This strange, timeless atmosphere is heightened by the lack of any introductory exposition. The story begins in the middle of things; the boy is already lost, deep in the wilderness. Although the story is marked as a type of fairy tale by its subtitle, it does not follow the rules of a traditional fairy tale. There is no "once upon a time." Elements of the fairy tale, such as metamorphosis and magic, are present, but Benedict's "bedtime story" is clearly one that moves below the surface of a safe and comforting child's tale.

The tale of the panther suggests other fictional legends of great beasts that seem to live forever despite human efforts to destroy them. If they were to vanish from the wilderness, these creatures would take a large part of the landscape's mystery and power with them. One is reminded of Faulkner's "The Bear." The panther seems as old as the land, pitted with scars and ancient wounds that the boy imagines were inflicted by spears. Yet it is proving itself mortal; it is "a hunter gone sheep-stealer," weakened by age. You might want to call attention to the author's decision to make the panther female. How might this affect students' perceptions of the ancient mountain cat?

"The Panther" will give you many opportunities to discuss an author's stylistic choices. Students should sense the story's eerie and unusual atmosphere. After reading, you might ask how Pinckney Benedict achieves this effect. Neither the place, the boy, nor the woman is named. The narrative does not race along, despite the immediate danger of the situation; rather, the boy seems to move in the slow motion of dreams. You might point out the climactic scene where the woman undergoes a transformation into a catamount. Even here, Benedict uses long sentences instead of short, clipped phrases that would hurry the action along. By not enclosing dialogue with quotation marks, he lends the text a sense of unreality, as if there is no record of the incident ever occurring. This technique is also reminiscent of the oral tradition, in which a story is usually told aloud by one voice. The story's timeless quality is emphasized by the absence of any social constructs—it lacks civilization, other characters, and a link with current events.

Benedict's use of colloquial language does give a suggestion of place. Dialogue such as "Thankee" and "Get you some eat" are indicative of Benedict's home locale, the Appalachians of West Virginia. Even today, certain enclaves of Appalachian people remain isolated by language and culture from the rest of the country. Many people in the region still speak a dialect that preserves characteristics of the Scots-Irish languages, blended with English and German. They are the descendants of the Scots-Irish immigrants who were among the first to enter the Southern frontier. Students may want to learn how this unique way of speaking has evolved.

The oral tradition still flourishes in the United States, particularly in the Appalachian region. Professor Cratis Williams, an expert on Appalachian speech, considers the Appalachian people the best storytellers in the world. Every year, the National Association for the Preservation and Perpetuation of Storytelling sponsors a festival in Jonesborough, Tennessee. Thousands of people attend to hear storytellers practice their craft. Stories are passed down within families and among professional storytellers, who embellish, alter, and add their own personal flair to the tales. One of these tellers is Ray Hicks, who comes down from his home in the Appalachian Mountains to perform at the festival every year. Hicks recounts "Jack Tales"—Scottish stories about a character such as the boy in "Jack and the Beanstalk"—that he learned from his grandfather. Professional storytellers perform in every state, and there are over 100 storytelling associations in the United States. Students might want to research storytelling in this country and elsewhere.

PRESENTATION

You will almost certainly want to read this story aloud. Before reading, ask students to name familiar stories, including ones that might have been told to them as "bedtime stories." Have them jot down some thoughts in response to the prereading question on page 14. That "The Panther" is subtitled "A Bedtime Story" may confuse some students. Ask them to consider what the purpose of a bedtime story might be. Many old fairy tales were told to warn children of dangers, whether natural or supernatural. Children's bedtime stories now are usually told to soothe a child to sleep. Do they find this story to be a peaceful tale, or does it strike them more as a horror story? What elements make it soothing or horrifying?

Fables and bedtime stories are often told to impart a lesson. In this tale, Benedict may be making a point about the merits of good manners. Since the boy has respect for the wild, aged creature, and does not carry a rifle into her camp, he is granted the opportunity to witness something miraculous. The woman tells him that he has good manners, and lets him in on her secret. Benedict may be suggesting here that wild, ancient things demand respect—that good actions can bring us closer to the hidden mysteries of the world.

After addressing the discussion questions, direct students to the writing assignment on page 19, A Well-Known Tale, and to the Speaking and Listening assignment. Challenge students to add their own creative flair to well-known fairy tales, make up their own tales, and interpret a story orally for the class. You will want to address the questions under Oral Tradition on page 18. See if students can think of any other tales in which an animal is transformed into a human, or vice versa. Some examples are "East of the Sun and West of the Moon," in which a woman's husband is a man by night and a bear by day, and "The Six Swans," a Brothers Grimm tale in which six brothers are enchanted by an evil stepmother and transformed into swans.

Ask students to identify places in the story where the author uses the idiom of his native region. This may lead to a discussion of dialect in different parts of the country. See if students can contribute any colloquialisms from a particular area; for example, "soda" is usually called "pop" in the Midwest. Can they trace how any of these expressions might have developed? Names for animals also differ according to region. At one point in "The Panther," Benedict calls the panther a catamount, one name common to the area. In other regions, the same cat is called a mountain lion, mountain cat, puma, cougar, and painter.

CHECKING UP (True/False) *Page 17*

T 1. The boy has lost the panther he had been trailing.

T 2. The boy cannot find his way down the mountain.

F 3. The boy is not surprised that the horse struck out at the old woman.

F 4. The old woman is wearing a tattered cotton dress.

F 5. The boy carries his rifle into the old woman's camp.

TALKING IT OVER *Page 17*

1. How do the boy's actions and speech show that he is considerate of others? The boy sympathizes with his lame horse's pain and tries to comfort him by putting his face against the horse's neck. The boy quickly apologizes to the woman when the horse strikes out at her. He does not bring his rifle into the old woman's camp, and he refrains from drawing his gun at the climax of the story, even though the strange transformation of the woman must frighten him. **How are his "good manners" important to the story?** The woman notes that he has good manners, and invites him to share in her meal. Because he does not threaten the old woman, she allows him to witness her miraculous transformation. One might surmise that if the boy had not been polite, he would have been attacked by the mountain cat.

2. *Atmosphere* is the overall mood or feeling that a story creates. What are some of the details that help create an atmosphere of mystery and eeriness? Details that students may cite include the lameness of the horse, the fact that the boy is lost on the mountainside, the approach of nightfall, and the old woman's strange appearance and behavior.

3. What connection does the boy see between his family's sheep and the lamb in the woman's pot? The boy realizes that the old woman is cooking one of his father's lambs. **Why does this connection turn out to be important?** It is important because it shows that the old woman and the panther are one and the same.

4. What does the old woman mean when she says, "And no more hunting the panther 'cause it ain't what you think it is, and it's the last one of them left"? The woman's remark conveys the idea that the panther is a magical, mysterious creature, not a mere beast. The story's conclusion suggests that the old woman has lived for centuries and has suffered persecution and injury. Note that the boy imagines that some of her scars "were the marks of the darts and spears of ancient savages." However, the woman is old and has resorted to stealing lambs to survive. She naturally has an interest in self-preservation, and perhaps she can no longer evade the hunters.

5. A number of clues throughout the story serve to hint at, or *foreshadow*, the ending. For example, the horse strikes out at the woman because it recognizes her as the panther. What other examples of foreshadowing can you find? Answers will vary. One clue is the ghostly way in which the old woman appears and disappears on the mountain. Another clue is the woman's emphasis on the rifle and on the boy's not hunting the panther.

6. The subtitle of "The Panther" is "A Bedtime Story." Do you consider this tale a kind of bedtime story? Why or why not? Answers will vary. Some students may argue that the tale would make a good bedtime story because of the eerie atmosphere and the elements of metamorphosis and magic. Some may make connections with other fairy tales that have similar elements. Other students may think that the story is too disturbing, especially for young children.

ORAL TRADITION *Page 18*

1. There are at least two references to oral tradition in "The Panther." The first is the subtitle. Where else in the story does Benedict refer to oral tradition? In the next-to-last paragraph, the boy thinks about "how he would tell his children and perhaps his grandchildren about the gray-yellow color of that hide."

2. Why do you think Benedict doesn't use quotation marks for the dialogue in this story? Answers will vary. Some students may suggest that the omission of quotation marks points to the oral quality of the story. The author signals that the dialogue may not be the exact words of each character, but rather the approximate words. Leaving the quotation marks out also enhances the eerie, surreal quality of the text.

3. What kinds of changes do you think tend to occur as a story is retold numerous times? Students may suggest that several important changes normally occur when a story is retold: for example, the omission, expansion, or exaggeration of certain incidents; shifts in dialogue; and even alterations in setting or in tone. Remind students that the numerous versions of ballads and traditional songs furnish good examples of the kinds of changes effected by oral tradition. Encourage students to discuss specific examples of repeated or retold stories from their own experience. **What elements of such a story might tend to become exaggerated?** Students may suggest story motifs concerned with feats of strength or eerie phenomena, as well as story details such as large numbers or unusual weather conditions. Encourage students to give examples, such as the size of the proverbial "fish that got away."

UNDERSTANDING THE WORDS IN THE STORY (Matching Columns) *Page 18*

1. reek	**c.** strong, offensive smell
2. writhed	**e.** squirmed in agony
3. forage	**j.** food for animals
4. cinched	**f.** bound or fastened firmly
5. shunted	**i.** moved or turned to one side
6. strove	**a.** struggled with great effort
7. shy	**g.** to move away suddenly
8. canteen	**d.** small metal flask
9. hurtled	**h.** moved fast with great force
10. briers	**b.** prickly thorns

WRITING IT DOWN

A Well-Known Tale *Page 19*

The suggested collaborative writing activity encourages students to experience firsthand how stories are altered through individual retelling. Many storytellers, when unable to recall details of a story, will employ their imaginations to invent their own. Students may be surprised to learn that it is sometimes a failure of memory that inspires creativity. Working together to list well-known stories, they will recognize how many stories are shared within a culture and, perhaps, across cultures as well.

SPEAKING AND LISTENING

Retelling the Tale *Page 19*

The speaking and listening assignment expands on the writing assignment by having students share their stories with the rest of the class. It may be instructive for them to hear the variations in each tale and will give them an idea of how the oral tradition works.

AN ASTROLOGER'S DAY

R. K. Narayan **Page 20**

INTRODUCING THE SELECTION

Like many of Narayan's short stories, "An Astrologer's Day" is built around simple irony of circumstance. By chance, the fraudulent astrologer encounters the very man he had nearly murdered years earlier. He turns the situation to his advantage by cautioning the man never to leave his home village again. Because the astrologer has been so accurate—and with good reason—the man accepts his pronouncements without question. Students should be pleased by the clever turnaround that Narayan employs in this story.

Narayan has written other tales of mistaken or false identity. One of his most popular novels, *The Guide*, tells the story of Raju, a former convict who is mistaken by villagers for a holy man. Unable to convince the villagers of his true identity, he finally adopts the role they give him. After his death, he is lauded as a saint. Narayan himself was once mistaken for an astrologer of sorts. In *Reluctant Guru*, he tells about a trip to a Midwestern college, where he is to be a visiting professor. Although his specialty is literature, students immediately assume he is an expert on mysticism. He knows very little about yoga, levitation, or psychic predictions, yet he is continually asked to speak on these subjects. In "An Astrologer's Day" Narayan may be making a comment about people who fall prey to their own beliefs. Part of the humor derives from the astrologer's deception of average citizens.

People have always been fascinated by the notion that we might be able to predict future events and "read" people's personalities. The popularity of horoscopes is often due to their flattering, vague generalities. The astrologer in the story makes accurate assessments of people's personalities on the basis of what he knows of human nature. He succeeds not because he has any paranormal powers, but because he makes an effort to understand people. Narayan characterizes him as a businessman who earns an honest living. Do students agree?

PRESENTATION

After assigning the story to be read in class or at home, you might want to gauge students' immediate reactions. Were they happy with the outcome of the story? Even though the astrologer is a fraud and a near-murderer, many readers may feel pleased that he "got away with it." Ask those who have this reaction why they feel this way. Responses might include the observation that the astrologer is clever and quick-witted. Like the trickster-hero of many folk tales, he may not be a thoroughly honest or respectable character, but he is talented enough to weasel his way out of a predicament. In many cases a trickster-hero means no real harm, but is just looking out for his own best interests. We can admire him for his cleverness despite his lack of principles. Direct students to the Speaking and Listening activity to further this discussion.

Address the questions under Surprise Ending on page 26. Were any students able to guess the outcome of the story? See if anyone can locate the brief clues that Narayan provides: "The astrologer sent up a prayer to heaven as the other lit a cheroot. The astrologer caught a glimpse of his face by the matchlight." Though at first desperate for a stroke of luck, the astrologer adjusts his behavior after seeing the man's face. Did any of the students guess that he recognized the stranger?

Another story in which someone's face is revealed by matchlight is O. Henry's "After Twenty Years." In this tale, two friends who meet in a prearranged spot after twenty years discover new truths about each other. Students may want to read this story to compare plot, character, and outcome with similar elements in "An Astrologer's Day." O. Henry is the master of the ironic "tale with a twist," as students will discover when they read "The Gift of the Magi" (page 403) later in this anthology.

Students may enjoy the colorful descriptions of the Town Hall Park in the story. Ask them if they have attended any street fairs or festivals. What kinds of performances, vendors, and special presentations did they see there? Perhaps students have attended an ethnic festival, where they were exposed to the diverse arts of another country or culture. As a writing exercise you might ask them to try to recall as many sensory images from the experience as they can. What did they see, hear, touch, smell, and taste? Have them freewrite on the subject for a few minutes.

CHECKING UP (Multiple-Choice) *Page 25*

1. People are attracted to the astrologer because of his
   a. reputation
   (b.) appearance
   c. reasonable prices
2. The vendors' shops are set up
   (a.) on a narrow road
   b. on the main street
   c. at the marketplace
3. The astrologer had left his village
   a. with plans to marry
   b. to study philosophy
   (c.) without a plan
4. The astrologer advises Guru Nayak to
   a. seek a promotion
   (b.) return home
   c. travel abroad
5. Who was waiting for the astrologer when he returned home?
   a. the customer
   b. his mother
   (c.) his wife

TALKING IT OVER *Page 25*

1. The story's opening passages form the *exposition*, the part of a story that provides important background information. At what point does the actual *narrative* begin? The narrative begins with the passage "The nuts vendor blew out his flare and rose to go home" (page 22). Until this point, we understand that the narrator is describing things that *always* happen. He now shifts his focus to a single incident in a single day.

2. The astrologer knows nothing about either the stars or the future, yet his customers are always satisfied with the advice he gives. How does he manage to say things that "pleased and astonished everyone"? The astrologer is a capable student of human nature. He ensures his own success by using general statements and questions, such as asking clients if they are getting sufficient results for their efforts. He also makes comments that appeal in a calculated fashion to a client's vanity.

3. The author describes in detail the way the various small shops are lit up at night. How is the effect of this lighting advantageous to the astrologer? The bizarre lighting contributes to the enchanting, mysterious atmosphere that the astrologer wants to promote. **How is the shop's lighting important to the story?** The light is so diffuse and cross-hatched with shadows that the astrologer's face is not clearly visible at night. This enables him to see Guru Nayak by matchlight while the other cannot see him at all.

4. What coincidence becomes apparent to the astrologer when the customer's face is revealed by matchlight? The coincidence is that Guru Nayak and the astrologer have met before. The astrologer had attacked Guru Nayak years earlier and left him for dead in a well. **How does the astrologer turn this coincidence to his own advantage?** The astrologer builds on Guru Nayak's failure to recognize him. He tells Guru Nayak that the man he has been seeking has been killed by a lorry and that Guru Nayak should return without delay to his village if he wishes to safeguard his life.

5. How would you describe the astrologer's character? Is he clever? imaginative? hardworking? reckless? Support your answer with examples from the story. Answers will vary. Some students might suggest that the astrologer is quick-witted and clever; others might characterize him as deceptive and underhanded.

6. Something said by a character that is the opposite of what readers expect or think appropriate is considered *ironic*. At the end of the story, what is ironic about the astrologer's complaint that Guru Nayak has cheated him? It is ironic when we consider that the astrologer is the one who cheated Guru Nayak. Guru Nayak has spent years hoping to avenge a crime, but the astrologer deliberately misleads him. It is also ironic that Guru Nayak pays the astrologer much more than he is accustomed to receiving, even if it is not the amount agreed upon.

SURPRISE ENDING *Page 26*

1. What information in the story hints at, or foreshadows, the story's ending? Information that prepares us for the surprise ending is the fact that the astrologer had to leave his native village suddenly, without telling anyone, and that he traveled a couple of hundred miles before he could rest. In addition, he offers Guru Nayak more than his usual vague advice.

2. Early in the story we are told that the astrologer "knew no more of what was going to happen to others than he knew what was going to happen to himself next minute." How, then, does he manage to solve his problem and thus "write" the ending of his own story? At first the astrologer is terribly nervous, but then he realizes Guru Nayak has not recognized him. He understands that he has a rare opportunity to halt Guru Nayak's pursuit forever. Since he is able to impress Guru Nayak with details about his life, including knowing his name, Guru Nayak is inclined to believe whatever the astrologer advises. This includes the command to return to his native village and never venture forth again.

UNDERSTANDING THE WORDS IN THE STORY (Matching Columns) *Page 26*

1. punctually	g. on time
2. resplendent	f. dazzling; shining
3. enhanced	j. made greater; improved
4. vendor	h. seller
5. shrewd	i. clever; cunning
6. perception	e. insight; understanding
7. impetuous	b. hasty; impulsive
8. forbidding	a. dangerous; threatening
9. piqued	d. resentful; offended
10. gratified	c. pleased; satisfied

WRITING IT DOWN

A Description *Page 27*

The suggested writing assignment asks students to describe a character. This brief assignment will develop skills that students will need when they attempt to write a short story, and can be used in conjunction with other writing exercises in *Impact*.

SPEAKING AND LISTENING

Discussing a Story *Page 27*

The Speaking and Listening assignment addresses many of the issues discussed in the Presentation section of this manual. This may be an ideal occasion for students to practice developing an argument and persuading the opposition, as there is likely to be some disagreement.

THE COLOMBER

Dino Buzzati **Page 28**

INTRODUCING THE SELECTION

"The Colomber" may be read as an allegory about the choices one makes in life. An **allegory** can be defined as a story in which the characters, places, and events are used to symbolize larger, abstract ideas. One famous allegorical work is Dante's *Inferno,* in which the poet uses the framework of a journey through Hell to condemn immorality and corruption. We assume that the events described in an allegorical tale are not to be taken at face value; they are representative of a larger truth. In "The Colomber," Buzzati does not tell readers whether they should view the events as realistic or not, but he does make a point about human choices. Stefano Roi's simultaneous pursuit of and flight from the colomber could be interpreted as a human need to seek out the dangerous, darker side of life. Happiness could be his, but he does not choose it.

"The Colomber" is reminiscent of other tales about a character dogged by ill fortune at sea. One such story appears in Samuel Taylor Coleridge's "The Rime of the Ancient Mariner," in which the Mariner shoots the bird of good fortune, the Albatross. As penance, he and his crew suffer terrible thirst and are pursued by a ghost ship. In Herman Melville's *Moby-Dick* , the doomed Captain Ahab is determined to avenge himself upon the great white whale that maimed him. When one compares "The Colomber" with literary paradigms such as these, the irony of the story's conclusion is quite apparent. Students who are unfamiliar with the stories of Coleridge and Melville may be less struck by the irony of Buzzati's tale, although they will no doubt be surprised at the ending. They will most likely have a wealth of questions demanding "why?" to spark a discussion.

As indicated in the biography on page 38, Dino Buzzati was influenced by existentialist philosophy. Existentialism is a belief system that focuses on the isolation of human beings in a meaningless universe and emphasizes freedom of choice and personal responsibility. It regards human existence as inexplicable and without structure. The idea of waiting for something that never happens is intrinsic to much existentialist writing. Buzzati's novel *The Tartar Steppe* is an example. In Samuel Beckett's *Waiting for Godot,* two characters spend an entire play waiting for someone named Godot, who never arrives. Their conversation is essentially trivial and meaningless and is supposed to represent the human condition. In Jean-Paul Sartre's play *No Exit,* several characters are trapped in a single room together, making one another miserable. The door is always open, but none of them can exit. Existentialism suggests that we make our own choices for happiness or unhappiness—fate does not hand us our future blindly. Introducing students to these concepts may help them understand the meaning behind "The Colomber." Stefano believes that a horrible fate pursues him, and it is the belief itself that torments him. Remind students that, for Stefano, "the temptation of the abyss had always been greater for him than the joys of a prosperous and quiet life." Do they think Stefano is unusual? Are others, including fictional characters, drawn to a restless life?

PRESENTATION

You may want to assign "The Colomber" for at-home reading. You might begin discussion by addressing the questions in "Talking It Over" (page 34). The text should inspire lively debate. Students may want to challenge the text and may wonder why the author put Stefano into such a cruel predicament. The following questions could be a springboard to such a discussion: Does the fault lie with Stefano, or with his father and the other sailors who warn him of the colomber? Was the father right all along in predicting that the colomber would "devour" Stefano? Doesn't Stefano face his fear by returning to the sea, despite the warning? Suppose that Stefano had remained on land all his life and had never met the colomber—would life have been easier for him?

Call attention to the point of view and tone in the story. Until the final two paragraphs, the story's point of view is close to Stefano. After Stefano meets the colomber, the author adopts a detached tone. He discusses the colomber scientifically: "The colomber is a huge fish, frightening to behold and extremely rare." What does this shift do to students' perceptions of the story? Are they more or less inclined to believe that the colomber is a real creature? The author writes of the fish: "Some even maintain that it does not exist," a statement that implies the fish *does* exist. Do readers believe that the author is being tongue-in-cheek, or is he really asking them to suspend their disbelief? How does this shift in tone add yet another "twist" to the story?

CHECKING UP (Short Answer) *Page 34*

1. When Stefano turns twelve, what does he ask of his father as a birthday gift? He asks to be taken to sea.

2. According to Stefano's father, for how long does the colomber pursue its victim? The colomber will pursue its victim for his entire life.

3. What decision does Stefano make when he is twenty-two years old? He decides to follow his father's career as a sea captain.

4. To whom does Stefano reveal the story of the colomber? He tells the story of the colomber to his second officer.

5. What does the colomber give Stefano before it sinks into the black waters forever? The colomber gives Stefano a magnificent pearl that brings luck, power, love, and peace of mind to whoever possesses it.

TALKING IT OVER *Page 34*

1. After his father's death, Stefano decides to ignore the advice his father had given him and

become a sea captain. Why does he make this decision? Answers will vary. In general, students may note the importance of family tradition, as well as Stefano's fascination with the sea, which goes back to his childhood. Students should also note that by the age of twenty-two Stefano is already in the grip of his obsession with the colomber.

2. In the "twist" that ends this story, how does the colomber turn out to be quite different from what Stefano had been led to expect? Although Stefano had expected the colomber to be fierce and destructive, the beast turns out to be gentle and courteous.

3. Which passages depict the colomber as an animal waiting for its master? Students may cite the passage directly after Stefano is put ashore by his father, when the colomber is "obstinately waiting for him." They might also note that the fish is referred to as "his" colomber, as if it were Stefano's pet. Another passage describes the fish "raising its muzzle . . . as if it anxiously watched for whether Stefano was coming at last." **Which passages in the story show that Stefano, in a sense, identifies with the colomber?** Students may cite the following passages: Stefano's hurrying to the pier each time he returns home to see if the colomber still awaits him (page 30); Stefano's "indomitable impulse" to travel the oceans without rest, like the colomber (page 32); and Stefano's preparing to meet the colomber, claiming that he cannot betray it in its old age (page 32). **Could these passages be considered clues to the story's ending?** The colomber's lifelong devotion to Stefano suggest that its intentions may be positive. By characterizing it as a hopeful, faithful animal, the author prepares us for its gentle demeanor and generosity at the end of the story.

4. What evidence in the story suggests that the colomber may really be a part of Stefano's own nature? There are several hints in the story that the colomber is really a part of Stefano's own nature. For example, Stefano says that the creature has escorted him throughout his life "with a faithfulness that not even the noblest friend could have shown." In addition, the colomber is said to be terribly old and weary at the time when Stefano, also worn out by old age, is about to die. Finally, the story implies that Stefano and the colomber die simultaneously. **If the colomber exists only in Stefano's mind, is it any less "real," in your view?** Answers will vary. Most students will agree that the colomber can be "real" in a symbolic or psychological sense.

5. The narrator says of Stefano that "The temptation of the abyss had always been greater for him than the joys of a prosperous and quiet life." What does this comment reveal about Stefano's character? This remark implies that the qualities that have made Stefano highly successful—his courage, drive, and pursuit of adventure—have also led him into restless, self-destructive tendencies. For Stefano, a prosperous, quiet life would not be satisfying but dull and uninspiring. **How does this statement relate to the colomber's gift of the pearl at the end of the story?** The gift of the pearl, had it appeared earlier in Stefano's life, might have provided him with peace of mind and serenity. As it is, the gift arrives too late, because Stefano has misinterpreted the colomber's intentions.

6. Even when Stefano is in an inland city hundreds of kilometers from the sea, he worries about the colomber. Why is the colomber a source of torment for him even when he is far away from it? Since the colomber is in one sense an aspect of Stefano's own nature, he cannot escape it no matter where he goes. It is not the actual creature that haunts him, but his own terrible fear of it. **How has Stefano been "devoured" by the Colomber even though he has lived out his life?** The father's prediction has been borne out because Stefano suffered more than he would have if the colomber had simply devoured him in a literal sense. Instead, he is "devoured"—or consumed—in a figurative sense. His constant fear occupies his thoughts and drives his actions, and he can never forget the colomber's presence.

7. Do you think Stefano could have led a life of contentment and satisfaction? Or does the story suggest that some people are singled out by destiny and their own natures to lead lives of restless searching? Support your answer with details from the text. Answers will vary. Encourage students to discuss and support their opinions with specific references to the story.

FANTASY AND MAGICAL REALISM Page 35

1. What are some of the other elements of fantasy in the story? Elements of fantasy that students may mention include the physical appearance of the colomber, the reference to the King of the Sea, and the beautifully phosphorescent *Perla del Mare.*

2. How does the story's final paragraph blend fantasy with reality? The final paragraph gives a parting description of the fantastic colomber in realistic terms, listing the alternate names by which it is known in various regions of the world. The author also remarks ironically that "naturalists strangely ignore it" and that "some even maintain that it does not exist."

3. Authors often use magical realism to write thought-provoking fantasies on serious themes. What do you think is the underlying message of this fantasy? Answers will vary. One possible statement of the message might run as follows: Some people spend their lives in the relentless pursuit of something—adventure, fame, or material wealth. In their race to escape fate or the inevitability of death, such people never realize the value of peace of mind until it is too late. **How is the colomber fantastic on one level and possibly very "real" on another?** The colomber's strange appearance and behavior make it fantastic on a literal level. On a psychological or symbolic level, however, the colomber is "real" in the sense that it represents an individual's nature or inescapable destiny.

UNDERSTANDING THE WORDS IN THE STORY (Matching Columns) Page 36

1. astern	f. at or to the rear of a ship
2. wake	h. ship's trail in the water
3. pretext	e. excuse
4. dissuaded	g. turned aside
5. intermittently	a. at intervals
6. indefinable	j. vague; unclear
7. scrutinized	c. examined carefully
8. expedient	b. means to an end
9. obsession	d. persisting concern or idea
10. ominously	i. threateningly

(Multiple-Choice) *Page 36*

1. Stefano's career shows the great attraction of the *abyss* for certain people.
   a. marketplace
   (b.) bottomless gulf
   c. sea
2. The colomber kept appearing with *inexorable* obstinacy.
   (a.) unrelenting
   b. noisy
   c. savage
3. Despite his crew's remarks, Stefano's will did not *slacken.*
   a. harden
   (b.) weaken
   c. alter
4. Stefano used his *patrimony* to acquire a freighter.
   a. bargaining skill
   b. credit
   (c.) inheritance
5. An *indomitable* impulse dragged Stefano from ocean to ocean.
   a. imaginary
   b. interesting
   (c.) unconquerable
6. Stefano proved his seaworthiness and his *intrepid* spirit.
   a. strong
   b. joking
   (c.) fearless
7. When Stefano set out in the rowboat, the sea was *placid.*
   (a.) calm
   b. misty
   c. choppy
8. The rowboat disappeared in the *nocturnal* shadows.
   (a.) nighttime
   b. thin
   c. nightmarish
9. The colomber's horrible *snout* suddenly appeared.
   a. tail
   (b.) muzzle
   c. fin
10. When Stefano raised his harpoon, the colomber groaned *imploringly.*
   a. loudly
   b. faintly
   (c.) pleadingly

WRITING IT DOWN

Notes for a Story *Page 37*

Encourage students to use their imaginations; their characters and events need not be bound by laws of nature. You may want to give some students more guidance about potential topics for their story. Ask them to freewrite two or three sentences on ten different incidents and then pick one to develop into a story.

Three Wise Guys

Un Cuento de Navidad/A Christmas Story

Sandra Cisneros

Page 39

INTRODUCING THE SELECTION

The pivotal object in the story "Three Wise Guys" is a large box that is given as a Christmas gift. Each member of the family imagines what the box contains; the mama, a portable washing machine; the papa, a record player, an ice chest, or an air conditioner; the children, toys. Each fantasizes about the gift that would bring him or her the most ease and pleasure, and even the neighbors join in to speculate. Readers, likewise, will want to complete the story to discover the box's secrets. When the gift is finally revealed, it proves to have value far beyond its material worth for at least one member of the family.

"Three Wise Guys" may be read as a type of **parable,** or tale from which a moral or spiritual lesson can be drawn. Some modern stories can be viewed as parables in that they teach simple and universal truths. The title alludes to the Biblical story of the three wise men, which can be found in the second chapter of Matthew. Their journey to bestow gifts of gold, frankincense, and myrrh on the Christ child heralded the tradition of gift giving at Christmas. In many countries, gifts are exchanged on January 6, the Day of the Epiphany, rather than on Christmas. In Christian tradition, the Epiphany is the feast that celebrates the revelation of Christ to the gentiles, as represented by the three wise men.

The word *epiphany* comes from the Greek *epiphaneia,* meaning "manifestation" or "to appear forth." The term **epiphany** is also used to refer to a moment of illumination or insight that occurs near the end of a work of fiction. When a character undergoes an epiphany, he or she comes to a sudden realization, understanding, or moment of emotional transformation. Near the end of "Three Wise Guys," the boy Ruben is suddenly overwhelmed by a flood of knowledge. He comes to understand the power of books, and in the final paragraph he contemplates the night sky with new eyes. You might ask how the Day of the Epiphany is an appropriate metaphor for Ruben's discovery of knowledge. How are the books a manifestation of knowledge? That the discovery is sudden, even accidental, makes Ruben's awareness of knowledge even more of an epiphany.

As a child, Sandra Cisneros also discovered that books could be useful things. She read constantly to escape from the painful shyness brought about by being constantly uprooted from her home. "Because we moved so much," she says, "and always in neighborhoods that appeared like France after World War II—empty lots and burned-out buildings—I retreated inside myself." Books became her solace. Throughout her childhood, she wrote poems and stories, later perfecting her craft at the prestigious University of Iowa Writers' Workshop. She tends to blend genres in her work, melding a poetic style with a fictional structure, or writing poetry that tells a story.

Cisneros experienced her own turning point in graduate school when she realized that her history was different from that of her classmates. Her literary obsessions began to develop out of this realization. In her writing, she focuses on her heritage as a Chicana, her childhood, and on all the women whom she believes are denied a voice in the world.

PRESENTATION

Before assigning the story, you may want to open with a discussion of Christmas, Hanukkah, Kwanzaa, and other holiday celebrations. Direct students to the activity that precedes the selection. Ask them what traditions they know of. How do traditions differ in other parts of the world? Students may be interested to note that many holiday celebrations occur in the heart of winter, when the days are short and the lack of light dampens people's spirits. A traditional celebration of food, light, and gifts is a natural counterpoint to the dreary season.

After reading the story, a discussion of gift giving might be a productive way to stimulate thinking. How would students go about choosing a gift for another person? How might the following factors influence their choice: wealth, gender, personality traits, age? What would they have chosen to give to the Gonzalez family?

While discussing this story, you might ask students about the role of learning in their own lives. Can they remember when they first picked up a book? How did they feel? Are they inspired more by novels and poetry, or by writings about history, science, and current events? Can they recall a turning point such as the one Ruben experiences with the encyclopedias? Point out the passage where the neighbor states, "A new TV would surely be the end to all your miseries." Do students agree at all with this statement? Point out that the gift of knowledge will prove to be more lasting for Ruben, and may help him to break out of the cycle of poverty.

CHECKING UP (Short Answer) *Page 44*

1. Who are the brothers Travis? Dwight Travis is the principal of the school that Ruben and Rosalinda attend. He and his brothers, Frank and Earl, give the Gonzalez family the Christmas gift.

2. When did the brothers first begin bringing gifts to the Gonzalez family? They began bringing gifts when the children started to earn high grades at school.

3. What does the comadre Elodia think the box contains? She suggests that the box holds a portable washing machine.

4. What does Rosalinda do with the books? Rosalinda colors and cuts out the pictures in the books. She also stacks them into spiral staircases for her paper dolls to descend.

5. Why does Ruben avoid Mr. Travis for several days after opening the gift? Ruben is afraid that he would not know how to respond if Mr. Travis asks him how he likes the gift.

TALKING IT OVER *Page 44*

1. Why does the mother insist that the family wait until January sixth to open the box? The mother was raised in Mexico, where gifts are customarily opened on the Día de los Reyes, or "Day of the Kings."

2. What details in the story show that, although the mother and father work hard, the family is not well off? Students may cite the family members' wishes for items that they cannot afford, such as a television set or a washing machine. They might also point out the practical gifts that the Travis brothers bring each holiday, which include food and clothing. Also, the mother and father sleep behind "plastic curtains," not in a separate bedroom.

3. Each member of the family is hoping that the box contains something different. How do these wishes reflect the needs and longings of each one? The mama hopes that the box contains a portable washing machine, since she spends her time boiling clothes in a big pot to clean them. The papa imagines a different gift every day according to his whims: a record player or an ice chest full of beer. Gradually, he wishes less for luxuries and more for necessities; as it gets hotter, he wants an air conditioner. The children hope the box is filled with toys, since it is unlikely their parents can afford such luxuries very often. Being poor, the family probably spends a lot of time imagining things they might like to own.

4. Why does the neighbor Cayetano think that a color television would be a good gift? Cayetano believes that the sagas of the rich on television soap operas could provide a distraction from their own troubles. Seeing the complex lives of these characters would make them thankful for the simplicity of their poverty.

5. How does the story suggest that the gift is a "turning point" in the life of Ruben? The story portrays Ruben as fascinated by the knowledge that the encyclopedias offer. The writer implies that the books have opened a new world to the boy. Education may make it possible for Ruben to change his circumstances and to leave behind the poverty of his childhood.

6. What do you think is the significance of the story's title? Answers will vary. The title is a reference to the three wise men who brought gifts to the Christ child. The presents—gold, frankincense, and myrrh—were gifts that were normally given to kings. The three wise men were acknowledging Christ as the king of the Jews. Thus, the encyclopedias brought by the three wise guys—the Travis brothers—is compared to a gift for a king. The gift is knowledge. **Who are the "three wise guys"?** The wise guys are the Travis brothers, who deliver the Christmas gift. The informal, colloquial tone of the title suggests that the story will be an updated version of the Biblical narrative. By referring to the Travises as "wise guys," Cisneros also suggests at the beginning of the story a flippant attitude toward the gift; this attitude is amusingly reversed at the end of the story, when the reader is led to recognize the gift as truly valuable.

UNDERSTANDING THE WORDS IN THE STORY (Matching Columns) *Page 45*

1. obstructed	**f.** blocked
2. portable	**j.** movable
3. distract	**g.** divert the attention of
4. plea	**e.** request
5. prophecy	**a.** prediction
6. sashaying	**h.** gliding
7. squat	**c.** short and thick
8. pillars	**b.** columns
9. improvised	**g.** created on the spot
10. descend	**d.** go downward

PARABLE *Page 45*

The moral of a parable is usually left unstated. How would you state the lesson of "Three Wise Guys" in your own words? One statement of the lesson is as follows: Knowledge is a more precious, lasting gift than any material thing.

WRITING IT DOWN

A Report on an Interview *Page 46*

Conducting an interview should give students practice in speaking and listening, as well as provide rich material for their own fiction. Remind them that a successful interview often depends on the ability of the interviewer to listen carefully and be prepared to modify his or her questions.

THE TROUT

Sean O'Faolain

Page 48

INTRODUCING THE SELECTION

Sean O'Faolain is one among three Irish writers in this anthology, a group that includes his contemporaries Liam O'Flaherty, author of "The Sniper" (page 213), and Michael McLaverty, author of "The Wild Duck's Nest" (page 230). Although O'Faolain shared an intense interest in Irish political struggles and Irish heritage with O'Flaherty, this story, with its understanding of children and the natural world, is akin to the work of the more introspective McLaverty. O'Faolain has been regarded as one of modern Ireland's greatest chroniclers.

Ask students to locate on a map the city of Cork in County Cork in the south of Ireland, where Sean O'Faolain was born, and Dublin, midway down the eastern coast on the Irish Sea, where he earned his M.A. degree at the National University of Ireland. He studied Gaelic, the ancient language of the Celts in Ireland and the Scottish Highlands, and changed his name to the Gaelic form. As a Commonwealth Fellow at Harvard (1926–1928) and as a Harvard Fellow (1928–1929), he taught Gaelic and Anglo-Irish literature. He was teaching in Ireland when the success of his *Midsummer Night Madness and Other Stories* (1932) and his novel *A Nest of Simple Folk* (1933) allowed him to quit teaching and devote himself full time to writing.

You might mention to students that "The Trout" has a twelve-year-old girl named Julia and her younger brother Stephen as central characters. Ask students to name other stories in which central characters are children. Ask students to decide if Julia and Stephen are as interesting and as real as students' favorite characters in other stories they have read.

PRESENTATION

After students have read "The Trout," proceed with the discussion questions and exercises.

The Dark Walk in "The Trout" may remind students of scary places of their own younger days. They may also have shared Julia's aversion to "a horrible old moral story." Perhaps they once had the experience of returning a wild creature to its habitat as Julia returns the trout. Encourage discussion of O'Faolain's understanding of child psychology and his appreciation of nature.

CHECKING UP (Short Answer) *Page 51*

1. Who is the main character of the story? The main character is Julia, an adolescent girl.

2. At what time of year does the story take place? The story takes place in early summer.

3. Who discovers the trout? Julia discovers the trout.

4. What story does Julia's mother tell about the trout? Julia's mother tells a tale about a naughty fish that grows too big for the water; it is then rescued by a fairy godmother who sends rain to flood it out.

5. How does Julia rescue the trout? Julia takes the trout from the well and empties it into a river.

TALKING IT OVER *Page 52*

1. Why does Julia enjoy racing through The Dark Walk? She likes to scare herself in the cool darkness of the long tunnel and then emerge victoriously at the end of the tunnel. **How do you know that she feels possessive about this place?** She shows it to her younger brother and teases him when he is afraid. She is unwilling to admit that the tunnel could include a well that she hasn't discovered for herself. She feels that the trout she finds there belongs to her, along with everything else about the tunnel.

2. In what way does Stephen serve as a contrast to Julia? Being younger, Stephen cannot run as fast as Julia or take the lead in their activities. He is more interested in their mother's stories about the trout than in the actual trout. Julia is critical of the stories and is more concerned for the trout's well-being.

3. Julia becomes preoccupied with the trout. How does the trout interfere with her vacation? She spends much of her time visiting the trout, wondering how he became trapped in the well and worrying about his predicament. She lies awake at night thinking about him.

4. Julia's mother tells Stephen a make-believe story about the trout. How does this story provide an incentive for Julia to act? When Julia hears the story with "one ear cocked," she objects to the idea that the "naughty fish who would not stay at home" would be punished by having the water diminish. She also realizes that no fairy godmother will come to the trout's rescue. She decides that she must save the trout herself before it is caught by an angler or dies in the dwindling water.

5. At the end of the story, why do you think Julia doesn't give her little brother a straight answer? Julia is possessive about her secrets, and she doesn't want to share the private wonder she has experienced. She has undergone a transformation of sorts and now feels superior to her baby brother, who still believes in such things as fairy godmothers.

6. How does Julia, in effect, write her own ending to the story of the trout? As she lies in bed, Julia imagines the trout gasping out its life. Realizing that no magical power will save it, she takes this duty upon herself. Her inspiration may have come from her mother's fanciful story of the water washing the trout down to the river. **How might this episode be taken as a "turning point," or sign of her growing up?** Julia no longer believes that luck and magic will solve her problems; she understands that she must take decisive action to solve them herself. Saving the trout is a selfless gesture, indicative of her growing maturity. She is able to reach out to the world at large.

7. Are the games and stories of childhood a preparation for life? Consider the events of O'Faolain's story in your answer. Yes. The children brave the darkness of the tunnel in preparation for facing other fears and challenges in adulthood. They consider the make-believe stories about the trout, but Julia devises a better story ending of her own. Julia's games with her brother and her concern for the trout will translate into adult work and responsibility for other people and other living creatures.

UNDERSTANDING THE WORDS IN THE STORY (Matching Columns) *Page 52*

1. lofty	g. rising high in the air
2. sinewy	d. tough
3. ordeal	a. trial
4. squabbled	j. quarreled noisily
5. incredulous	h. not ready to believe
6. haughtily	b. arrogantly
7. spawn	i. eggs
8. resolutely	e. steadily
9. ewer	c. jug
10. scuttled	f. moved swiftly

WRITING IT DOWN

Updating a Fairy Tale *Page 52*

The assignment to update a fairy tale asks students to interpret a preexisting story. Students may want to modernize their tale with references to recent technology and current events. They can use also use modern language and slang terms. Comparing different versions in class may prove interesting.

A Narrative *Page 53*

The assignment to write a narrative asks students to use personal experience and also provides a chance for them to weave in knowledge about the story. They may want to remark on similarities and differences between Julia's experience and their own.

THE NO-GUITAR BLUES

Gary Soto

Page 54

INTRODUCING THE SELECTION

Many children hope to become rock stars, and Fausto is among them. The appeal of being a rock musician often lies in money, fame, and applause, rather than in the long, hard hours of practice required. Seeing Los Lobos, a Hispanic group, on American Bandstand ignites Fausto's fervor to become a star. In the process of pursuing his dream, he accidentally discovers something about himself and makes a change for the better.

In many of his stories, Gary Soto captures the essence of what it means to be young. All the traumas of youth—trying to get a first date, hoping to change one's appearance, wanting to be talented and popular—are treated sympathetically. Soto effectively maintains the point of view of teenagers, refusing to regard their troubles as petty or banal. Students may find that the circumstances of "The No-Guitar Blues" ring true, even if they have not been in Fausto's predicament themselves.

Soto believes that young writers can find the seeds for stories in their own lives. Although we may believe that interesting things happen only to other people in other places, he says, our lives too can be a source of inspiration. He encourages writers to think back on their childhood memories and stories. Students may want to respond to Soto's remarks. What past incidents do they remember most clearly?

PRESENTATION

Have students read the first two paragraphs of the story and then ask them to recall a time when they wanted something as badly as Fausto did. After they write a sentence or two about the item's importance, you might ask them to list emotions, things, or ideas associated with that particular item. For example, under "Guitar," Fausto might list the following words: friends, fame, money, stylish clothes. What emotions are connected with each of the words on their list? Ask them to consider the essence of the thing itself: in Fausto's case, a guitar. Is the object still good on its own, without the addition of all the other benefits? Fausto gets a taste of this at the end of "The No-Guitar Blues" when he finally gets his guitarron and hears that the strings "sounded beautiful, deep and eerie."

After this discussion, proceed with the story and address the questions that follow. The writing exercises, A Journal Entry and Writing Dialogue (Page 62), should give students practice in writing about realistic people and events.

Ask students if they think Fausto's character is effectively portrayed. Do they believe in his actions? Do they imagine that this will prove to be a great turning point in Fausto's life—one on which he will look back for years? Why or why not?

Ask any Spanish-speaking students in the class to help others with pronunciation of foreign words. These include *conjunto, empanada, papas, chorizo con huevos, hijo, enchiladas.* Since several of these are Mexican dishes, ask the students to describe what these meals are like for those who haven't tasted them.

CHECKING UP (True/False) *Page 60*

F 1. Fausto mowed lawns to earn money for a guitar.

T 2. Fausto fed the dog pieces of orange peel.

T 3. Fausto thought the dog belonged to rich people.

T 4. Fausto felt guilty about having deceived the couple.

F 5. Fausto's grandfather bought him a new guitar.

TALKING IT OVER *Page 61*

1. Why did Fausto think his parents would not want to get him a guitar? He knew that they would respond by saying they didn't have the money to buy one. Also, they hated rock music.

2. How did Fausto try to earn the money to buy a guitar? First he had the idea to mow lawns, then he went door-to-door hoping to get paid for raking leaves. **What idea came to him when he saw the "fancy" dog?** Fausto realized that the dog belonged to rich people, so he planned to take it back to them, claim that it was lost, and collect a reward.

3. *Internal conflict* is a character's struggle within himself or herself. At what points in the story does Fausto face internal conflict? He begins to feel guilty about his deception when the man hands him a twenty-dollar bill. His internal conflict steadily intensifies until he donates the bill to the church.

4. A statement is considered ironic when it points out the difference between appearance and reality. Why is it ironic that the woman calls Fausto a "lovely child?" The woman calls Fausto a "lovely child" at the very moment when he is sinking into remorse for being dishonest. Presumably, Roger's owners don't suspect that Fausto might have lied to them. **Why is it ironic that Fausto's mother is proud of him for going to church?** Fausto's mother is unaware that he wants to attend church to assuage his guilt.

5. How might this episode be a "turning point" in Fausto's life? Answers will vary. Fausto might decide that dishonesty is not worth the price one has to pay in guilt. He may resolve to do things in a straightforward manner from now on, particularly with people who are so generous and kind to him. Also, he may value his first guitar more since he came by it honestly.

REALISM *Page 61*

1. How is Fausto presented as an ordinary teenager? In what way are his thoughts and actions realistic? Answers will vary. Like many teenagers, Fausto has dreams of fame and popularity. He is frustrated by obstacles in his life, such as the fact that he has no money and has to ask his parents for a guitar. He is still childlike and makes errors in judgment, but he can also make a mature decision.

2. The use of *dialogue*, or conversation between characters, contributes to the realistic quality of a story. Is the dialogue between Fausto and his mother believable? Most students will say yes. Fausto and his mother talk casually, using short phrases. A son and his mother would naturally use informal speech, and money is a typical topic of conversation. **Did you consider the dialogue between Fausto and the husband and wife to be realistic? Explain your answers.** Again, students will probably think their conversation is realistic. Like many teenagers, Fausto keeps many of his thoughts to himself. The husband and wife are considerate and welcoming, and appear to understand that Fausto might be shy and uncomfortable. Their dialogue sounds like the language real people actually speak in an informal setting, and reflects their backgrounds and where they live. For example, Fausto does not know what a turnover is because his family does not eat them.

3. What details about the setting help make the story true to life? Answers will vary. Students may cite the description of the interior of the house that Fausto visits, with the copper pans, the bright yellow wallpaper, and the perpetual clock. They may also note that Fausto's neighborhood is a realistic and typical one.

UNDERSTANDING THE WORDS IN THE STORY (Completion) *Page 62*

1. The baby started to cry, but I distracted him with a cookie.
2. He always said that the best kind of charity is giving without being asked.
3. Since he remembered the pain from the last shot he received, Pablo entered the doctor's office reluctantly.
4. Ludmila fidgeted so much that her mother couldn't fasten the back of her dress.
5. Since there was no other explanation for the disappearance of the trunk, we realized that the porter had been deceitful.

WRITING IT DOWN

A Journal Entry *Page 62*

The first writing assignment calls for students to employ imagination as well as knowledge of the story. Remind them that journals can be written in a more informal style than papers written with a specific audience in mind.

Writing Dialogue *Page 62*

Students are asked to listen to what is going on around them and to practice writing authentic speech. They may find the seeds for future stories in the conversations they overhear and take part in. Remind them that dialogue is an effective way of conveying character and moving the action of a story along. You can challenge them to translate their dialogue into a dramatic scene.

I Confess

Wei Wenjuan

Page 64

INTRODUCING THE SELECTION

"I Confess" is a story with a significant turning point for one character, Mr. Wei. The portrayal of the teacher marks the story as a type of **satire**, or literary work that reveals human weakness, folly, and vice. Satire employs irony, humor, and derision to expose a character's flaws. In the case of "I Confess," Mr. Wei's mistake is brought to light through the use of irony. At first a loud, unforgiving disciplinarian, Mr. Wei is humbled by the revelation that he was once at fault himself. The fact that he has entirely misjudged young Wang Wei makes his predicament even more humiliating. He saves himself from being a completely foolish, satirical figure through his ability to change and admit his wrongs. It is ironic that these positive traits are precisely the ones that Mr. Wei believes to be "the sign of a good student."

Mr. Wei notes that the characters carved in the desk are written in Song-dynasty style. The Song Dynasty (960–1279) marked China's movement away from medieval thought and practices and heralded its entrance into the modern era. It was a time of scholarship, technological breakthroughs, and a flowering of the fine arts.

The most remarkable achievements in technology were in the fields of ship-building and firearms. Watertight and efficient seagoing junks, man-powered paddleboats, and the innovative sternpost rudder all came into being during this time. The mariner's compass, with its floating needle, was in use by around 990. Gunpowder was also perfected by the Song, who used it successfully in a grenade battle in 1161.

Landscape was a major theme in art, and scroll-work paintings of landscapes showed a progression and an unfolding theme that Western art, with a fixed vanishing point, could not. The great Song artists were influenced by Daoist and Buddhist philosophy. If students are interested, they may want to do some research to compare Western and Asian art.

PRESENTATION

The brevity of "I Confess" makes it ideal for oral reading and discussion in one class period. After First Response and Checking Up, address the questions under Talking it Over. The activity on page 68 challenges students to adapt the story as a play.

Because the story is told in the first-person point of view, it is a type of "confession" itself. Ask students what the story might have been like if it had not been told by Mr. Wei. If the tale had been told by an outside party, we might have been less inclined to forgive Mr. Wei. What if the story were told from the point of view of Wang Wei, the student who is falsely accused? He certainly might have portrayed Mr. Wei in an unflattering light. Ask students to think of an alternate title for the same story told from a new point of view. How does a story's title set their expectations before they begin to read?

CHECKING UP (True/False) *Page 67*

F 1. Mr. Wei had been teaching for many years.

T 2. Mr. Wei had been encouraged to be firm with the children.

T 3. Wang Wei is terrified as Mr. Wei questions him.

F 4. Wang Wei identifies the characters carved on the desk.

T 5. Mr. Wei is ashamed when he realizes that he had carved the characters himself.

TALKING IT OVER *Page 67*

1. Why is Mr. Wei so upset about the carvings on the desk? He has set high standards for his classroom, and is distressed to learn that his strict discipline has not been successful.

2. How does Wang Wei react to Mr. Wei's questioning? Wang Wei trembles, stammers, and finally begins to cry. **Why do you think he responds as he does?** Wang Wei is intimidated by Mr. Wei, a teacher who is known for strict, authoritarian methods.

3. Why doesn't Mr. Wei allow Wang Wei to defend himself? Mr. Wei has been taught not to allow children the slightest leverage. He believes that if he lets Wang Wei argue, he might lose his tight control over the situation.

4. What evidence in the story *foreshadows*, or hints at, the story's conclusion? Students may cite the fact that Wang Wei and Mr. Wei share the same name; also, Wang Wei's denial seems authentic. Some students might think that Mr. Wei's blustering, stern attitude seems to deserve some sort of reprisal at the end.

5. An experience that causes a person to admit a mistake and change his or her ways can be considered a "turning point." How might the incident with Wang Wei be a turning point in Mr. Wei's teaching career? Answers will vary. Having been humbled by his experience, Mr. Wei might be less inclined to judge students so harshly. He will probably be able to see the students' point of view, and to listen to all sides of an issue before jumping to a hasty conclusion. Students might note that although Mr. Wei has lost face among his students, they might respect him more for his honesty and ability to admit his wrongdoing.

UNDERSTANDING THE WORDS IN THE STORY (Completion) *Page 67*

1. We resolved the problem by leaving a day earlier.
2. It was easy for him to articulate what was on his mind.
3. The amount was incorrect by hundreds of dollars, but I was not registering that fact.
4. Paco had to reimburse his sister for the money he had borrowed.
5. Sally tried to write in the snow, but her letters were indistinct.
6. Mother left the table abruptly when she heard the baby cry.
7. The nurse monitored the patient's progress.
8. The teacher was careful to keep reserves of pens in her desk.
9. Surprised and unable to speak, he stammered for a few moments.
10. Father did not chastise the children for getting home late.

WRITING IT DOWN

A Personal Essay *Page 68*

The suggested essay-writing assignment asks students to look critically at the text, and to imaginatively predict what might occur in the future. Students might exchange these essays for peer review.

A Play *Page 68*

"I Confess" makes an ideal source for play-writing practice because of its brevity and simplicity. Students should work in groups, share their ideas with the class, and eventually perform their scenes.

WAR

Luigi Pirandello

Page 70

INTRODUCING THE SELECTION

Luigi Pirandello's "War" is a story we might prefer to examine from a distance—there seems to be nothing special about the unattractive people in their smoky, second-class carriage, waiting to depart from Fabriano. Yet despite our effort to remain uninvolved, we are drawn into the controversy of these travel-worn parents who want to plumb the depths of their feelings for sons at war. When the exemplary pride of the fat man disintegrates into harrowing sobs of grief for his dead son, we share his utter misery.

Students may have difficulty understanding why the fat man wishes to deny the loss of his son. The following statement by Pirandello may cast light on the theme of the story. Read the statement aloud to the class and ask students to speculate about the character of the man who wrote it. What is his attitude toward self-deception?

> I think that life is a very sad piece of buffoonery; because we have in ourselves, without

being able to know why, wherefore, or whence, the need to deceive ourselves constantly by creating a reality (one for each and never the same for all), which from time to time is discovered to be vain and illusory. . . My art is full of bitter compassion for all those who deceive themselves, but this compassion cannot fail to be followed by the ferocious derision of destiny which condemns man to deception.

Refer students to the writer's biography on page 76 of *Impact.* Have them note that the Italian Fascist dictator Mussolini objected to Pirandello's moody studies of human personality. Ask what kind of writing such a dictator would prefer. Would he extol sagas of shining heroes fighting evil foes for the sublime glory of the fatherland? Why would he wish to restrain thoughts of despairing parents crying in a dingy railroad carriage?

PRESENTATION

Ask students if they would be satisfied to read only those war stories in which an admirable hero defeats terrible foes and survives unscathed. Why should we consider other views of war, even views that depress us? Stories that portray the tragic side of war have the power to enlighten and educate readers. Ultimately, these stories may affect peoples' attitudes toward war. Challenge students to make their reading of Pirandello's "War" something more than a depressing experience.

After the reading proceed with the discussion questions and the exercises.

Students will be exposed to several different treatments of war in this anthology. You might discuss the attitudes expressed in the stories by Knight, O'Flaherty, Twain, O'Brien, and Ngugi before completing the study of Pirandello's "War." Do all contain some truth about war? Explain.

CHECKING UP (True/False) — *Page 74*

F 1. The people in this story are being evacuated from Rome during wartime.

F 2. The couple who board the train at the opening of the story have just lost their only son.

T 3. The characters present different points of view about losing sons in warfare.

T 4. The fat man argues that a parent should be comforted by a son's heroic death.

T 5. At the end of the story, the fat man is overwhelmed by grief.

TALKING IT OVER — *Page 74*

1. **What is the *setting* of this story?** The setting is a smoky second-class carriage at the small station of Fabriano, Italy, in wartime. **How does it serve to bring together the different characters?** They must wait for their train to depart, and they have time to exchange views about their sons who have gone to the war.

2. **The major *conflict* in the story is the differing attitudes toward a specific subject. What is the subject of discussion?** The characters are discussing their various attitudes toward the military service of their sons. **What are the different points of view of the characters?** The big woman, as her tiny husband explains, is overcome with grief because their only son has just been called to the front. Another passenger claims they are fortunate because his son has been twice wounded and sent back to the front again. Still another man argues that he has two sons and three nephews at the front and that he loves each son as much as parents love an only child. The fat man says that he is proud and thankful that his son died serving his country.

3. **How does the fat man's description of his son's noble and heroic death affect the woman whose only son has gone to war?** The woman is both stunned and heartened by the man's words. She has spent months wondering why no one can understand her grief; she now realizes that she has not considered the nobility of her son's duty to his country.

4. **The *climax*, or point of greatest intensity, occurs when the woman asks a "silly" question. What does the fat man realize at that moment?** He realizes that his son is gone forever. None of his noble statements about his son's glory can assuage his grief. **How does his reaction to the question suggest that this episode may be a "turning point" in his life?** Answers will vary. Students may suggest that the man is able to have an authentic, emotional reaction to his son's death, instead of posturing for the benefit of onlookers. He may suffer more, but he will gain insight and strength by facing the truth head-on.

5. **Why do you suppose the author did not identify his characters by name?** They are intended to represent all parents whose sons have gone to war. **Is the story's impact heightened or lessened by this anonymity?** It is heightened.

6. Do you think the author has chosen a good title for his story? Give reasons to support your answer. Answers may differ, but many readers will most likely deem the title appropriate. In every war there are parents with strong feelings about their sons' service. At the heart of the anguish caused by war is the loss of loved ones.

UNDERSTANDING THE WORDS IN THE STORY (Matching Columns) *Page 75*

1. plight	**g.** unfortunate condition
2. excessive	**d.** too much
3. paternal	**i.** characteristic of a father
4. console	**a.** comfort or help
5. spurt	**c.** gush forth
6. livid	**j.** grayish or pale
7. stoically	**b.** unflinchingly
8. incongruous	**f.** not fitting
9. distorted	**h.** twisted
10. harrowing	**e.** distressing

WRITING IT DOWN

A Monologue *Page 75*

The writing assignment asks students to take on the persona of a character in the story. Remind them that it might be a challenge to play the role of a character with whom they would not ordinarily agree.

SPEAKING AND LISTENING

Evaluating the Impact of War *Page 75*

This assignment should draw students into a spirited discussion. You may want to organize this as a debate, particularly if current events are relevant. For example, ask the students to evaluate the impact of a specific war or conflict taking place somewhere in the world today. This may help them make a connection between the large, seemingly impersonal issues of war and the personal, devastating loss that occurs among individuals.

HOME

Gwendolyn Brooks

Page 77

INTRODUCING THE SELECTION

Rare are the writers with Gwendolyn Brooks's power of evoking a scene, a time, and a people with just a few words. Her poems and stories involve us as movingly, it seems, as the drama of our own lives.

You might arrange in advance for a student to report on the life and writings of Gwendolyn Brooks, who won the Pulitzer Prize for *Annie Allen* in 1950 and who was chosen as the poet laureate of Illinois in 1968. Your students should be familiar with her poetry from their previous English classes. Some of her best poems have appeared in *The Bean Eaters* (1960) and *In the Mecca* (1968).

As stated in Brooks's biography on page 82 of *Impact,* the short story "Home" is from her novel *Maud Martha,* which tells about a girl growing up in Chicago.

PRESENTATION

Challenge your students to perceive the differences in the reactions of Maud Martha, Helen, and Mama as they face the threat of losing their home. The story is a fine one for oral reading.

Follow the reading with a discussion based on the questions in *Impact.* The strong values of characterization, story problem, and setting will be evident.

CHECKING UP (True/False) *Page 79*

T 1. Maud Martha is unhappy about leaving the old house.

F 2. The family plans to rent out rooms in the house.

F 3. Papa wants to move into a better neighborhood.

F 4. Helen is tired of starting the fire in the house.

T 5. Papa gets an extension on his loan.

TALKING IT OVER *Page 79*

1. In this story we see how the members of a family react to the threat of losing their home. How do Mama and Helen react? What defenses do these characters use against disappointment? They talk as though they expect to move to a better place where Helen can entertain her friends and Mama won't have to fire the furnace. Helen says it will be a relief to move, and Mama says the move might be an act of God. They are trying to pretend they do not care about their old house.

2. How does Maud Martha's reaction differ from the reactions of Mama and Helen? Maud Martha says that she and Harry have been helping with the firing, and that sometimes they have been able to build a little fire in the fireplace. She says, with a touch of impudence, that her mother always says that God knows best. **What are the things she feels she will miss?** She thinks to herself how she will miss her tree and the birds and the sunset.

3. What evidence is there that Maud Martha and Helen value different things? Helen first talks as if she has been ashamed to invite her friends to this old house; later, when she knows the family will not have to move, she plans to give a party so that her friends can "just casually see that we're homeowners." Helen values material things and social success; Maud Martha values everyday aesthetic pleasures and family doings.

4. How does the author heighten suspense at the end of the story? When Papa returns with the news, there is no way to tell from his demeanor whether it is good or bad. The reader is kept waiting, as are the women, while Papa makes his progress down the street.

5. How is the problem the family faces resolved? Papa comes home from the Home Owners' Loan office, says "Hello" to the family, and then goes into the house. Mama follows him in and soon returns with her eyes like "lamps turned on." Papa has been able to secure the loan.

6. If Papa had not been successful, which family member do you think would have taken the blow hardest of all? Explain your answer. Answers will vary. Many students will think that Maud Martha would have taken the news hardest, because of her strong, emotional reactions to sensory details around her and her struggle to keep from crying. Helen and Mama seem to anticipate the changes they view as inevitable, whereas Maud Martha does not. Some students may even say that Papa would have taken the news hardest, because of Maud Martha's outburst about how much he loves the house and how it would kill him to lose it. However, they might sense that perhaps Maud Martha really means to say how much *she* loves the house.

7. Reread the first paragraph of the story. What things about their home are at "the heart of the matter" for Maud Martha and her family? The heart of the matter is not so much the house as the elements of their lives in that place: the garden plants, the soft voices of the women, and the irreplaceable view from the porch. The women realize that the view of the light's particular angle on the iron fence and the poplar tree may soon belong to other eyes. Much of their distress at the thought of leaving comes from never wanting their discussions on the porch to draw to an end. "Home" has come to embody the familiar, repetitious, and comforting events of everyday life within a family.

SKETCH — *Page 80*

1. How do the details in the opening paragraph of "Home" quickly establish a sense of place? The place is presented as the women on the porch see it. Immediately, a reader senses the emotion invested in the place by these women who want "this always to last." The narrator remarks on the quality of the afternoon light as it strikes the poplar tree and the iron fence, and uses specific names for the plants, precisely noting their location on the porch. A phrase such as "friendly door" implies that this home is a welcoming, safe haven.

2. What is the *atmosphere*, or mood, in most of this sketch? Students may respond that the mood is one of wistful melancholy and loss. Others may suggest that the mood is tense, since the women are awaiting an answer.

3. Explain how the subject matter of this sketch makes the scene important and memorable. "Home," the title of the piece, is a word with much more significance than "house." A house is a shelter, whereas a home is a safe haven to which one can always return and a place to build memories with loved ones. The subject of this sketch is one of the most important concerns of any family: their ability to keep their home. When they are threatened with an involuntary move, the family must confront the prospect of having to give up all the things they have loved about their home.

UNDERSTANDING THE WORDS IN THE STORY (Matching Columns) — *Page 80*

1. obstinate	**g.** hard to control
2. emphatic	**i.** striking
3. shafts	**e.** slender rays
4. possessively	**f.** as an owner
5. extension	**j.** additional time
6. flat	**h.** apartment
7. burdens	**c.** troubles
8. suspect	**a.** arousing suspicion
9. staccato	**d.** short and abrupt
10. emerged	**b.** came out

WRITING IT DOWN

A Description — *Page 81*

The suggested writing exercise asks students to take careful note of sensory details. This may help them to think more carefully and avoid generalized, vague abstractions in their writing.

SUCCESS STORY

James Gould Cozzens

Page 83

INTRODUCING THE SELECTION

There is enough truth in "Success Story" to make most readers smile wryly. Students anticipating engineering or business careers should be eager to discuss Richards' formula for success. You and they will need to examine it critically.

Cozzens' knowledge of Cuba, the setting for "Success Story," came partly from a year he spent there as a teacher after leaving Harvard. See his biography on page 91 of *Impact*. Some of his sympathetic fellow writers have claimed that Cozzens' emphasis on conservative social values in his novels of professional people delayed critical recognition of the literary merit of his work. He did, however, receive the Pulitzer Prize in 1948 for *Guard of Honor*. After his *By Love Possessed* (1957) became a best-seller, his earlier novels were reprinted and more widely read and appreciated.

You might ask your students how many of them are considering careers in engineering or in business administration. Ask interested students to define each of these career fields in general terms. Engineering has numerous branches (including civil, mechanical, electrical and electronics, chemical, and aerospace). Business administration is, in general terms, the art of organizing, conducting, and supervising a business organization for profitable service and/or production.

Mention that in Cozzens' story, two young American civil engineers are working in Cuba for a company named Panamerica Steel & Structure. They are quite different from each other in their personalities and skills. Ask students to determine which one is more successful and why.

PRESENTATION

After students have read the story, use the text questions to guide discussion. Obviously, Richards, with his superior knowledge of human nature and psychology, emerges with a higher position in the corporate structure. The narrator, though proud of his engineering knowledge and skill, makes a poor impression on other people, even on Richards, who cheerfully exploits him. There is ironic humor in the outcome of "Success Story."

Readers interested only in the literary experience may want to leave the story at this point. Some students may be interested in carrying their analysis further. Do the successful engineers of students' acquaintance necessarily aspire to upper management levels of their organizations? Aren't there some who really prefer to be practicing engineers? They can make a good living, enjoy a well-earned reputation, and avoid some of the vexations of the rat race. On the other hand, if an engineer does aspire to upper management levels, will he not need to prove himself as a competent engineer on every intervening level? Good human relations contribute to the success of engineers and corporate executives, but obviously so do knowledge and expertise.

Students may show some understandable cynicism in view of media coverage of company politics, ruthless international competition, takeovers, mergers, and bankruptcies. In such operations, an executive like Richards is as likely to lose out as an honest engineer and is less likely to recoup his losses.

CHECKING UP (True/False) *Page 87*

F 1. The narrator and Richards both worked for United Sugar.

T 2. Farrell was construction manager for Panamerica Steel.

F 3. The narrator impressed Prossert with his intelligence and training.

F 4. Prossert easily saw through Richards' bluffing.

T 5. Richards was a poor engineer but a good judge of character.

TALKING IT OVER *Page 87*

1. This story gives us a picture of two young engineers at the start of their careers. How are they different in attitude and ability? The narrator prides himself on his intelligence and knowledge of engineering. He is arrogant, prickly, tactless, and reticent with everyone except engineers. Richards is deficient in engineering skills, but he is clever, humorous, ambitious, ingratiating, and resourceful.

2. Richards claims that he is the "executive type." How does the incident with Prossert demonstrate what he means? He puts on a convincing act as a somewhat bashful engineer who has been working out many problems on his own. He glibly supplies plausible (though fabricated) answers to Prossert's questions and makes a fine impression on the executive, who will certainly remember him as an up-and-coming young man.

3. When the outcome of a situation is the opposite of what we were expecting, we say that it is *ironic*. In what way is the outcome of "Success Story" ironic? Richards is not found out as a fraud; the narrator is not discovered as a worthy engineer. Richards advances; the narrator does not. **Why is Richards a success?** He tells Prossert and probably other people later whatever they want to hear. They think of him as a bright young man and promote him again and again.

4. Consider the author's attitude toward the characters and events in the story. Do you think his attitude is realistic? pessimistic? scornful? Give reasons for your answer. Answers may vary. A possible interpretation is that the author's attitude is all three—realistic, pessimistic, and scornful. He knows that manipulative, unscrupulous, amiable people sometimes succeed more than competent, honest, but uncongenial people. Such a state of affairs makes the author pessimistic about corporations and scornful of the inadequacies of both Richards and the narrator. Even so, the author enjoys the ironic humor of the outcome. We infer the author's attitudes from the characters' words, their actions, and their destinies.

5. In the second paragraph of the story, the narrator says about Richards, ". . . I couldn't then imagine how he had managed to get his job. I have an idea now." What has the narrator figured out? The narrator has discovered that the qualities needed to be a successful executive are not always honesty, talent, and intelligence. Richards probably got his first job using the same attributes that later ensure his success: manipulation, dishonesty, and a pleasant exterior.

THE AUTHOR AND THE NARRATOR *Page 87*

1. The narrator of "Success Story" says about Richards, "I liked him a lot, once I was sure that he wasn't going to outshine me." What does this remark suggest about the narrator's confidence in his ability? He is not confident. Rather, his remark suggests that he is relatively insecure and on guard against any threat posed by a rival.

2. The narrator says to Richards, "Boy, you are undoubtedly the dumbest man in Santa Clara province. If you don't buck up, Farrell will see you never get another job down here." What does this comment reveal about the narrator's attitude toward interacting with other people? The comment reveals that the narrator is judgmental and tactless. He imagines that he is more talented, and that he can readily predict someone's success or failure on the basis of his own standards.

3. Richards' faults are obvious, because the narrator points them out to us. By allowing the narrator to speak and think in a certain way, however, the author indirectly points to the narrator's shortcomings. What are these shortcomings? Answers will vary. Some students may criticize the narrator as conceited, insecure, naive, narrow-minded, and self-righteous.

UNDERSTANDING THE WORDS IN THE STORY (Completion) *Page 88*

1. The children liked to visit the old man because he didn't patronize them or talk down to them.
2. Since Fiona had already been hired for the job, she knew that the next interview was merely a formality.
3. We were scornful of those who disagreed with us.
4. Everyone knew that Allie's father considered all politicians stupid, so it came as no surprise when he pronounced the mayor's speech asinine from beginning to end.
5. Because the director had such a ponderous way of answering questions, everyone tried to avoid asking them.
6. Even though Ronan feared meeting Spaulding's mother, her affable manner set him at ease right away.
7. He was a short, stout man with a hearty appetite.
8. On a weekend jaunt through Michigan, they stopped to visit some friends.
9. Nominally at work on an urban renewal project, Cheever took advantage of the city's numerous movie theaters.
10. Magda hung her poster in such an inconspicuous spot that weeks passed before her family noticed it.

WRITING IT DOWN

A Persuasive Essay *Page 89*

The suggested writing exercise challenges students to formulate a persuasive essay. These writing skills may prove useful outside of the classroom.

A Personal Essay *Page 90*

This writing exercise asks students to apply the events of the story to real life. How will the lessons learned in the story translate into their own attitudes toward jobs and success later in life?

SPEAKING AND LISTENING

A Group Discussion *Page 91*

The speaking and listening exercise asks students to compare and contrast the two main characters in the story. Group discussion should be lively, since both characters are complex enough to have positive and negative attributes.

THE MAN TO SEND RAINCLOUDS

Leslie Marmon Silko **Page 92**

INTRODUCING THE SELECTION

"The Man to Send Rainclouds" is about a meeting of two cultures, that of the Native Americans who live in the Southwest and that of the Christians who live among them. The events surrounding the death of Teofilo, an old sheep herder, prove to be the common ground on which the two cultures meet. The story suggests that the outward trappings of ceremony may be different, but not incompatible.

You might want to point out that, although Leslie Marmon Silko is a Laguna Pueblo, the Native Americans in the story are not specifically identified as Laguna. However, it is likely that Silko is writing about her own people and traditions in this story.

Much in the narrative is stated indirectly. The story implies that Teofilo's death, occurring just when spring returns to renew and nourish the land, brings a promise of rain for the people. Many Native Americans traditionally divide the calendar in two—winter and summer, barren time and growing season. At the end of the long winter, the people await a promise of new life. Paradoxically, the old man's peaceful death brings them hope. The story suggests that death and life are part of the natural cycle. The Native American cultures tend to regard time as circular rather than linear; nature's seasonal, circular return is very much a part of their daily lives.

Water has a strong symbolic importance in the story. The people of both cultures use water in religious ceremonies. Christians use holy water for baptism and purification of sins. The Native American view of water as a means to life and a good harvest is inherently religious. The Pueblo have traditionally held ceremonies throughout the year to summon rain and to make their crops grow. The story reaches its emotional height when the priest sprinkles holy water on Teofilo's grave. This action may be a nominal gesture for the priest, who has not performed the Last Rites, but to Teofilo's friends and family it brings the promise of thunderclouds.

Leslie Marmon Silko grew up on a Laguna Pueblo Reservation in New Mexico. As a child, she heard the songs and stories of her ancestors. Several of the story-poems and stories in her collection *Storyteller,* from which "The Man to Send Rainclouds" is taken, are recountings of traditional tales told to her by her Aunt Susie and other relatives. These stories do not always have a clearly defined beginning, middle, and end. They sometimes end unexpectedly, or make self-conscious connections with the present and with real people. These stories often explain oddities of the landscape and the relationships between people and animals.

When she reads her work aloud, Silko can turn her poetry and stories into songs or chants, bringing the oral tradition fully alive. As she tells her stories, she may modulate her voice to interject explanations for the listener unschooled in Laguna myths, or she may descend into a low, sing-song chant to convey a character's grief. She has said, however, that her duty is not to preserve the oral tradition in a vacuum. Stories forgotten by their people, she has said, should be allowed to vanish quietly.

PRESENTATION

It may take you more than one class period to discuss "The Man to Send Rainclouds." Refer to the prereading question to get the discussion off the ground. How have students been affected by cultures other than their own? There may be a broad mix of different cultures in your school and community. How do they interact? What does each culture contribute to the others? What are some ways in which students can be exposed to other cultures?

You might want to organize a classroom display or a series of presentations on Native American culture. Before reading, ask students to discuss briefly what they already know about Native Americans. Following their reading of the selection, students could present oral reports on aspects of Native American culture. You may want to limit their study to the Laguna Pueblo or to Indians from the Southwestern states. After students have done some research, you can spark a discussion by asking the following questions: In general, how do Native Americans respond to nature? the weather? What is their relationship to the land? their ancestors? animals? What rituals do they observe in their day-to-day lives?

"The Man to Send Rainclouds" concerns the meeting of two cultures, but it is also about the human response to nature and natural events. Ask students to consider how people are affected by their environment—particularly farmers, fishermen, loggers, and others who rely on nature for their livelihood. Then ask them how they perceive the natural world. How does the climate they live in affect their lives? Students may remember an outing being postponed because of rain, or a day of sledding abandoned because of insufficient snowfall. Some students may be familiar with snow, whereas others may have had to contend with floods or even hurricanes. If you have time, you may want to direct students to a creative activity that helps them focus on the climate and environment in which they live. This might take the form of an observational sketch about their neighborhood, a poem about the weather, or an artistic rendering of a landscape.

CHECKING UP (True/False) *Page 97*

T 1. Teofilo had been herding sheep before he died.

F 2. Leon and Ken wrapped Teofilo's body in an old sheet.

T 3. Leon and Ken wanted holy water for Teofilo's grave.

F 4. The priest offered to sprinkle holy water on the grave.

T 5. The neighbors and clanspeople came to comfort Teofilo's family and leave food on the table.

TALKING IT OVER *Page 97*

1. The season of the year in which a story takes place is sometimes an important part of the story's *setting*. At what time of year does "The Man to Send Rainclouds" take place? The story takes place in early spring. **How is the season important to the story?** Spring is traditionally a time of renewal and rebirth; it is then that rain begins to nourish new growth. Teofilo's death is symbolic of the eternal return of the seasons and a new beginning.

2. To prepare Teofilo's body for burial, Leon and Ken perform a traditional ceremony. Why do they perform this ritual? This traditional ritual is performed in order to ensure a good rainfall. After painting Teofilo's face, Leon and Ken ask him to send them rain clouds.

3. Father Paul tells Leon and Ken that they shouldn't allow Teofilo to stay at the sheep camp alone. Why is their response *ironic*, or the opposite of what we would expect? Leon and Ken use words in a double sense when they answer Father Paul. They leave the priest with the impression that Teofilo is alive, even though they have just discovered his body. **Why do you think they mislead the priest?** Leon and Ken want time to prepare for Teofilo's burial according to their own traditions and rituals.

4. For both the Native American people and the Franciscan priest, water is an important part of the burial ceremony. Why do Leon and Ken change their minds about involving Father Paul? For the Native American culture in arid New Mexico, water represents life and fertility. It is important to Leon and Ken that Father Paul perform the gesture of sprinkling holy water on the grave. They connect the holy water with rain, and they imagine that it will slake Teofilo's thirst.

5. When Father Paul sprinkles the holy water on the grave, it falls "through the light from sundown like August rain. . . ." How does this image *symbolize*, or represent, the events of the story? Leon and Ken hope that Teofilo will become "the man to send rainclouds," ensuring them a good harvest. In this arid landscape, rain may be as sparse as the droplets from the jar of holy water that almost evaporate before reaching the parched earth. The holy water is representative of their peoples' communal hope for rain. It is also a poignant image of the end of a life—the water quickly vanishes under the light from the sunset.

6. What evidence in the story suggests that the Native Americans move in two worlds—the world of the Christian workers and that of their traditional culture? One major example is the wish of the old man's family for both Native American and Christian rituals at Teofilo's burial. Teofilo's family has adopted some Christian practices, such as going to Mass, while maintaining their own traditions. **What does the story suggest lies at "the heart of the matter" for the Native American characters?** The story suggests that these characters place great value on being true to their ancient cultural traditions.

7. What is the narrator's attitude toward these characters and their differing cultures? Do you think the story is told with sympathy for all the characters? Answers will vary. Some will say that the narrator seems more sympathetic toward the Native Americans and somewhat critical of Father Paul. Note, for example, that Teofilo's family is depicted as strong because they live close to their cultural roots. Father Paul, on the other hand, has to remind himself that he is in New Mexico. Although he is shown to be kind and dedicated, he has trouble departing from his usual ways and seems uncomfortable in the dual-culture setting. For example, he sees only "a pile of jackets, gloves, and scarves" when he looks at the Native American people in the graveyard.

UNDERSTANDING THE WORDS IN THE STORY (Completion) *Page 98*

1. A *tarp* is used to
   a. start an engine
   (b.) cover and protect something
   c. decorate a building
2. To *embrace* is to
   a. visit
   b. move
   (c.) hug
3. A *mesa* is a
   (a.) high, flat plateau
   b. heavy downpour
   c. sharp rock
4. A *glossy* magazine is
   a. filled with pictures
   b. large and colorful
   (c.) smooth and shiny
5. A *perverse* trick might be described as
   (a.) improper and contrary
   b. amusing and ingenious
   c. grim and repulsive

WRITING IT DOWN *Page 98*

The writing exercise provides a graphic organizer for students to structure their own personal narratives. The topic, ceremonies, should help them relate the rituals in their own lives to those in the story.

DEAD MEN'S PATH

Chinua Achebe

Page 101

INTRODUCING THE SELECTION

In many of his works, Chinua Achebe focuses on the conflict created by the Europeans' intrusion into African society and consciousness. "Dead Men's Path" is structured around the clash of "modern," Western ideals with traditional African beliefs. However, in this story it is not the outsider who brings trouble, but a native Nigerian, Michael Obi. Obi brings the ethical, religious, and societal values of the modern world to a village still steeped in ancestor worship and traditional beliefs. Achebe makes the point that although the two systems could peaceably coexist, they do not. Michael Obi's "misguided zeal" prevents this from happening. Both of Achebe's stated literary aims, to teach and to satirize, come into play in this story.

The child of a Christian missionary, Achebe faced religious conflict in his own village. Although conflict between ideals never escalated into violence, there were certain differences that had to be contended with. For example, the young Achebe was often forbidden to eat food at the houses of "heathen" villagers, since the food was purportedly prepared for the native gods and idols.

Students may be curious to learn more about Nigeria and the Ibo, or Igbo, people. Situated on the southern coast of western Africa, Nigeria has the largest population of any African state—over one hundred million. A central hub for migration routes between continents, it is now a melting pot of at least 250 ethnic groups. Many citizens speak some English as well as one or two other languages. The population is roughly one-half Muslim and one-third Christian. Many Nigerians continue to practice animism, which is a belief in the existence of spirits. In "Dead Men's Path," the villagers practice an animistic religion. They believe that the spirits of ancestors and unborn children still tread the path.

Nigeria became a British colony in 1886. In 1960, it became independent and joined the United Nations. At that time, however, the Ibo people decided to form their own nation of Biafra. They lost a civil war for independence fought during the years 1967–1970 and were eventually reintegrated into Nigerian society. A world map on the wall of your classroom will help students to pinpoint the location of Nigeria and other African nations.

PRESENTATION

One way to draw students into the story is to have them discuss a problem that would affect them as a group. Perhaps there is an upcoming decision affecting the school. If not, you might pose a hypothetical problem for them to solve. Divide the class into two groups and ask each to take a position on the issue. Then have each group draft a list of supporting arguments. Is there a way to compromise and make both groups happy, or are the two positions incompatible? The prereading question is another way to get students thinking about divisive issues that have affected them in the past. After a brief discussion, have students read the story in class or at home. How do they feel about the earlier classroom debate? Does the outcome of the story change their stance at all?

Some students may have difficulty relating to the unfamiliar setting of the story. Remind them that although the details of the issue may be unusual, "the heart of the matter" is the same as it would be anywhere. Ask them to cite instances, including their own debates and discussion, in which ideals came into conflict. Writing It Down and Speaking and Listening should help draw students into the scene at the Ndume School. Direct students to the exercise on page 106, which asks them to compare this story with "The Man to Send Rainclouds" (page 92), another story that concerns a conflict between cultures.

CHECKING UP (Short Answer) *Page 104*

1. What does Michael Obi hope to accomplish as headmaster of Ndume Central School? He hopes to bring modern ideals and high teaching standards to a "backward school," as well as to beautify the school compound.

2. What news comes as a disappointment to his wife? She learns that she will not have the companionship of other wives, since all of Obi's colleagues are young and unmarried.

3. Why is Obi anxious to close the path right away? Obi knows that the Government Education Officer is coming to inspect the school in one week.

4. What event causes the villagers to seek revenge? A woman's death in childbirth causes the villagers to seek revenge.

5. How do the villagers take revenge? The villagers destroy all the hedges, trample the flowerbeds, and tear down one of the school buildings.

TALKING IT OVER *Page 105*

1. What is Michael Obi's attitude toward the beliefs of the villagers? He considers the villagers' beliefs backward and primitive, and he refuses to take their traditions seriously.

2. In the discussion between Obi and the village priest, which of the two shows more tolerance for the other's beliefs? The village priest shows more tolerance for the beliefs of others. **What is the meaning of the proverb the priest recites to Obi?** His statement "Let the hawk perch and let the eagle perch" is another way of saying "To each his own." The two powerful birds in the proverb—the hawk and the eagle—represent people with different, strongly held beliefs. By asserting that both birds have a right to perch, the proverb signifies that two people with different opinions can accept each other's right to exist.

3. According to the priest, why is the path important to the life of the village? The villagers believe that the path is a thoroughfare for dead relatives, ancestors, and children coming to be born. It is the bridge between the spirit world and the physical world. **Why is the death of the young woman so significant?** The woman's death is a sign to the villagers that the baby's spirit was barred from coming down the path. They decide to avenge the spirits by undoing some of Michael Obi's modern trappings.

4. A situation is *ironic* when the outcome is the opposite of what was expected. What is ironic about Obi's closing the path with heavy sticks and barbed wire? Obi's barrier is ironic because one of his goals is to beautify the school compound. The sticks and wire are, undoubtedly, very ugly. Moreover, rather than keeping the villagers off the path, the barrier incites them to damage the school property. **In light of Obi's ambitions, why is the conclusion of the story ironic?** Obi hoped to bring enlightenment to a "backward" institution and reap glory for himself. However, he manages only to cause trouble between the villagers and the school.

5. In what sense was the headmaster's zeal "misguided"? Obi is misguided because his zeal does not allow him flexibility. He is so obsessed with rules, regulations, and modernization that he cannot acknowledge the beliefs of others. What seems "backward" to Obi is a fervently held belief by the villagers.

6. Is the main conflict in this story a clash between characters, between generations, or between ideas? Explain. Answers will vary. In some ways, the conflict embraces all three. The character of Michael Obi is responsible for the "tribal-war" situation that begins to develop at the end of the story, and he comes into direct conflict with the priest, who acts as the representative of the villagers. The story is also a conflict between generations. Obi is young and energetic and hopes to bring modern enlightenment to a village steeped in the traditions of its ancestors. Mostly, however, the story is a conflict of ideas. The villagers believe that the ancestors and all others deserve respect; the world of the spirits is eminently real to them. Obi does not grant them the freedom to practice their beliefs, so caught up is he in modern ideas of progress and scientific truth. To Obi, the beliefs of the villagers are merely backward superstitions.

UNDERSTANDING THE WORDS IN THE STORY (Matching Columns) *Page 105*

1. thoroughfare	**g.** public way or passage
2. pivotal	**h.** central; crucial
3. designated	**b.** named; appointed
4. skirting	**f.** passing along the edge of
5. downcast	**j.** sad; depressed
6. cordialities	**i.** friendly warmth
7. detour	**a.** deviation from the direct way
8. rank	**c.** overgrown; coarse
9. zeal	**d.** intense enthusiasm
10. eradicate	**e.** to root out; eliminate

WRITING IT DOWN

A Letter to a Colleague *Page 106*

The suggested writing assignment asks students to think imaginatively as well as to analyze the actions of the main character in the story, Michael Obi. In a similar situation, what might they have done differently?

SPEAKING AND LISTENING

Improvising a Scene *Page 106*

The speaking and listening exercise gives students a chance to explore dramatic skills. They may wish to work in small groups.

Comparing Two Stories *Page 106*

The exercise asks students to compare two stories in *Impact.* Students must look at how the theme of cultural conflict is handled by two different authors, particularly through tone.

THE BRACELET

Yoshiko Uchida

Page 108

INTRODUCING THE SELECTION

Like many others of Japanese descent, Uchida wrote out of her personal recollections of a painful episode in American history. Shortly after Japan bombed Pearl Harbor on December 7, 1941, all Americans of Japanese descent living on the West Coast were ordered to relocate to internment camps. Uchida and her family were among those evacuated from their homes. Government policy did not exclude those Japanese Americans who professed loyalty to the country; they were under suspicion, even if they had led very ordinary lives. In her book *Desert Exile,* Uchida writes:

> The ultimate tragedy of that mistake, I believe, was that our government betrayed not only the Japanese people but all Americans, for in its flagrant violation of our Constitution, it damaged the essence of the democratic beliefs on which this country was founded.

Uchida recounts her evacuation and internment experiences in *Desert Exile.* Many of the events in "The Bracelet" are based on her own experience. You may want to share the following passage, which shows obvious similarities with Ruri's narrative in "The Bracelet":

> Barrack 16 was not a barrack at all, but a long stable raised a few feet off the ground with a broad ramp the horses had used to reach their stalls. Each stall was now numbered and ours was number 40. That the stalls should have been called "apartments" was a euphemism so ludicrous it was comical. When we reached stall number 40, we pushed open the door and looked uneasily into the vacant darkness. The stall was about ten by twenty feet and empty except for three folded army cots lying on the floor. Dust, dirt, and wood shavings covered the linoleum that had been laid over manure-covered boards, the smell of horses hung in the air, and the whitened corpses of many insects still clung to the hastily whitewashed walls. High on either side of our entrance were two small windows which were our only source of daylight. The stall was divided into two sections by Dutch doors worn down by teeth marks, and each stall in the stable was separated from the adjoining one by only rough partitions that stopped a foot short of the sloping roof.

Uchida also writes of her father's penchant for gardening; *Desert Exile* opens with descriptions of the sweetpeas, chrysanthemums, and blackberry bushes that grew behind her childhood home. Ask students to compare the autobiographical passage with the fictional account in "The Bracelet." What details from the original experience has Uchida discarded, elaborated on, or kept the same? How does she modify her language to suit the audience for each selection? You might refer students back to the discussion of fiction on page 5 that accompanies "A Tiger in the House."

After their detainment at the Tanforan stables for several months, Uchida's family was relocated to a camp in Topaz, Utah, a place she dubbed the "city of dust." Uchida wrote of this experience in *Journey to Topaz.* It was there that she witnessed her grandfather's death. A guard who observed him hunting for arrowheads along the perimeter of the camp assumed he was trying to escape, and shot him. Although the internment camps for the Japanese in no way resembled the Nazi death camps of World War II, cruelties were, in fact, visited upon the Japanese Americans detained there. Limits were placed upon freedoms; letters from Uchida's father arrived perforated with holes by the censors, who zealously snipped out all "dangerous" material.

You might ask students to compare "The Bracelet" with Dwight Okita's poem "Executive Order Number 9066." Both pieces of literature are portrayals of children confronting the injustice of wartime events. In addition, students might attempt a creative exercise in connection with these pieces. Ask them to read a news story or watch a broadcast about a current political or wartime situation. Then have them write a short piece personalizing the events or incident captured in the news story. They might want to invent a fictional character who witnesses these events.

PRESENTATION

You should be able to cover "The Bracelet" in one class period. Although the story has a simple structure, the underlying issues are complex. You will want to outline the historical background of "The Bracelet" before or after reading, and give students a chance to discuss the ethical issues that arise.

Students may want to do further research on World War II or on the Japanese American evacuation and resettlement policy. Ask them to discuss the fact that Americans of Italian and German descent were not imprisoned, although the United States was at war with Italy and Germany.

After discussing the issues surrounding the story, you can address the questions about imagery, irony, and plot in Talking It Over (page 113). Ask students how an audience affects an author's tone, method, and language. How, also, does genre influence style? Do students prefer fiction or nonfiction? What are the merits of each?

You can urge students to make connections with "Home," another story in this unit. In both cases, "the heart of the matter" concerns the love and family ties that will remain no matter what becomes of the physical house. Losing one's home can be devastating, and Ruri and her family are not as lucky as the women in Gwendolyn Brooks's story. However, they do come to recognize that their greatest treasures are not material things.

CHECKING UP (Short Answer) *Page 113*

1. How long had Ruri's mother lived in the house? She had lived there for fifteen years.

2. Which family members are leaving with Ruri? Her mother and her sister, Keiko, are leaving with Ruri.

3. Where had Ruri's father been sent? He had already been sent to a prisoner-of-war camp in Montana.

4. Why does Ruri wear the bracelet instead of packing it? She doesn't have any room left in her suitcase, since they have been instructed to bring only what they can carry.

5. Who drives Ruri and her family to the Civil Control Station? A neighbor drives them to the station.

TALKING IT OVER *Page 113*

1. How do Ruri's descriptions of her empty room and the abandoned garden help establish the mood of the story? The descriptions create a melancholy mood. Comparing the house to a "gift box after the nice thing inside was gone" and describing the garden as "shabby and forsaken" remind us that Ruri's time there is over.

2. A *symbol* can be an object or a place that stands for a larger idea. How is the garden a symbol of Ruri's feelings? The garden, in its full bloom, represents the love between members of Ruri's family. Papa used to lavish care on the flowers and give them as gifts to Ruri's mother. Now the empty, neglected garden is representative of the disintegration of their home; Papa has been separated from them and they are losing their home. Like the garden, Ruri feels abandoned.

3. *Irony* is a situation or idea that is the reverse of our expectations. Why is there irony in the message of the sign hanging on the Japanese food store that the family passes? The sign's statement, "We are loyal Americans," calls attention to the blind insensitivity of the evacuation policy. By emphasizing the loyalty of Japanese American citizens and long-time residents, the sign serves as an eloquent commentary on the government's assumption that everyone of Japanese descent must be treated as a potential spy or traitor.

4. Why is Ruri excited at first about living in an apartment? How are her hopes cruelly disappointed? Ruri assumes that the family's "apartment" at Tanforan will be like her music teacher's apartment in a large building in San Francisco. However, the family finds that instead of having an elevator and thick carpeted hallways, their new lodging is in a narrow, dark horse stall located in an ugly barracks.

5. Despite the sadness in this story, Mama manages to console Ruri by reminding her of what things are truly valuable. Why, according to Mama, are physical "things" not necessary for remembering people and places we have loved? The finest treasure is the memories of their friends, their home, and their possessions—rather than any material object. No one can take away the memories that the family members carry in their hearts.

UNDERSTANDING THE WORDS IN THE STORY *Page 114*

Jumble solutions are as follows:

1. eventually 2. interned 3. looming
4. forsaken 5. evacuated

WRITING IT DOWN *Page 114*

The writing exercise asks students to analyze the stories as they relate to the unit's theme. A chart is provided to help students organize their thoughts. They are then asked to write a book review comparing two of the stories in the unit.

The Revolt of the Evil Fairies

Ted Poston **Page 117**

INTRODUCING THE SELECTION

The autobiographical story "The Revolt of the Evil Fairies" is an illuminating portrait of the effects of intraracial prejudice. Students may empathize with the frustrations of the narrator who, though talented and studious, can never fill the role of Prince Charming. The favoritism shown to the light-skinned "yallers" causes readers not only to sympathize with the evil fairies, but to cheer them on as they seek their revenge in the third act. The fact that Leonardius has done nothing to merit the narrator's anger does not diminish our vicarious pleasure at seeing him and the others "dethroned." You may want to ask students to evaluate their emotional response. Who is at fault in the story? Who merits our anger? Students may see how much easier it is to blame those who "come out on top" than to blame the system that fosters such inequality. Note that the dark-skinned blacks have, in retaliation, developed their own degrading, racist term—"yallers"—for the lighter-skinned blacks. Underneath the story's amusing, entertaining tone are bitter truths about injustice.

Students will find that Poston uses terms that are no longer current. Explain that the word *colored* was in widespread use at one time, as was *Negro.* The words that are preferred today are *African American* and *black.*

Ted Poston earned recognition as a reporter while he was working for the *New York Post.* He said that he chose the job by closing his eyes and thrusting a pin at the telephone listings of New York newspapers. As he tells it, the pin struck the *Post,* so he went there the next day to apply for a job. The editors accepted him on the condition that he unearth a front-page story that day. Chance intervened. Poston fell asleep on the subway ride to Harlem and awoke to a dispute between a white man and a group of angry blacks outside the subway car. He soon discovered that the white man was trying to serve notice of a lawsuit against Father Divine, a well-known black preacher. Supporters of Father Divine, known as his "angels," were trying to protect their mentor and to prevent the summons from being served. Poston wrote the story and it was accepted for front-page publication in the *Post* the next day.

PRESENTATION

You can assign "The Revolt of the Evil Fairies" to be read silently in class or at home. Poston's enthusiasm for storytelling and his well-wrought prose should hold almost any student's interest. Ask students to evaluate their response after they read. When did they sense the pace quickening? When was their interest most piqued? You will want to refer them to the discussion of **exposition** and **conflict** on page 122, after covering the questions under Talking It Over.

Call attention to Poston's tone and his use of language in the story. He often uses humor to expose the pretensions and hypocrisy of the people he is writing about. One method is his use of circumlocution. For example, the narrator's statement that he "expired according to specifications" is an overstated, formal way of saying that he "died as he was told." By phrasing his words politely, he avoids a harsh, condemnatory tone. The narrator's words have a stronger impact because he "keeps his cool"—despite his anger at the situation, he does not scream and rail against injustice. He shows that he can laugh at his circumstances, no matter how disheartening they are. Statements such as "I would be leading the forces of darkness and skulking back in the shadows" give the narrator a sense of power—he may be cast as an Evil Fairy, but he will make the most of it. Poston also employs sarcasm. Quiet, cynical phrases such as "the grand dramatic offering" ring hollow under scrutiny. Miss LaPrade may view her play as a grand theatrical spectacle, but we know it to be a pretentious and superficial display. Ask students why humor can sometimes be more effective than a solemn or argumentative tack.

You may consider this an appropriate time to broach the issue of racism with students. Are there any current issues that can be brought to bear upon

Poston's story? In the story, racism occurs not only between whites and blacks but also within the black community. Have students encountered other situations in which someone was discriminated against for a small, subtle difference?

CHECKING UP (True/False) *Page 121*

F 1. Miss LaPrade used the same script each year.

T 2. The narrator made the best grades in his class.

T 3. The narrator's disappointment was shared by his classmates.

F 4. The teachers were unaware of the narrator's resentment.

T 5. The audience thought that the fight was part of the play.

TALKING IT OVER *Page 122*

1. What is the narrator's "personal tragedy"? Although the narrator is an outstanding student and debater and comes from a respected family, he can never be Prince Charming because he is dark-skinned.

2. What do you think the character of Rat Joiner contributes to the story? How does he serve as a contrast to the narrator? Answers will vary. In general, Rat Joiner contributes a realistic, even humorously cynical perspective. He views their situation pragmatically, stating that "If you black, you black." His comment about the narrator's romantic infatuation with Sarah Williams and his pitching in to settle some "old scores" during the fight are humorous and lively.

3. The *climax* of a story is its turning point, or moment of greatest intensity. What is the climax of this story? Explain your answer. The climax of the story begins when the narrator throws a punch at Leonardius, an action that propels the drama on stage into utter chaos. This fight is the story's climax because all the events of the story build up to it. It finally allows the narrator and the other "Evil Fairies" to release the frustration caused by favoritism.

4. How does the narrator prolong the *suspense*, or feeling of tension and excitement, as he describes the third act? The narrator hints that he attacked Leonardius without actually saying so right away. Leading statements such as "and then it happened" (page 120) heighten suspense, since we anticipate the narrator's final revelation.

5. Miss LaPrade refers to the production as a "modern morality play." How could this description apply to the story itself? Answers will vary. The story might be described as a modern morality play because it portrays the divisive effects of racism and discrimination.

6. The *tone* of this story—its overall mood, or atmosphere—is humorous. What examples of humor can you find in the story? Answers will vary. Most students will cite the descriptions of the fight, including Sleeping Beauty "streaking for the wings" and the forces of Good and Evil "locked in combat." Other instances include the narrator's overly formal tone when he describes how he "expired according to specifications." Some subtler, more cynical instances of humor include the narrator's tongue-in-cheek reference to the play as the "grand dramatic offering."

PLOT

Exposition and Conflict *Page 122*

1. Reread the exposition in the first five paragraphs of "The Revolt of the Evil Fairies." Where does the story take place? What event is at the center of the story? Who is telling the story? The story takes place at an elementary school in Hopkinsville, Kentucky, and it centers around the annual school play which is based on the story of Prince Charming and the Sleeping Beauty. The narrator is an adult who relates his childhood experiences at the school.

2. What external conflict does the narrator face? The narrator wants to play the lead role of Prince Charming, but because he is dark-skinned he is always cast as an Evil Fairy. **How does this conflict reflect the larger conflict within the community?** This conflict is related to the broader division in the community between light-skinned blacks, or yallers, who are the elite and have the best jobs, and dark-skinned blacks, who are considered inferior.

3. What internal conflict does the narrator experience? He is struggling with his resentment at being prevented from playing the role of Prince Charming because of his skin color.

UNDERSTANDING THE WORDS IN THE STORY (Multiple-Choice) *Page 123*

1. An *intervening* row is one that is
   a. off to the side
   (b.) between other rows
   c. blocked off

2. Mr. Ed Smith's *garb* refers to his
   (a.) clothing
   b. facial expression
   c. prudent behavior
3. A *scion* of a family is one of the family's
   a. friends
   b. critics
   (c.) descendants
4. If you *rationalize* a situation, you
   (a.) find ways to explain it
   b. reject it
   c. get angry at it
5. If you are a member of the *elite,* you are in
   a. trouble
   (b.) the top rank of society
   c. a dilemma
6. You *declaim* when you
   a. apologize
   b. back down
   (c.) speak eloquently
7. To *purloin* something is to
   a. analyze it
   (b.) steal it
   c. respect it
8. If people behave *tactfully,* they may be said to act
   (a.) diplomatically
   b. outrageously
   c. shyly
9. Leonardius' *impromptu* rapping in the second act was
   a. improper
   (b.) unrehearsed
   c. malicious
10. When the narrator *expired* on stage, he pretended to
    a. catch his breath
    b. fight back
    (c.) die

WRITING IT DOWN

A List of Story Conflicts *Page 124*

The assignment follows the literary element exercise on exposition and conflict. The graphic organizer will help students to distinguish types of external and internal conflict and to recognize these conflicts when they encounter them in their reading. It may also be a good source for beginning their own short stories.

THE DINNER PARTY

Mona Gardner

Page 126

INTRODUCING THE SELECTION

In "The Dinner Party," we have a short short story remarkable for its brevity and impact. The present-tense narration makes us feel that we are on the scene in a spacious dining room in colonial India. The author tells us all we need to know, yet wastes no words.

The dinner guests are arguing this question: How does a woman behave in a crisis? Immediately a real crisis looms—in the form of a deadly but unseen cobra. Suspense mounts. Then both the crisis and the argument are neatly resolved.

Before presenting the story to the students, you will want to look it over for possible obstacles. If vocabulary might impede the reading, write the less familiar words on the chalkboard: *colonial official, attachés, naturalist, veranda, colonel, contracting,* and *rupees.*

If you have a world map on the classroom wall, you might comment that "The Dinner Party" takes place in southern Asia. Ask a student volunteer to point out the modern nations of India, Pakistan, and Bangladesh on the world map. Discuss the fact that most of the densely populated Indian subcontinent was a British colony for nearly a century before gaining independence in 1947. The British officials and army officers and their families who lived in colonial India in the days of the British Empire found problems and hazards as well as advantages in their privileged position. Ask students what they have learned about colonial India from such films as *Gandhi* and *A Passage to India* and from such books as Rudyard Kipling's *Kim* and *The Jungle Books.* Find out if any member of the class can tell more about India from family travel or family acquaintances. Remind students that two other stories that take place in India, "A Tiger in the House" (page 1) and "An

Astrologer's Day" (page 20), can be found in the first unit of this anthology.

PRESENTATION

Build suspense during the preliminary discussion by keeping books closed. Ask any students who have read the story previously not to give away the secret of the danger that threatens the dinner party. Suggest that during the reading of the story students try to imagine themselves in the same terrifying situation. What would they do?

The students' first response to the last line of the story is likely to be delighted horror. You may want to show a picture of the Indian cobra (*Naja naja*) with its spectacle markings and its neck ribs expanded to form a wide hood. These Indian cobras, which are more than five feet long, often enter houses at dusk in search of rats. They kill thousands of people every year. Ask students if they would have been able to sit as quietly as the hostess. Have any of them ever been frightened by a poisonous snake? After a brief discussion, promise that students will have an opportunity later to read more about poisonous snakes or to tell a personal experience. Continue with the questions under Talking It Over and Plot (page 128).

In the midst of a story discussion, students sometimes display astonishing insight. One such possibility is a comment on the "invisible man" at the dinner party—the native boy who hears the hostess' whispered command to bring a bowl of milk. The boy's eyes widen because he comprehends that a cobra is present, but he obeys the hostess despite the danger to himself. Although no one in the story notices or commends the Indian boy's self-control and courage, a perceptive student reader might do so.

At some point in the discussion, students may prolong the argument begun by the colonel and the young girl. Is self-control a matter of one's gender or one's individual character and training? How would members of the class behave if a bumblebee buzzed around the room or a spider dangled on a web from the ceiling?

Use the interest created by discussion of "The Dinner Party" as a stimulus for one of the suggested writing assignments.

CHECKING UP (Multiple-Choice) *Page 127*

1. Which of the following statements would the colonel agree with?
   a. "Women never show courage."
   (b.) "Men show greater self-control than women."
   c. "Men do not experience fear."
2. The naturalist knows that there is a snake in the room because
   a. he sees a strange expression on his hostess' face
   b. the native boy's eyes widen in alarm
   (c.) a bowl of milk is placed on the veranda
3. The naturalist gets everyone to sit still by
   a. warning them about the snake
   (b.) challenging the guests to test their self-control
   c. offering to pay each guest money
4. We can assume that the cobra did not strike Mrs. Wynnes because
   (a.) she kept her body absolutely still
   b. cobras do not attack women
   c. it wasn't hungry

TALKING IT OVER *Page 128*

1. The first sentence of the story tells us that the action takes place in India. Why is this information important to the story? India is one of the countries in which cobras live.

2. The American is identified as a *naturalist*. How does his training as a scientist show itself in his behavior? His training shows itself in his keen observation of the hostess and the native boy. He is the only guest who sees a "strange expression come over the face of the hostess" before she whispers to the boy, whose "eyes widen." When the alert scientist sees the boy place a bowl of milk on the veranda, he realizes it is intended for a snake. The scientist's disciplined mind enables him to act rationally to save the guests from provoking the snake to attack.

3. The colonel believes that men always show greater self-control than women. What do the events of the story show about his belief? The events show that a woman may show great self-control in a dangerous situation. When the cobra crawls across the hostess' foot, she maintains her poise and quietly orders a bowl of milk to draw the cobra away to the veranda.

4. A situation is said to be *ironic* when the outcome of events is the opposite of what is expected or believed to be true. Why is the twist at the end of this story ironic? The host exclaims that the colonel's belief has been proved true: "A man has just shown us an example of perfect control." Ironically, the colonel's belief is disproved by the revelation that a woman has given an example of self-control arguably greater than the man's.

PLOT

Climax and Resolution *Page 128*

1. What is the climax of this story? The story's climax occurs when the cobra emerges from under the table.

2. How is the conflict resolved? The hostess manages to overturn the notion that a man has greater nerve control than a woman. **Do you think that the resolution is a fitting conclusion to the story?** Answers will vary.

UNDERSTANDING THE WORDS IN THE STORY (Multiple-Choice) *Page 129*

1. A *spacious* dining room is
   (a.) large and comfortable
   b. well decorated
   c. huge and impressive
2. The *rafters* of a house are
   a. tiles decorating the walls
   (b.) beams supporting the roof
   c. ceiling fans
3. A *veranda* is
   (a.) an open porch
   b. a screen door
   c. a circular staircase
4. A *spirited* discussion is
   a. an angry quarrel
   (b.) a lively conversation
   c. a seance with a medium
5. An *unfailing* reaction is one that is
   a. unfavorable
   (b.) certain
   c. unfeeling
6. When the muscles of her face *contract,* the hostess
   a. smiles broadly
   b. opens her eyes in alarm
   (c.) draws her brows together
7. When the hostess *summons* the native boy, she
   (a.) orders him to approach
   b. criticizes him
   c. reports him to the police
8. A *commotion* is
   (a.) noisy
   b. quiet
   c. stealthy
9. If the guests who move *forfeit* fifty rupees, they will
   (a.) surrender the money as a penalty
   b. lend the money to the hostess
   c. give the money as a reward to the native boy
10. When the American sees the cobra *emerge,* the snake
    a. rises up to strike
    (b.) becomes visible
    c. weaves across the room

WRITING IT DOWN

An Incident for a Story Plot *Page 130*

Have students use the chart on page 130 to plan the plot of a story. Encourage them to examine their own lives for incidents that might lend themselves to a good story and to expand on one of them.

A Dialogue *Page 131*

Asking students to write a dialogue about an imaginary scene helps them imagine what happens to the characters after the story ends. Because "The Dinner Party" ends with such an ironic punch, students may have already started to imagine the colonel's reaction. You might ask them to adapt their scenes for dramatic performances.

STOLEN DAY

Sherwood Anderson

Page 132

INTRODUCING THE SELECTION

Sherwood Anderson's story of a small boy who steals a day from school to go fishing evokes reminiscences and daydreams. Who has not played truant at least once? Who wouldn't like to steal a day away from the rigors of school or work? As the small boy in Anderson's story discovers, the stolen day has its complications, dismaying to him and amusing to readers.

One day in 1912 Sherwood Anderson himself decided he had had enough of his duties as a paint manufacturer in Elyria, Ohio. He left his office and dropped out of sight for four days. When he was found in Cleveland, unkempt and distraught, he said he wanted to devote his life to writing, not business. Although he had to return to business to support himself, he continued to write and eventually sold enough fiction to devote all of his time to a literary career. Anderson wrote several novels, but he is admired most for his autobiographical sketches and his short stories, which influenced such writers as William Faulkner and Ernest Hemingway to explore the psychological depths of ordinary small-town people.

PRESENTATION

If you are planning to follow this story with the writing assignment on page 138 of *Impact,* you might mention it to students before they read "Stolen Day." Perhaps their stolen day will turn out more successfully than the small boy's.

Reading the story should be an easy and pleasant experience for most students. Continue with the discussion questions and exercises. When your class discusses the flashback in "Stolen Day," you might suggest a use for flashbacks in students' stories. The pleasures of their stolen day might be heightened by a flashback to the episode that prompted the theft.

CHECKING UP

(Putting Events in Order) *Page 136*

The narrator sees Walter fishing at the pond.
The narrator's legs and back begin to hurt.
The narrator begins to cry during recess.
The narrator's mother sends him upstairs to bed.
The narrator gets his fishing pole and heads for the pool.
The narrator gets a bite on his line.
The narrator wrestles with the fish.
Mother puts the big carp in the washtub.
The narrator's father asks him why he left school.
The narrator tells his family that he has inflammatory rheumatism.

TALKING IT OVER

Page 137

1. **This story is told by an adult who remembers an episode in his childhood. He opens the narrative by saying, "It must be that all children are actors." How do the events of the story show this to have been true in his own case?** The boy imitates Walter by convincing himself that his legs and back hurt so that he can be excused from school. Although the boy rallies from his imagined illness enough to go fishing and catch a big carp, he continues to fantasize about the way his mother would respond to his death if he succumbed to the illness or drowned in the pool. Even as a hero bringing home his big fish, he still imagines himself as having inflammatory rheumatism and incautiously tells his family so.

2. **How does the narrator convince himself that he has inflammatory rheumatism?** When he sees Walter fishing, he realizes the advantage of having the illness; then his legs and back start aching, too. **What do you suppose is his motivation?** He wants to receive special attention and to be allowed to go fishing instead of attending school.

3. **Why does the narrator become angry at his mother?** He thinks she should have been more concerned about the illness he has imagined himself as having. **What dramatic scene does he imagine as punishment for her?** He imagines how she will act when his drowned body is discovered in the pool.

4. **In what way is the narrator's day "stolen"?** The narrator has stolen the day away from his school responsibilities. In another sense, the glory of his day of catching the big carp is stolen when his family shouts with laughter at the suggestion that he has inflammatory rheumatism.

5. What kind of ache does the narrator have at the end of the story? The narrator is referring to the "ache" of humiliation, since he knows that the family won't let him forget his embarrassing revelation.

PLOT

Flashback *Page 137*

1. What causes the narrator to remember the death of the Wyatt child? The narrator feels that his mother has paid too little attention to him, and he wonders what she would do if he died of his illness and fell into the pool. He is reminded of the Wyatt child who drowned in a spring and who was discovered there by the narrator's mother.

2. How does this memory stimulate him to imagine the effect of his own death? The narrator thinks that his absence would cause great alarm, and that his mother would pick up his body and run home with him as she ran with the Wyatt child. He enjoys imagining how sorry his mother would be for what he considers her neglect of him.

WRITING IT DOWN

An Anecdote *Page 138*

Many students should be able to come up with lively anecdotes to fulfill this writing assignment. Ask them to recall techniques they or others have used to get themselves out of trouble or to achieve their desires. Was the motivation for their "acting" a positive one? You might ask students to share their stories with the class.

WHO'S THERE?

Arthur C. Clarke

Page 139

INTRODUCING THE SELECTION

Clarke's "Who's There?" is a suspenseful story that will appeal to a broad range of readers. The title, the astronaut's predicament, and the flawless imagery are irresistible. Readers identify with the narrator gliding through the abyss of space and share his crescendo of fear of the strange scrabbling noises in his spacesuit. Who is the invader—what alien or ghostly being?

It is interesting to note that this credible story of space adventure, set in the 1980s, was first published in 1958. Such successful prophecies of scientific marvels are not at all unusual in Arthur C. Clarke's fiction and nonfiction. In 1945 he wrote a magazine article titled "Extra-Terrestrial Relays," proposing the construction of communication satellites that could hover in stationary orbit twenty-two thousand miles from the Earth to relay radio and television signals around the world. Twenty years later NASA (the United States National Aeronautics and Space Administration), began building and launching such satellites. Clarke has received world recognition and many honors for his creative insight into the future of space.

Clarke himself marvels at the way "nature imitates art," and he enjoys the friendship and humor of astronauts. Here is a relevant passage from one of his books.

> *2001* was written in an age that now lies beyond one of the Great Divides in human history; we are sundered from it forever by the moment when Neil Armstrong set foot upon the Moon. July 20, 1969 was still half a decade in the future when Stanley Kubrick and I started thinking about the "proverbial good science-fiction movie" (his phrase). Now history and fiction have become inextricably intertwined.
>
> The Apollo astronauts had already seen the film when they left for the Moon. The crew of *Apollo 8,* who at Christmas, 1968, became the first men ever to set eyes upon the Lunar Farside, told me that they had been tempted to radio back the discovery of a large black monolith: alas, discretion prevailed.
>
> And there were later, almost uncanny instances of nature imitating art. Strangest of all was the saga of *Apollo 13* in 1970.
>
> As a good opening, the Command Module, which houses the crew, had been christened *Odyssey.* Just before the explosion of the oxygen tank that caused the mission to be aborted, the crew had been playing

> Richard Strauss' *Zarathustra* theme, now universally identified with the movie. Immediately after the loss of power, Jack Swigert radioed back to Mission Control: "Houston, we've had a problem." The words that Hal used to astronaut Frank Poole on a similar occasion were "Sorry to interrupt the festivities, but we have a problem."
>
> When the report of the *Apollo 13* mission was later published, NASA Administrator Tom Paine sent me a copy, and noted under Swigert's words: "Just as you always said it would be, Arthur." I still get a very strange feeling when I contemplate this whole series of events—almost, indeed, as if I share a certain responsibility.

In a quite positive way, Arthur C. Clarke has always been willing to share "a certain responsibility" for space happenings. Students will be interested in learning how Clarke became a space prophet.

As a boy in Minehead, Somerset, England, Clarke visited Woolworth stores to buy cheap science-fiction magazines that had been shipped across the Atlantic as ballast. He read every word he could find about space science and even built a small telescope to study the moon. He joined an exclusive group named the British Interplanetary Society.

Clarke began his successful writing of science fiction while he was serving as a radar instructor in the Royal Air Force in World War II. In his long and distinguished career he has written fifty books of fiction and nonfiction printed in over thirty languages and sold to more than twenty million readers around the world.

Like Mona Gardner, author of "The Dinner Party," Clarke has an Indian connection. Since the 1950s he has had a home in Colombo, Sri Lanka (formerly Ceylon), now an independent Commonwealth republic. Ask for a volunteer to point out on a world map the large island of Sri Lanka, just off the extreme southeast coast of India. Clarke's *The Coast of Coral* and several other books are based on his experiences as a skin diver and photographer in the Indian Ocean and other oceans.

How can a science-fiction writer living in Sri Lanka communicate with his publishers in New York? Clarke explains in the Acknowledgments for *2010: Odyssey Two,* page 291:

> This book was written on an Archives III microcomputer with WordStar software and sent from Colombo to New York on one five-inch diskette. Last-minute corrections were transmitted through the Padukka Earth Station and the Indian Ocean Intelsat V.

You might ask students how they can keep up with the Space Age and its rapidly growing vocabulary. They will surely recommend wide reading and careful listening, use of context clues, and recourse to an up-to-date dictionary. In reading "Who's There?" they will have the benefits of footnotes, the glossary, and vocabulary exercises.

PRESENTATION

You may need to allow two class periods for the reading of "Who's There?" and related discussion and writing. If you assign "Who's There?" for silent reading in class, you can allow for differences in reading speed by having students proceed to Checking Up and the vocabulary exercise.

When all students have completed the reading, guide discussion with the questions in the anthology and review the vocabulary exercise. A profitable extension of discussion may result from students' interest in space exploration. You might ask students if, like Arthur C. Clarke, they regard the moon landing as "one of the Great Divides in human history." What has been their special experience in the Space Age?

Perhaps students will recall times when they watched television cartoons about space heroes, heroines, and monsters, and played with such space toys as rocket guns, light swords, and transformers. Many students will have played computer space games. Nearly all will mention favorite programs and movies that are frequently shown on television—old favorites such as *Star Trek, Star Wars, 2001: A Space Odyssey, 2010: Odyssey Two, Close Encounters of the Third Kind, E.T., Space, The Right Stuff, Cosmos, Nova,* or the like—as well as current first-run productions.

When you ask students to name their favorite science-fiction authors, they are almost certain to mention the two represented in *Impact*—Clarke and Ray Bradbury (page 203). Students may enjoy drawing up a list of science-fiction conventions. Ask them to find elements that are common to stories, films, and television shows.

If you or your students have visited a space center or attended an actual launching, be sure to share observations and feelings. What are we learning from space shuttle experiments and ongoing satellite probes? Why is peaceful exploration of space important to all people on Earth? What are the possibilities of space-related careers?

To capitalize on the interest created, you may want to check out science-fiction books to students from the library or plan a trip to the library for reports on space. The suggested writing assignments are well worth additional time and effort.

CHECKING UP (Short Answer) *Page 144*

1. Why does the narrator leave the space station? He leaves the station to retrieve a stray satellite.

2. Why doesn't the narrator check the suit's internal lockers? The lockers are used for food and special equipment, and the narrator is going on a short trip.

3. Why is the sun an enemy to those traveling in space? In space, the sun is so bright it can blind a person within seconds.

4. What causes the narrator to yell into the microphone? The narrator is overwhelmed with fear and wants to know if the suit he is wearing once belonged to another astronaut who was killed.

5. What are the doctors busy doing when the narrator regains consciousness? The doctors are playing with three newly born kittens.

TALKING IT OVER *Page 144*

1. The *exposition* of a story gives the reader important background information. Where does the action of this story take place? The action takes place in and near a space station in orbit twenty-thousand miles above the Earth. **What details are used to create a sense of place?** The "Observation Bubble" in which the narrator is working is described as a "glass-domed office that juts out from the axis of the Space Station like the hubcap of a wheel." The construction teams are "performing their slow-motion ballet." The narrator looks down on "the blue-green glory of the full Earth, floating against the raveled star clouds of the Milky Way." Many other details also create a sense of place.

2. Why does the narrator decide that he is the person to retrieve the space traveler? He cannot release anyone else from the closely knit teams building the global communication system. A single day of delay would cost a million dollars.

3. What preparations are necessary for using the spacesuit? After getting inside the spacesuit, the narrator switches on the power and checks the gauges. He uses the acronym FORB to remind himself to check the fuel, oxygen, radio, and batteries. He then seals himself into the suit. **What omission in the narrator's preparations has frightening consequences?** The narrator fails to check the suit's internal lockers because his trip will be brief. Tommy, the ship's cat, has recently given birth to three kittens and secluded them in one of the lockers.

4. What possibilities does the narrator consider and reject in attempting to explain the noise in his spacesuit? The possibilities are a faulty mechanism, insanity, and invasion of the suit by something from space, possibly the ghost of Bernie Summers, the dead astronaut.

5. The action in a story is often built around some kind of *conflict*. What is the major conflict in this story? There seems to be an external conflict between the astronaut and an invader. The major conflict, however, is the internal conflict between the astronaut's reason and his fear.

PLOT

Suspense and Foreshadowing *Page 145*

1. What details in "Who's There?" create suspense? Suspense is created by the mysterious sounds such as "muffled thudding" and "purposeful scrabbling"; by the narrator's instincts flashing alarm signals and his body whirling madly in the harness; and by his increasingly frenzied questions such as "Are you still here, Bernie?" Many other suspenseful details could be cited.

2. At what point in the story did you experience the greatest suspense? Answers will vary. For some readers, this will be the moment when the narrator yells desperately into the microphone.

3. What hints does Clarke use to prepare you for the ending of the story? A cat has recently been acquired by the astronauts. The narrator doesn't bother to check the suit's internal lockers. "An intermittent, muffled thudding" could be small creatures in a weightless environment. The "scraping noise, as of metal upon metal" could be the kittens' nails on the locker walls. Other sounds are also kittenlike: "unmistakable stirrings of life," "purposeful scrabbling," and "scratchings and soft fumblings." The soft pat on the back of the narrator's neck is, of course, a kitten's paw. Despite all these details, Clarke's suspenseful narrative distracts us from the truth.

UNDERSTANDING THE WORDS IN THE STORY (Matching Columns) *Page 145*

1. confirm — g. establish as true
2. plaintively — i. sadly or sorrowfully
3. clambered — e. climbed clumsily

4. gyrated — b. moved in a circular path
5. acceleration — a. an increase in speed
6. reverberate — j. re-echo
7. void — d. total emptiness
8. impending — c. about to happen
9. lunged — f. plunged forward
10. seclusion — h. isolation from others

WRITING IT DOWN

A Critical Review *Page 146*

The suggested writing exercise encourages students to be critical of entertainment and books that they watch and read in their spare time. Instead of taking everything at face value, students may begin to appreciate artistic craft and to recognize when a suspenseful episode of a book, movie, or show is poorly written or executed. This exercise will also encourage them to make connections with art forms other than literature.

SPEAKING AND LISTENING

Focusing on Suspenseful Details *Page 146*

The Speaking and Listening exercise asks students to work in groups and analyze the structure of a movie or television show. By breaking a show's elements down into parts, students may be able to see the series of plot twists and details that contribute to the piece as a whole. Students are asked to make their summaries clear and precise.

THE INTERLOPERS

Saki (H. H. Munro)

Page 148

INTRODUCING THE SELECTION

This famous story resembles a fairy tale in several ways. Like many fairy stories, it has a remote setting, and the coincidence and unexpected events of nature that shape the plot create an atmosphere of mystery. The style of the narrative has an old-fashioned charm, and there is even mention of castles and bands of foresters. You might tell your students that the approach to a story like "The Interlopers" should be different from the approach to a realistic, "true-to-life" story.

Saki is best known for his witty, bizarre short stories, many of which satirize pretentious upper-class English life and which feature stern aunts and precocious children. Well-known examples include "The Open Window" and "The Storyteller." Although this theme is not found in "The Interlopers," the story does contain a literary element Saki used frequently, the ironic twist.

Saki was born in Burma as H. H. Munro and received his education in England. While in his early twenties he returned to Burma and for a year served with the Burmese police. He then left for London, where he began his career as a political satirist. At that time he chose the pseudonym Saki—the name of the cupbearer in *The Rubáiyát* by Omar Khayyám. Saki also wrote novels and plays and a book on Russian history.

PRESENTATION

To prepare your students for "The Interlopers," you might briefly review the meaning of the term *feud* and ask if they can think of any examples of a feud from literature, television, or real life. The best known feud in literature is, of course, between the Montagues and Capulets in Shakespeare's *Romeo and Juliet.* A few students may have heard of the Hatfields and the McCoys, the famous feuding families of American legend.

After the students have read "The Interlopers," you can use the First Response question to open a discussion of the story. Ask your students if they were surprised by the outcome of the story and allow them to tell you how they were expecting the story to end. Have them describe their reactions.

CHECKING UP (Short Answer) *Page 154*

1. What is the reason for the quarrel between Ulrich von Gradwitz and George Znaeym? The quarrel is caused by a property dispute.

2. Why do the enemies hesitate to shoot each other down when they meet? They wait to shoot because it would be improper not to speak first.

3. At what point does Ulrich experience a change of feeling toward his old enemy? He experiences a change in feeling when he begins drinking from his wine-flask.

4. What plans do the men make for resolving their conflict? They will make peace between themselves and their families, they will be guests at each other's castles, and they will hunt together.

5. Who are the interlopers? The interlopers are wolves.

TALKING IT OVER *Page 154*

1. The *exposition* at the opening of the story gives readers important background information. What do you learn about the conflict between the main characters? The conflict is caused by a boundary dispute and has lasted for three generations. The conflict between the main characters has become personal; they wish to take each other's lives.

2. Given the time and place of the story, is the accident in the woods believable? The accident in the woods is believable because the story takes place in the mountains in wintertime.

3. Did you find the sudden change of heart in the two enemies believable? Some students might say that the sudden change of heart is believable—that with death so close, they realize the foolishness of their conflict. Others might argue that since the hatred runs so deep, such a sudden change of heart would be unlikely. **If they had been rescued, would they have remained friends?** Some students will answer yes, that the ordeal has truly changed them. Others may say no, that once they are out of danger they will resume their former ways.

4. Note the number of times the word *interlopers* appears in the story. How does the word become ironic at the end of the story? The interlopers turn out to be wolves.

5. Suppose the story had been called "The Feud." Would that have been as effective a title as "The Interlopers"? No; "The Interlopers" is a more effective title because it emphasizes the story's ironic ending.

PLOT

Coincidence *Page 154*

Have the class point out events in the story that appear to be coincidental. These strangely timed occurrences—the meeting of Ulrich and George in the woods, the breaking of the storm, and the coming of the wolves—actually form the plot of the story. The way these events come together in an almost supernatural way adds to the story's effectiveness.

UNDERSTANDING THE WORDS IN THE STORY (Analogy) *Page 155*

1. joy : sadness :: *languor* :
   - a. happiness
   - b. effort
   - c. weariness
   - (d.) energy
2. eat : devour :: *acquiesce* :
   - (a.) assent
   - b. attack
   - c. assist
   - d. fix
3. thief : steal :: *marauder* :
   - a. villain
   - (b.) raid
   - c. flee
   - d. citizen
4. obstacle : barrier :: *succour* :
   - a. hindrance
   - (b.) relief
   - c. encouragement
   - d. justice
5. mean: cruel :: *pious* :
   - a. angry
   - b. fascinated
   - c. anxious
   - (d.) devout

WRITING IT DOWN

A Radio Play *Page 156*

Adapting "The Interlopers" for stage or screen will allow the students a great deal of freedom to be creative.

GENTLEMAN OF RÍO EN MEDIO

Juan A. A. Sedillo **Page 159**

INTRODUCING THE SELECTION

In "Gentleman of Río en Medio," Juan A. A. Sedillo portrays a memorable Mexican American. Ask Hispanic Americans or Spanish-language students to help with words like *Río en Medio,* "river in the middle"; *buena gente,* "good people"; *sobrinos,* "nephews and nieces"; and *nietos,* "grandchildren." Even though these words are explained by footnotes or context clues, have students share any Spanish they know. Ask students to locate the historic town of Santa Fe, New Mexico, on a map. Share pictures of the town, adobe houses, and the Sangre de Cristo (Blood of Christ) Range. Perhaps students can bring such pictures, or you can borrow them from the library or media center.

Tell students that the story will introduce them to an old gentleman whose ideas may be different from their own. These ideas cause the lawyer-narrator some unusual problems. The selection is short enough to be read aloud and discussed in a single class period.

PRESENTATION

After students have read the story, use the questions on pages 162 and 163 of the anthology to discuss the title character and Sedillo's methods of characterizing him.

You may want to use some of the following questions as guides to further discussion: How do you know that the narrator in the story is a man of honor? What most impresses you about Don Anselmo? In what ways does he deserve the respect of the other people of his village? Does Don Anselmo remind you of anyone you know? If so, why? Has anyone ever planted a tree especially for you? Would this be a good custom for other people to adopt? Why or why not? You have probably heard the saying, "Clothes make the man." In what ways is this saying true or untrue of Don Anselmo?

Ask students how the author, Juan A. A. Sedillo, could write so knowledgeably about a Mexican American. The *Impact* biography (page 165), provides answers. Your students might be interested in discussing nationalities and family traditions represented in their own heritage. How is this cultural diversity beneficial to America?

CHECKING UP (True/False) *Page 162*

F 1. Don Anselmo has no intention of selling his land.

F 2. Don Anselmo demands an outrageous price for his land.

T 3. Good manners are important to Don Anselmo.

F 4. The lawyer tries to cheat Don Anselmo and the Americans who wish to buy his property.

F 5. Don Anselmo is a shrewd and practical businessman.

T 6. Don Anselmo lives in the mountains.

T 7. The children of the village come every day to play under the trees.

F 8. The children of the village are rude to the new owners of the orchard.

F 9. Don Anselmo offers to keep the children of Río en Medio out of the orchard.

F 10. The owners feel they have been tricked by Don Anselmo.

TALKING IT OVER *Page 162*

1. **What details describe Don Anselmo's appearance when he first comes to the office?** Don Anselmo wears a Prince Albert coat, torn gloves, and a hat, and he carries the cane of a worn-out umbrella. **What details describe his behavior?** His behavior is formal and old-fashioned: he bows to everyone, slowly removes his hat and gloves, converses about the weather and his family, and finally discusses business in a gracious and honorable way. **How does his behavior contrast with his appearance?** Although his clothes may be faded and shabby, his manners are impeccable.

2. Look up the word *gentleman* in a dictionary. In *The American Heritage Dictionary* the word *gentleman* is defined as "**1.** A man of gentle or noble birth or superior social position. **2.** A well-mannered and considerate man with high standards of proper behavior. **3.** A man of independent means who does not need to have a wage-paying job."[1] **In what way is this word an accurate description of Don Anselmo's character and manners?** As the patriarch of a family that has lived many hundreds of years on the same land, he is proud, dignified, courteous, generous, and honorable. Although he tills the land and earns little money, he is in all important ways a gentleman.

3. Don Anselmo lives by a code that the Americans find surprising. Why does he refuse to accept more money for his property? He agreed earlier to sell his house and land for twelve hundred dollars, and he feels the offer of a higher price insults his honor. **Why does he believe that he does not own the trees in the orchard?** Each time a descendant has been born, he has planted a tree for the child. He feels that the trees belong to the children, not to him.

4. Despite his new wealth, Don Anselmo is still wearing the same old clothes a month after the sale of his land. What does this reveal about him? Don Anselmo's values go deeper than new clothes or money. He has lived his whole life according to a certain set of values, and he will not change now.

5. Are the descendants of Don Anselmo entitled to the money they receive for the trees? Give reasons for your answer. Legally, the descendants have no claim to the money. However, the American owners of the house and the lawyer know how scrupulously Don Anselmo has kept his code of honor, not accepting more money for his land and not giving away the trees he planted for the children. Some readers will feel that the descendants of Don Anselmo are entitled to the money from the sale of the trees by simple standards of human decency.

1. From entry for "gentleman" from *The American Heritage Dictionary of the English Language,* Third Edition. Copyright © 1992 by Houghton Mifflin Company. Reprinted by permission of ***Houghton Mifflin Company.***

CHARACTER

Direct and Indirect Characterization *Page 163*

Find other passages in the story that reveal the character of Don Anselmo indirectly. In each case, tell what conclusion you have drawn. The explanation and examples of direct and indirect characterization on page 163 of *Impact* will prepare students to find other passages that develop the character of Don Anselmo indirectly. For example, the fifth paragraph of the story (page 160) shows Don Anselmo's actions (bowing his head, standing up, and staring at the lawyer) and his words in response to the offer of more money for his land. Obviously he believes his original contract should be strictly observed. He is a man of honor.

UNDERSTANDING THE WORDS IN THE STORY (Matching Columns) *Page 164*

1. quaint	c. pleasingly old-fashioned
2. kin	e. blood relatives
3. broached	f. mentioned
4. survey	i. determine land boundaries
5. adobe	h. sun-dried brick
6. innumerable	a. without number
7. gnarled	g. knotty and twisted
8. negotiation	j. bargaining
9. preliminary	b. introductory
10. real property	d. land and houses

WRITING IT DOWN

A Character Sketch *Page 164*

Making a character wheel encourages students to move from the general to the specific when developing a rounded fictional character. Students list general personality traits in the spokes of the wheel and then cite specific incidents or clues that illustrate those traits. As a preliminary exercise, you can suggest that they fill out a character wheel for another short story they have read in *Impact*. They may want to try a rough draft of an original short story or character sketch so they have material to work with before completing the character wheel. These pieces can later be revised and polished.

THANK YOU, M'AM

Langston Hughes

Page 166

INTRODUCING THE SELECTION

This well-known story introduces us to a strong, no-nonsense woman who knows exactly what to do with a purse snatcher. Students should have no difficulty reading this plainly written story, and they will find subject matter for lively discussion and debate.

Find out if students have read any of Langston Hughes's prose and poetry in other books. After noting the *Impact* biography on page 172, you might assign an interested student a special report on this versatile American writer.

Born in Joplin, Missouri, Hughes moved with his hard-working mother to several other cities. He graduated from high school in Cleveland, Ohio. Influenced by the work of Carl Sandburg and Vachel Lindsay, he wrote poetry that attracted favorable attention even before he studied at Columbia University in New York City and Lincoln University in Pennsylvania. He worked his way to Africa as a steward on a freighter, and he lived for a time in Paris and Rome; he felt most strongly attracted to New York City's Harlem, which he called "the great dark city." His later travels took him to Japan, Russia, and Haiti, and he served as an American newspaper correspondent during the Spanish Civil War.

The variety of Hughes's work is impressive: poetry, short stories, autobiographies, children's books, African American history and folklore, plays, opera lyrics, translations of Spanish poetry, and newspaper columns. He is renowned not only as an interpreter of African American experience in America but also as an interpreter of human experience everywhere. Students should perceive that a story like "Thank You, M'am" has universal appeal and significance.

Before students read the story, you might ask them if there is much difference in the replies "Yes'm" and "Thank you, m'am." The first is a conventional reply that may sound grudging or mocking. "Thank you, m'am" is a personal response that is likely to be sincere, courteous, and heartfelt. There is a big difference between "breath honor" and true respect.

PRESENTATION

The class can easily read this story aloud and discuss it in a single class period. The questions on pages 170 and 171 will help students focus on the author's skill in portraying the characters realistically. Class discussion sometimes digresses from the story. A student may mention the danger of opposing a street criminal who is armed, ruthless, and possibly crazed by drugs. The question of what an individual and society should do about such a criminal is worth class concern and study. Help students see, however, that the undernourished boy in Hughes's story is so inexperienced in purse snatching that he falls on his back. He is no match for the redoubtable Mrs. Jones. Her methods might work with many a young delinquent.

CHECKING UP

(Putting Events in Order) *Page 169*

The boy snatches the woman's purse.
The woman grabs the boy by his shirt front.
The woman drags the boy up the street.
The woman turns the boy loose.
The boy washes his face.
The boy offers to go to the store.
The woman cooks dinner.
The woman tells the boy about her job in a hotel beauty shop.
The woman gives the boy money to buy a pair of blue suede shoes.
The boy thanks the woman.

TALKING IT OVER *Page 170*

1. Why do you think Mrs. Jones takes Roger home with her instead of calling the police? Answers will vary. Possible answer: She wants to teach him a lesson, but she wants to do so in her own way, combining sternness with kindness.

2. After she releases Roger, Mrs. Jones leaves her door open and the purse on the bed. Why does she do this? She gives Roger a second chance to judge right from wrong. She wants him to make a conscious decision to do the right thing in the face of temptation. **Why doesn't Roger take the purse and run?** Roger wants to be trustworthy. He is beginning to respond positively to Mrs. Jones's influence.

3. How does Mrs. Jones show that she does not want to embarrass Roger or hurt his feelings?

She does not ask him questions about his family or where he lives.

4. Why do you think Mrs. Jones gives Roger the ten dollars? Answers will vary. Possible answer: Mrs. Jones has grown fond of Roger, and she also wants to teach him that it is possible for him to come by the shoes through honest, rather than "devilish," means.

5. What do you think Roger has learned from Mrs. Jones? Answers will vary. Possible answer: He has learned the values of honesty, dignity, kindness, and self-respect.

CHARACTER

Credibility, Consistency, and Motivation — *Page 170*

1. How does Langston Hughes make Mrs. Jones a true-to-life character? Many details could be cited. Her purse is a large one that has "everything in it but hammer and nails." She responds to the outrage of having the purse snatched by kicking the boy and shaking him. She calls him "a lie." She has the impulse to take the neglected boy home and wash his face. As she talks with him, she admits that she is far from perfect; she has done things she wouldn't tell the boy or God "if he didn't already know."

2. While he is in Mrs. Jones's apartment, Roger has an opportunity to steal her purse and run, but he does not do so. Is his behavior consistent? Give reasons for your answer. Yes, his behavior is consistent. Since entering her room, Roger has washed his face, has heard that Mrs. Jones intends to feed him instead of taking him to jail, has confessed that he wanted blue suede shoes, has thought about Mrs. Jones's discussion of right and wrong in her own life, and has seen her lay her purse on the daybed instead of hiding it. He is now feeling better about himself and wants to merit her trust.

3. Why does Mrs. Jones take Roger into her home? Although she disapproved of Roger's attempt to steal her purse, Mrs. Jones can see that he is confused, scared, dirty, and undernourished. When he tells her there is nobody at home to tell him to wash his face, she decides to take him to her own apartment. She remarks, "You ought to be my son. I would teach you right from wrong." **Why does she cook for him and give him money?** She wants to attend to his physical needs and to give him a chance to think about his own conduct. She wants to give him the opportunity to behave himself in the future. **Are her motives believable? Give reasons for your answer.** Answers will vary. As a self-supporting person who has learned much from her life's experiences, she is strong and perceptive enough to be able to help a young person like Roger. She probably has a maternal feeling for the "frail and willow-wild" boy and takes personal satisfaction in befriending him.

WRITING IT DOWN

Notes for a Retelling — *Page 171*

Many students may respond to the writing prompt by suggesting that the incident was a major turning point for Roger. Encourage them to delve into the emotions a neglected boy might feel when confronted with generosity and love. What does the final statement in the story, "And he never saw her again," mean to them in the persona of "Roger"? Remind them that, as Roger, their choice to tell the story to their children must mean that it had some lasting impact. Do they intend to express regret, entertain, or teach a lesson?

SPEAKING AND LISTENING

Relating an Incident — *Page 171*

The speaking and listening assignment builds on the writing exercise by asking students to share their interpretations of Roger as an adult.

ALL THE YEARS OF HER LIFE

Morley Callaghan

Page 173

INTRODUCING THE SELECTION

This short story builds to what James Joyce called an *epiphany*—a sudden moment of revelation. Alfred Higgins, an adolescent, assumes that his mother is a strong person who will always save him from the consequences of his actions. At the end of the story, a sudden glimpse of his mother's "frightened, broken face" reveals that behind her facade of strength she has been exhausted by her trials for "all the years of her life." The move toward a climax of revelation is characteristic of the modern short story. James Joyce, Anton Chekhov, and Katherine Mansfield, among others, have written distinguished examples. "All the Years of Her Life" should prepare students for other stories that focus on moments of insight and revelation rather than on twists of plot.

The Canadian author Morley Callaghan, whose biography appears on page 183 of *Impact,* is noted for unsparingly realistic portrayals of urban people. A theme in his later novels and short stories is Christian love as the answer to social injustice.

You might introduce "All the Years of Her Life" by asking students if it is possible for people to live in the same family in the same house for years without really looking at each other. What kinds of experiences might cause teenagers to observe their parents?

Mention that Alfred Higgins has come to a crisis in his life. How will his parents react? With this question in mind, students should read the story thoughtfully.

PRESENTATION

Following the reading, use the questions in the anthology to stimulate accurate interpretation of the plot and of the characters.

You will probably find that some students are impatient with Alfred Higgins and curious about his future. Although Morley Callaghan has ended the story in a way that is artistically and psychologically appropriate, students may not be satisfied to leave it there. If so, this would be a good opportunity for improvisation and role playing.

Some students may show interest in becoming better acquainted with their own parents after reading "All the Years of Her Life" and other stories of family life in *Impact.*

The following comments by James Squire on "All the Years of Her Life" might be helpful in planning your discussion and evaluating your class's awareness of the subtleties of character in the story. The remarks are based on Mr. Squire's work with students at Technical High School, Oakland, California.

> In this story the behavior of the mother shifts dramatically and is virtually inexplicable until the final paragraph. Initially expected by her son to be enraged by his apprehension for stealing, she is poised, considerate, and well-mannered in securing his release. On reaching the privacy of their home, she turns on him vehemently and bewails his actions, but is later observed by the boy to be in a state of nervous exhaustion—alone, frightened, and "broken"—and it seems to him "that this was the first time he had ever looked upon his mother." Student readers who are willing to withhold final assessment of the mother until the conclusion of the story experience much less difficulty in comprehending this selection than do those who seem certain of her nature following the initial sequence in the drugstore. For example, a boy who reacts to the initial passage with the qualified judgment, "The mother seems pretty nice in here, but you don't know what she will be like when she gets home" is much better prepared for the surprising but consistent shift in her behavior than is a reader who initially pictures her as "just what a mother ought to be." Because their judgments crystallize too soon in reading fiction, readers of the latter type appear unable to follow the logical development of a characterization and hence either misinterpret situations in stories or lose much of the potential value in the experience of responding to fiction.
>
> One characteristic many searchers for certainty seem to share is a fixation on the obvious features of a plot. They insist on completeness and lack of ambiguity in all aspects of the narrative, even in those strands which are unrelated to the central problem of the story. They almost always misinterpret literature which derives its primary value from the experiences and feelings of the characters rather than from the narrative exposition of the plot. Thus

the ending of "All the Years of Her Life" is almost universally condemned by these readers who want to know what happened. Essentially, the story is the expression of a boy's experience in understanding for the first time the real motivations of his mother. Viewed in terms of these purposes, the selection is complete and unified. However, individuals who respond primarily at the narrative level are often distracted from a more profound analysis of the selection by their insistence that even obscure strands of the narrative be completed. Thus they express interest in such questions as: Did Alfred reform? What happened when his father came home? Did his mother "apologize" for talking to him that way? All are questions unrelated to the essential experience the author is trying to convey. Quite possibly, in a regular classroom situation the easiest method of identifying readers who fail to develop an exploratory and tentative approach to weighing evidence is to study those persons who perpetually express an interest in establishing the finality of unimportant strands of the plot.

CHECKING UP (Multiple-Choice) *Page 178*

1. Alfred Higgins has been working for Sam Carr
- **a.** since he left school
- **(b.)** for six months
- **c.** for a few weeks

2. When he is questioned by his employer, Alfred
- **(a.)** at first denies that he has anything in his pockets
- **b.** calls Mr. Carr a liar
- **c.** immediately returns the stolen items

3. Alfred is guilty of
- **a.** robbery
- **b.** burglary
- **(c.)** petty theft

4. From evidence in the story we know that Alfred
- **a.** is bored with his job
- **b.** enjoys getting into trouble
- **(c.)** can't keep a job

5. From Mr. Carr's actions we can conclude that he
- **(a.)** is hesitant to call the police
- **b.** is eager to have Alfred locked up
- **c.** will let Alfred have his job back

6. Alfred expects his mother to
- **(a.)** rush into the drugstore in a rage
- **b.** beg Mr. Carr to give her son another chance
- **c.** urge Mr. Carr to call the police

7. Mrs. Higgins surprises both Alfred and Mr. Carr by
- **(a.)** her calm manner
- **b.** her stern looks
- **c.** the way she is dressed

8. Mrs. Higgins convinces Mr. Carr that
- **a.** she will punish Alfred severely
- **b.** Alfred is innocent
- **(c.)** what Alfred needs is good advice

9. Alfred's reaction to the incident is
- **a.** anger at Mr. Carr
- **(b.)** admiration for his mother's strength
- **c.** shame and guilt

10. At the end of the story, Alfred realizes that his mother is
- **a.** fatally ill
- **b.** filled with self-pity
- **(c.)** broken in spirit

TALKING IT OVER *Page 179*

1. What do we learn about Alfred's life ever since he left school? How does his behavior reveal that he is immature and irresponsible? He has been repeatedly in trouble and has failed to keep a job, even though his parents depend on his earnings. At Mr. Carr's drugstore, he is guilty of petty theft and lying.

2. Why is Mr. Carr reluctant to call the police? Mr. Carr seems to want to help Alfred because he likes him. He wants to talk over the problem with Alfred's father or mother.

3. Alfred is surprised by his mother's behavior in the drugstore. What has he come to expect? He expects that his mother will come rushing in with her eyes blazing. Instead, Mrs. Higgins is calm and dignified.

4. How does Mrs. Higgins win Mr. Carr's respect and confidence? She is friendly and earnest. She reassures Mr. Carr that the best way to handle Alfred is to set him straight with some good advice.

5. At what point in the story does Alfred become aware of the consequences of his actions? As he watches his mother's broken face when she tremblingly pours her tea in the kitchen, Alfred realizes that his irresponsible behavior has made his mother worry about him for a long time.

6. What does Alfred finally realize about his mother? How is he changed by this new understanding? Alfred finally realizes that his mother has grown old loving and caring for him. Alfred realizes that his own youth is over. He must face the future with more maturity and responsibility.

CHARACTER

Static and Dynamic Characters *Page 180*

How does his [Alfred's] understanding of his mother cause Alfred to change? Find the passage that tells you. The last paragraph of the story implies that Alfred's new perception of his mother's long ordeal changes him from a boy to a man.

UNDERSTANDING THE WORDS IN THE STORY (Multiple-Choice) *Page 180*

1. When one speaks *brusquely,* one
   a. hesitates over each word
   b. shouts angrily
   (c.) is blunt to the point of rudeness
2. The person most likely to *bluster* is
   a. an infant
   (b.) a bully
   c. a librarian
3. *Indignation* results from
   (a.) anger at some injustice
   b. jealousy over possessions
   c. rivalry in sports
4. Something that is *blurted out* is
   (a.) spoken before thinking
   b. expressed calmly
   c. whispered brokenly
5. To behave *arrogantly* is to
   a. pay attention to other people's ideas
   (b.) act superior to other people
   c. submit willingly to criticism
6. To *swagger* is to
   a. drink thirstily
   b. stagger along
   (c.) show off
7. One feels *contempt* for someone or something that is
   (a.) despised
   b. far away
   c. precious
8. When one speaks *crisply,* one's words are
   a. harsh and angry
   (b.) short and forceful
   c. gentle and flattering
9. Eyes that *waver*
   a. stare fixedly at an object
   b. grow tearful
   (c.) show indecision
10. The *proprietor* of a store is
    (a.) its owner
    b. a janitor
    c. the salesperson

(Matching Columns) *Page 182*

1. gravely	d. seriously
2. humility	j. modesty
3. falter	e. hesitate
4. composure	c. calmness
5. tolerance	a. respect for others' beliefs
6. assured	i. confident
7. dominant	h. most important
8. repose	g. quietness
9. groping	f. reaching for uncertainly
10. doggedly	b. stubbornly

WRITING IT DOWN

An Opinion *Page 182*

The first writing assignment asks students to analyze the story and its outcome.

A Conversation *Page 182*

The assignment will give students practice in writing dialogue, comparing and contrasting, and imagining familiar characters in new circumstances.

A Comparison *Page 182*

A graphic organizer is provided to help students compare and contrast characters from two different stories. Make sure that students know the difference between a static and a dynamic character. A static character, often a stock character or a stereotype, does not change throughout the course of a story, whereas a dynamic character is fully rounded and capable of change.

THE RIFLES OF THE REGIMENT

Eric Knight

Page 185

INTRODUCING THE SELECTION

Although young Americans are amply supplied with books and movies about World War II, both factual and romanticized, they seldom encounter a war hero as memorable as Colonel Heathergall. At first they may be puzzled by the monocle, which they probably associate with caricatures of society matrons and Nazi generals, but they will soon see that the colonel adjusts it to read maps or to get a better look at Fear. They may be surprised to learn that the colonel is leading a retreat instead of an advance and that he is on speaking terms with Fear. By the end of the story, however, they may agree with his regiment that "Old Glass-eye" deserves to be a legend in his time.

Eric Knight himself, as the text biography (page 193) shows, was a Yorkshire-born Englishman who became a Canadian Army soldier in World War I and a United States Army major in World War II. He was one of the more than fifty million service personnel and civilians of the warring nations who were killed in World War II.

"The Rifles of the Regiment" does not, however, dwell on the carnage of global war. It concerns the plight of one British regiment trapped in France after the evacuation of Dunkirk.

Students may have some knowledge of the Dunkirk crisis from their history books and grandparents' recollections. More than 300,000 Allied troops had been cut off from retreat over land by Nazi breakthroughs to French ports on the English Channel. To rescue the troops and bring them across the Channel, the British sent every available Royal Navy craft, and thousands of civilians manned their own boats while the Royal Air Force provided fighter cover. The heroic evacuation lasted from May 26 until June 4, 1940.

In Knight's story, nearly two weeks after the Dunkirk evacuation, Colonel Heathergall and his regiment are still fighting their way toward the Channel. They are trapped near the fictional town of Ste. Marguerite-en-Vaux.

Before the reading, ask students if they think people who act bravely ever feel afraid. Tell them that Colonel Heathergall is an experienced military leader who has fought bravely in previous wars, but who is now trapped with his men in a perilous situation. What can he do? How does he feel?

Remind students to use the helpful footnotes to interpret British military jargon as they read "The Rifles of the Regiment."

PRESENTATION

After students have completed their reading, use the questions on pages 190–191 of *Impact* to guide discussion of the story, and of the terms *stock characters* and *personification.* Continue with vocabulary study and the writing assignment.

This may be an appropriate time to recommend books for outside reading. Students who have enjoyed *Lassie Come-Home* in novel and movie forms may be interested in Knight's appealing characters, local color, and genial humor. James Herriot, a Yorkshire veterinary surgeon, is another popular author with his true stories, found in *All Creatures Great and Small* and other books.

CHECKING UP (True/False) *Page 190*

F 1. Colonel Heathergall has only one eye.

F 2. The colonel will not permit the regiment to get rid of its equipment.

T 3. The regiment is trapped on a cliff beside the English Channel.

T 4. The men use the rifles to escape from the Germans.

F 5. The British troops are rescued by American soldiers.

TALKING IT OVER *Page 190*

1. How did Colonel Heathergall get the nickname "Old Glass-eye"? His men nicknamed him "Old Glass-eye" because he wears a monocle. **Does this name show the men's affection or disrespect for their leader? Explain your answer.** The name shows their affection since they also say he is a Pukka Sahib (good sir).

2. We are told early in the story that Colonel Heathergall was the "type brought up not to know Fear." Explain what this statement means, using what you know about the colonel's background, education, and military career. Heathergall has been brought up in the tradition of a "bygone day," as he calls it: to keep on trying and never to surrender. He has been brought up to think of Fear as "a cad—you just don't recognize the bounder." He has not met Fear in the World War I battle on the Somme or in his service in India and Palestine. The code may be arrogant and aristocratic, but it is a guiding force in the colonel's career.

3. The colonel insists that the men carry out all their rifles. What does this tell you about his feeling for army tradition? He feels a strong loyalty to military tradition. After battles the regiment leaves its dead behind but never fails to carry all the rifles out as the colonel orders.

4. At what point does the colonel first experience fear? He faces Fear for the first time when he is alone in his cliff-top headquarters above the sea. The regiment is hemmed in by the Germans, who will make their final attack at dawn. **Why do you think the author represents the colonel's inner conflict as a conversation between two characters?** Fear is alien to the colonel's character and upbringing. Making Fear a separate personality dramatizes the conflict between the colonel's customary courage and the unwanted Fear. **How does the colonel master his fear?** He calls Fear a "bloody civilian" and a "slimy brute." He refuses to surrender and asserts that bringing out the rifles is everything. He tells Fear that the regiment is more important than any of the persons in it: the regiment goes on living.

5. How is the colonel's escape solution logical and consistent with his character? He receives with gratitude the news that naval vessels have signaled below the cliff. He ingeniously uses the rifle slings as a chain to descend the cliff and is the last person to go down to the waiting ships, as is customary for an honorable colonel. The rifles have been thrown from the cliff and, even though many are shattered on the beach below, they are taken to the ships with the regiment. Heathergall has caused Fear to flee and he has saved his men and his pride.

6. Why do you think Knight chose the title "The Rifles of the Regiment" for this story instead of naming it for Colonel Heathergall, the hero? Besides becoming an important symbol of duty in the story, the rifles are the ingenious means for the men's escape down the cliff face. In addition, a title that refers to the rifles rather than to the man is consistent with Colonel Heathergall's own philosophy when he stresses that the regiment is "bigger than me—it's bigger than the men." Note that the nickname for the regiment, in fact, is the "Loyal Rifles."

CHARACTER

Stock Characters *Page 190*

1. What details in the story make the colonel's experience of fear vivid and persuasive? He knows that his men are terribly tired from all the marching and fighting they have been forced to do. They have had to jettison all their equipment except for their rifles. They have lost many of their number in repeated battles. The regiment is trapped on a high cliff overlooking the channel, and the Germans who have surrounded them are waiting for daylight before attacking.

2. How does the colonel show his desperation? He thinks the navy will come to rescue the regiment, but he doesn't know how his men can descend the cliff. He thinks of trying to cut south to find a better spot, even though his men are hopelessly outnumbered by the enemy. Notice that Knight twice uses the adverb *desperately* to describe the colonel when he speaks to Fear.

3. What doubts does he express about his abilities as a leader? He wonders if he and his kind are outmoded and incompetent representatives of a "bygone day."

Personification *Page 191*

1. What physical characteristics are given to Fear? Fear has a leprous face, wears damp white robes, and smells of stale sweat.

2. How do these characteristics suggest a nightmarish vision? In the colonel's exhausted and anxious state, he could visualize such a monstrous Fear.

3. How does the personification of Fear make the colonel's experience of terror convincing? Fear's dreadful appearance, his derisive laughter, his insistence that surrender is the only alternative to useless sacrifice of the men, and his attack on the colonel's "well-bred polo-field kind of courage" make the colonel's terror convincing.

UNDERSTANDING THE WORDS IN THE STORY (Jumbles) *Page 192*

Jumble solutions are as follows:

1. incompetent 2. foresight 3. aristocratic
4. arrogant 5. outmoded

FOR WRITING

A Character Analysis *Page 192*

Students should have little difficulty completing the exercise on locating and describing stock characters. As a further assignment, you might ask the students to read their paragraphs aloud in class to see whether they agree or disagree with one another's assessments.

If you wish to extend the discussion of personification, you may have students reread "Appointment in Samarra," which appears in the introduction to *Impact* (page xi). Do they consider personification an effective method of characterization?

CHARLES

Shirley Jackson

Page 194

INTRODUCING THE SELECTION

This short story is emblematic of the delightful stories Shirley Jackson wrote of her family life in the 1950s. She and her husband, the literary critic Stanley Edgar Hyman, needed all their intelligence and humor to bring up their spirited children—Laurie (alias Charles), Jannie, Sally, and Barry. As mentioned in her biography on page 201 of *Impact,* Jackson related the many family misadventures in *Life Among the Savages* and *Raising Demons.* If your students, like many other teenagers, are fond of the television reruns of family shows of the fifties, they may enjoy reading these entertaining books.

Shirley Jackson is even better known for her chilling novels and stories of witchcraft and superstition. In a posthumous edition of her work, her husband comments on its variety:

> People often expressed surprise at the difference between Shirley Jackson's appearance and manner, and the violent and terrifying nature of her fiction. Thus many of the obituaries played up the contrast between a "motherly-looking" woman, gentle and humorous, and that "chillingly horrifying short story 'The Lottery'" and similar works. When Shirley Jackson, who was my wife, published two light-hearted volumes about the spirited doings of our children, *Life Among the Savages* and *Raising Demons,* it seemed to surprise people that the author of her grim and disturbing fiction should be a wife and mother at all, let alone a gay and apparently happy one.
>
> This seems to me to be the most elementary misunderstanding of what a writer is and how a writer works, on the order of expecting Herman Melville to be a big white whale. Shirley Jackson, like many writers, worked in a number of forms and styles, and she exploited each of them as fully as she could. When she wrote a novel about the disintegration of a personality, *The Bird's Nest,* it was fittingly macabre and chilling; when she wrote a funny account of "My Life with R. H. Macy," it was fittingly uproarious. Everything she wrote was written with absolute seriousness and integrity, with all the craft she could muster; nothing was ever careless or dashed off; but she did not believe that serious purpose necessarily required a serious tone.
>
> Shirley Jackson wrote in a variety of forms and styles because she was, like everyone else, a complex human being, confronting the world in many different roles and moods. She tried to express as much of herself as possible in her work, and to express each aspect as fully and purely as possible. While she wanted the fullest self-expression consistent with the limits of literary form, at the same time she wanted the widest possible audience for that self-expression; she wanted, in short, a public, sales, "success." For her entire adult life she regarded herself as a professional writer, one who made a living by the craft of writing, and as she did not see that vocation as incompatible with being a wife and mother, so she did not see her dedication to art as incompatible with producing art in salable forms. In this, as in other respects, she was curiously old-fashioned.
>
> Despite a fair degree of popularity—reviews of her books were generally enthusiastic, reprints and foreign publications

were numerous, and her last two novels, *The Haunting of Hill House* and *We Have Always Lived in the Castle,* became modest best-sellers—Shirley Jackson's work and its nature and purpose have been very little understood. Her fierce visions of dissociation and madness, of alienation and withdrawal, of cruelty and terror, have been taken to be personal, even neurotic, fantasies. Quite the reverse: they are a sensitive and faithful anatomy of our times, fitting symbols for our distressing world of the concentration camp and the Bomb. She was always proud that the Union of South Africa banned "The Lottery," and she felt that *they* at least understood the story.

Old and new generations of readers can profit from Mr. Hyman's thoughtful interpretation of his wife's literary purposes and accomplishments. Shirley Jackson, who "died peacefully of heart failure during a nap in her forty-sixth year," gave us many memorable short stories and twelve books.

PRESENTATION

The first day of school is so important in the lives of many children that they remember it for years. Ask students what they expected when they started kindergarten. What can they now recall about the teacher, the other pupils, and their activities? How did their parents feel about their entering school? Some students may not remember much about their first day and first year in school, but others may be able to tell of their experiences in vivid detail.

If you have already discussed Shirley Jackson's life and writing, you might mention that the story "Charles" tells about the kindergarten experiences of her eldest son, Laurie. Students will need to judge for themselves whether Charles was a bad influence on Laurie.

After reading the story, continue with the discussion questions and exercises. The suggestion for writing on page 201 may lead to further discussion of class members' recollections of "acting" when they were younger—or even recently. Almost everyone has told a "whopper" or acted a convincing role at some time in his or her life. This is excellent subject matter for creative writing.

CHECKING UP (True/False) *Page 198*

T **1.** When he begins attending kindergarten, Laurie becomes bold and disrespectful.

F **2.** Laurie claims that Charles is his best friend in school.

F **3.** According to Laurie, Charles is the teacher's pet.

T **4.** Laurie's parents are eager to meet Charles's mother.

T **5.** The teacher says there is no Charles in the kindergarten.

TALKING IT OVER *Page 199*

1. Laurie tells a great many stories about Charles's behavior in kindergarten. Whose behavior is he describing? Laurie is describing his own behavior. He has invented Charles to impress his family. **Is it likely that all these stories are true?** It is likely, since Laurie's behavior at home is suspiciously similar to that of the fictional Charles. Charles behaves badly, but he doesn't do anything completely outrageous or truly destructive. Still, it is also possible that Laurie has exaggerated for humorous effect. Having invented the irrepressible Charles, Laurie has no restrictions on the levels of badness to which Charles can descend.

2. Why do you suppose Laurie enjoys telling his family stories about Charles? Laurie wants to impress them, and he can see how fascinated they are. He secretly knows how horrified they would be to discover the truth, and he enjoys putting one over on them.

3. At what point in the story did you begin to suspect the true identity of Charles? Answers will vary. The author provides clues from the very beginning that Laurie is playing the role of a "swaggering character." Laurie's behavior at home is far from impeccable, and he takes a devilish pleasure in telling his parents about Charles's misdeeds. When Laurie's mother arrives at the P.T.A. meeting, she looks for Charles's mother in vain. **Why do you suppose Laurie's parents never catch on?** Answers will vary. Laurie's parents are finding it difficult to adjust to his new ways, but they naturally want to think their son is doing well in kindergarten, unlike the notorious Charles. Laurie's parents are new to the world of kindergarteners.

4. Why do you think the author does not move the action to the school until the end of the story? The author does not want to reveal Charles's true identity until the final moment in the story. This intensifies the ironic humor.

5. How does the author create humor in this story? Methods of creating humor include

Laurie's snappy dialogue and evident pleasure in "Charles's" misbehavior, the adults' naiveté, and the surprise ending.

6. In what way is the outcome of this story ironic? Laurie's parents have feared that Charles may be a bad influence on their son. Now they know that Charles is their own son, a bad influence on all the other children.

CHARACTER

Methods of Characterization *Page 199*

1. How does Laurie's style of dress reflect a change in his behavior and attitude? Laurie gives up the clothes of his babyhood—corduroy overalls—and begins to dress in blue jeans with a belt. His entrance into kindergarten makes him feel mature, confident, and independent, and he no longer wants to be mothered.

2. There is a sharp contrast between the way Laurie's mother and father think of him and the way he actually is. How does this contrast serve as a clue to the outcome of the story? Laurie's mother and father obviously dote on him. Even though his behavior is suspiciously rude at times—for example, he ignores and insults his father and pulls a wagonload of mud through the kitchen—his parents never dream that he might not be a model child at school. Insightful readers can sense Laurie's malicious glee in telling stories of Charles to his parents, but Laurie's parents are too naive to see that Laurie is not all sweetness and light. Their naiveté, contrasted with Laurie's deception, sets up the ironic outcome.

3. How is Laurie's behavior strikingly similar to Charles's? Answers may vary, but will include the following: Laurie deliberately uses poor grammar to irritate his parents; he shows bad manners at the table and speaks raucously; he leaves the room while he is being spoken to; he directs rude nonsense rhymes at his father; he pulls a wagonload of mud through the kitchen; and he takes great pleasure in repeating the "bad word" in his father's ear.

UNDERSTANDING THE WORDS IN THE STORY (Matching Columns) *Page 200*

1. renounced — **f.** gave up utterly
2. raucous — **j.** harsh and rough
3. swaggering — **h.** bold and self-important
4. insolently — **g.** disrespectfully
5. deprived of — **b.** denied
6. warily — **a.** cautiously
7. incredulously — **i.** in an unbelieving way
8. cynically — **c.** in a way that shows distrust
9. haggard — **e.** tired
10. primly — **d.** neatly and properly

WRITING IT DOWN

Another Point of View *Page 200*

The suggested exercise asks students to tell the story of Charles from another point of view. Since this story will change dramatically according to who tells it, students will learn how a shift in point of view can change almost every aspect of a story, including plot, structure, and tone.

A Comparison *Page 201*

You may want to refer students to the writing assignment for "Stolen Day" (page 132) in which they were asked to relate a personal experience about "acting" to achieve something or to avoid punishment. This may serve to inform their writing for a comparison-and-contrast essay on the stories "Charles" and "Stolen Day."

A Cartoon *Page 201*

Artistic and creative students will enjoy designing a cartoon strip about the irrepressible Charles.

All Summer in a Day

Ray Bradbury

Page 203

INTRODUCING THE SELECTION

If students have read other stories by the popular American science-fiction writer Ray Bradbury, they will probably look forward to reading "All Summer in a Day." You might comment that this is a story that will especially interest readers who like to imagine otherworldly settings.

Students may be interested in Bradbury's comments on life and writing as recorded in an interview for the Los Angeles Times News Service. Excerpts from the interview, reproduced here, relate an interesting encounter with a creative individual who has inspired many young people.

> Listen to Ray Bradbury tell about a recurring daily experience: "Early in the morning, in a half-awake, half-asleep state before I get out of bed, it often seems like my birthday or the Fourth of July. I'll hear characters talking. They live in a toy box in my imagination. They're usually part of a novel I'm writing, or part of a short story, a play, a poem. They tell me what has happened, and what's going to happen next. Then I rush to the typewriter and pound away as fast as I can."
>
> Speaking in low-pitched urgent tones, projecting a manner of awe, wonder, and boyish enthusiasm, he continues: "Sometimes like a fool I'll stay in bed too long and by the time I get up, the voices are gone, the images have vanished. It's important to rush to the typewriter and get those words on paper quickly."
>
> Pink-cheeked and husky, peering at the world through thick glasses, Bradbury is a fantasist and storyteller whose imagination runs cometlike across the skies. Out of his early morning journeys has come an impressive body of work: more than four hundred published short stories, plus novels, plays, and scripts for motion pictures and television. He has thrilled and chilled millions of readers with *The Martian Chronicles, Fahrenheit 451, The Illustrated Man,* and *Something Wicked This Way Comes.*
>
> Bradbury had his first close encounter with science fiction at the age of eight when he picked up a pulp magazine, *Amazing Stories,* and in terrified fascination read one titled "The World of Giant Ants." He also began collecting and pasting in scrapbooks the comic strip adventures of Tarzan, Buck Rogers, Flash Gordon, Prince Valiant. (Sentimental and retentive by nature, he keeps those comic strip collections to this day.)
>
> He soon grew enchanted with the science fiction of Jules Verne and H. G. Wells, the eerie fantasies of Edgar Allan Poe. After graduating from high school in Los Angeles, Bradbury hawked newspapers on a street corner four hours a day and divided his remaining time between writing stories and reading books.
>
> "I spent almost every night at the main library or branch libraries around town," he said. "My favorite pastime was wandering around in those libraries, just taking books off the shelves and falling in love with them, and sitting around the library and writing stories on those little bits of blank paper they have for reference notes. I was fairly poor, and all those nice little reference notes were there, so I'd write half a short story on those, and then take a stack of them home and type it all up.
>
> "There was something about the library that revved me up constantly. I loved being there. I couldn't afford to buy books. For three years, starting at age nineteen, I made about ten dollars a week by selling newspapers. I had few clothes, no car, and lived at home with my folks. I didn't see it as a terrible hardship because I knew where I wanted to go—I wanted to write. I kept writing, and at twenty-one I sold my first story. Gradually I began to sell more stories, though for years it all went to pulp magazines. Practically all the material in my later books, like *The Martian Chronicles* and *The Illustrated Man,* was first sold to the pulps for from twenty to eighty dollars a story. . . . By 1953, when I was thirty-three, I averaged a hundred and thirty dollars a week."

A turning point occurred that year when film director John Huston hired Bradbury to write the screenplay of *Moby Dick.* Huston's imprimatur, Bradbury said, "amounted to a signal to other producers and directors that I could write scripts for motion pictures and television, and it meant a sudden increase in income." Bradbury wrote a dozen scripts for *Alfred Hitchcock Presents,* and over the years he has occasionally written screenplays in addition to a steady outpour of books, short stories, and poems.

PRESENTATION

If time permits, you might have students read this story aloud. Afterward, guide the discussion of the story and its setting with the questions on page 209 in *Impact.* Let students find examples of Bradbury's sensory imagery.

Help students use images of sight, sound, touch, taste, and smell in their own writing. They will have an opportunity to use imagery in creative writing if you assign the first writing topic on page 211.

You may want to assign the second topic also—a factual essay about the planet Venus. Ray Bradbury's description of the atmosphere of Venus is imaginative, not factual. The surface temperature of the planet is so hot that liquid water could not exist anywhere except possibly right at the poles. Scientists are interested in further exploration of the Venus clouds and surface topography. There have been conjectures that some forms of life might exist somewhere in the atmosphere of our neighbor planet.

The second-brightest natural object (after the moon) in the night sky, Venus is a splendid setting for science and science fiction.

CHECKING UP (Multiple-Choice) *Page 209*

1. The author of this story imagines the planet Venus to be
   a. covered with forests and lakes
   (b.) a wetter place than Earth
   c. pitted with craters
2. The other children in the class resent Margot because she
   a. is the teacher's pet
   b. is a crybaby
   (c.) was born on Earth
3. The events of the story suggest that Margot probably will
   (a.) never adjust to life on Venus
   b. get even with her classmates
   c. make friends with the other children
4. The children lock Margot in the closet
   a. by accident
   (b.) to keep her from seeing the sun
   c. as a game
5. At the end of the story, the children feel
   (a.) ashamed of their behavior
   b. affection for Margot
   c. angry at their teacher

TALKING IT OVER *Page 209*

1. What are the climatic conditions the author imagines to exist on the planet Venus? He imagines constant rain with only two hours of sunshine every seven years. **What places on earth does the planet Venus most closely resemble?** As described by Bradbury, the climate of Venus is probably most like the equatorial rain climates in Africa, the Amazon Basin, and Indonesia. (The greatest amount of rainfall in one year was 905 inches in Cherrapunji, Assam, India, in 1861.) Jungles, hardwood forests, and swamps characterize these regions.

2. Although the story takes place in an alien world, the characters behave much the same way human beings behave on Earth. Why do the children pick on Margot? They pick on her because she is different. **In what ways is she different from them?** She is the only child who was born on Earth, and she is the only one with a real memory of the sun. She is pale and weak, and she will not join in their games. The other children are envious of her future, because her parents are planning to take her back to Earth.

3. Why do you suppose Margot makes no effort to join the children in their games or to respond to their taunts? She hates the rain and lives for the day when she can return to Ohio. Because she has seen the sun, she longs for it more fiercely than do the other children. She knows how dismal the endless rain is by comparison, and she cannot take much pleasure in her life on Venus. She knows that the other children do not understand her.

4. How are the children affected by their first experience of the sun? They run, laugh, stare at the jungle world around them, play games, breathe the fresh air, listen to the silence, and squint at the sun. They are amazed, excited, and happy.

5. Do you think that the children have a better understanding of Margot at the end of the story? Explain your answer. Yes. They are unhappy, pale, and solemn when the rain and lightning and thunder return. When they remember Margot in the closet, they hang their heads and cannot look at each other. They understand for the first time the experience that made her different from them.

SETTING

Background in a Story *Page 210*

Find details in the story that describe the climatic conditions and environment Bradbury imagines to exist on the planet Venus. How does the author make the setting convincing? Students will be able to cite many passages such as this: "the sweet crystal fall of showers and the concussion of storms so heavy they were tidal waves come over the islands" (page 203). There are other images of the rain on pages 204, 207, and 208. These images contrast strongly with Margot's memories of Earth's climate and the children's sensory experiences in their two hours of sunshine on Venus. The imagery makes the setting convincing.

UNDERSTANDING THE WORDS IN THE STORY (Matching Columns) *Page 210*

1. concussion	**h.** violent shaking
2. consequence	**e.** importance
3. muffling	**j.** deadening
4. repercussions	**a.** reflections of sound
5. resilient	**g.** springing back
6. savored	**b.** enjoyed
7. slackening	**c.** slowing down
8. solemn	**f.** serious
9. suspended	**d.** held in position
10. tumultuously	**i.** in a riotous way

FOR WRITING

Notes to Describe a Setting *Page 211*

The writing exercise asks that students carefully observe or visualize details about a real or an imaginary place. This will help teach them about how setting informs the tone and theme of a short story. They can later use this setting as the basis for one of their own stories.

THE SNIPER

Liam O'Flaherty

Page 213

INTRODUCING THE SELECTION

Students who have been waiting for a story with violent action will find it in Liam O'Flaherty's "The Sniper." The author, himself a veteran of the Irish Civil War, renders a Dublin street skirmish with grim naturalism. Readers may or may not be shocked by the ending of the story, a bitter experience known to other civil war soldiers, including Americans.

Refer students to the text biography of O'Flaherty (page 219) to note his service in World War I and the Irish Civil War. Ask students to use a wall map to point out the author's boyhood home, the Aran Islands, lying across the mouth of Galway Bay on the west coast of Ireland. These are the same desolate islands of John Millington Synge's play *Riders to the Sea.* Years later, O'Flaherty, too, portrayed rugged and courageous Irish people like the fisherfolk and farmers of his boyhood islands.

Between wars young O'Flaherty traveled widely, working his way to South America, the United States, Canada, and the Near East. Ask a student to point out Dublin, the Irish capital, on the east coast of Ireland by the Irish Sea. After a bombing incident that caused his arrest in Dublin, O'Flaherty moved to England and began a long and successful career as a novelist and short-story writer.

The impact of "The Sniper" will be greater for those students who do not expect its ending. You will want to be careful not to give any hints that could take away the element of surprise. Before the reading of the story, you might ask why a sniper would be positioned on a roof in a city occupied mainly by the enemy. What kind of person would be an efficient sniper? In a civil war what kind of motivation would make a sniper willing to kill men and women of his own country?

PRESENTATION

Suggest to the students that they visualize the Irish Civil War setting in their own minds as they read the story. Can they imagine themselves in the position of the sniper?

The fast-moving narrative is suitable for silent reading. Let students who complete the reading proceed with Checking Up and Understanding the Words in the Story. After everyone has finished reading the story, use the discussion questions and writing assignments to guide students in their analysis of "The Sniper."

CHECKING UP

(Putting Events in Order) *Page 217*

The sniper eats a sandwich.

The sniper strikes a match.

An armored car advances up the street.

The sniper kills the machine gunner.

The sniper shoots the informer.

The sniper is wounded.

The sniper lets his rifle drop to the street.

The sniper feels remorse.

The sniper crawls down through the skylight.

The sniper turns over the body of his enemy.

TALKING IT OVER *Page 217*

1. In this story O'Flaherty gives us a realistic account of the fighting in the Irish Civil War. What conclusions can you draw about the war from the events in the story? Fighting occurs in isolated pockets throughout the city of Dublin at any given time; O'Flaherty describes the sound of guns as spasmodic. The city is occupied mainly by the enemy, who drive tanks along the streets. Citizens of the same city have turned against each other to defend their ideals. In such a situation, families may be divided in their loyalties, and brothers will wage war on brothers.

2. The sniper is referred to as a *fanatic*. How do his actions show that he is obsessed with a cause? His eyes have a cold gleam, and he is used to looking at death. He has been too excited to eat since breakfast. **How does he show both courage and cunning?** He shows courage by keeping his vigil in an extremely dangerous place. He shows cunning by pretending to die and letting his rifle fall to the street. When the enemy sniper stands up, the protagonist shoots him.

3. What change becomes apparent in the sniper after he succeeds in killing his opponent? He becomes remorseful. **How do you explain this change?** Previously the sniper was in peril of his own life. Now he knows that an enemy soldier has died instead. He is feeling tired, sick from his wound, revolted by the "shattered mass of his dead enemy," and angry at the war.

4. What is the ironic twist at the end of the story? The man he has killed is his brother. **Do you consider this ending a logical outcome of the events? Explain.** Yes, in a civil war neighbors inform on neighbors, and brothers kill brothers.

5. The characters in this story are not identified by name, but by function. The old woman wearing a shawl is referred to as an informer, and the central character is known only as the sniper. What do you think is O'Flaherty's purpose in making his characters anonymous? O'Flaherty's anonymous characters show us that war dehumanizes people, making them working parts of a killing machine. This dehumanization is a universal problem of war. Human values are destroyed in any war.

6. What do the events of the story lead you to conclude about the author's attitude toward war? He views war as brutal and senseless, making victims of all who participate.

SETTING

Verisimilitude *Page 218*

Identify at least five details that establish the historical setting of "The Sniper." The author writes of the heavy guns roaring around the Four Courts, a Republican sniper on a rooftop near O'Connell Bridge, machine guns and rifles breaking the silence throughout Dublin, an armored car advancing up the street, and the spasmodic shooting by Republicans and Free Staters waging civil war. Students may cite additional details of the historical setting.

UNDERSTANDING THE WORDS IN THE STORY (Completion) *Page 219*

1. A person who gives information against others for pay is an informer.
2. To stagger or sway is to reel.
3. Regret for one's past actions is remorse.
4. To deny oneself comforts is to be ascetic.
5. A low protective railing or wall is a parapet.

6. The kick of a gun when it is fired is known as its recoil.
7. To look intently is to peer.
8. To besiege with armed forces is to beleaguer the enemy.
9. An action intended to mislead someone is a ruse.
10. The light in someone's eyes is a gleam.

WRITING IT DOWN

The Setting of a Historic Event *Page 219*

The suggested exercise will give students an opportunity to research and explore a historical event. You may want to encourage artistic presentations to highlight details of setting.

Too Soon a Woman

Dorothy M. Johnson

Page 221

INTRODUCING THE SELECTION

The hardships of pioneer life in the Old West made many an American girl "too soon a woman." In Dorothy M. Johnson's story a runaway girl named Mary insists on joining a destitute family's migration westward. An enigma to the family and to readers at first, Mary turns out to be the kind of pioneer woman who belongs in all American family sagas.

The author, whose biography appears on page 228 of *Impact,* excels in writing about the Native American leaders and the pioneers of the Old West. She has made the characters and the setting of "Too Soon a Woman" true to life. Since she has not specified an exact time and place, readers can choose any year during the westward migration—between about 1870 and 1900—and an expanse of prairie and mountains anywhere west of the Mississippi.

The boy in the story speaks of a grandfather who journeyed west in a Conestoga. By the middle of the nineteenth century, Conestogas were superseded by prairie schooners, or covered wagons. The family in "Too Soon a Woman" is traveling even more humbly, with one horse and a farm wagon. Although the author doesn't say so, Pa and the children are probably moving away from a worn-out farm or logging camp and the grave of a dead wife and mother. Their destination is a "little woods town" where Pa thinks he has an uncle who owns "a little two-bit sawmill." Like millions of other families before and after, they are migrating hopefully westward.

You might ask students if they would like to have lived in the Old West. Why or why not? What challenges and dangers would they have met? What adult responsibilities would they have had to assume in their teens? After a brief discussion, proceed to the reading.

PRESENTATION

"Too Soon a Woman" should stimulate thoughtful discussion and writing. Besides using the questions and exercises in the text, you may find that students are curious enough to explore other aspects of the story.

One interesting possibility is a closer study of the characters. Divide your class into small groups and assign each group one of the following: Pa; the boy narrator; Mary; or the two little girls, Elizabeth and Sarah. The group should look again at the story from the point of view of the assigned character(s) and then retell the story briefly from that point of view, preferably using the first-person pronoun. The students will see that the author has provided enough details for readers to perceive each character's motivations and feelings. Obviously, the point of view of the narrator who looks back on a boyhood experience is best for the author's purpose of gradually revealing Mary's qualities.

A second possibility is a project on the American West, which could be coordinated with one or more departments of your school. Consult the school administration and faculty, and consider involving the PTA and other community groups. The social studies department could assist with reports or research papers on aspects of the westward expansion. The science department could exhibit plants of the prairies and mountains, demonstrating what to eat and what to avoid on the hiking trail. The mathematics department could set up frontier survival simulation games on the computer. The art department could demonstrate pioneer crafts and exhibit art of the Old West. The music department could teach authentic songs of pioneer days, and the physical education department could demonstrate frontier games and dances. The home economics department could exhibit pioneer clothing and food preparation, and the industrial arts department could show pioneer hand tools and construction methods. The library and media center could work with the English, speech, and drama departments on a program featuring literature of and about the Old West. Properly planned and executed, such a project is an enjoyable educational experience with beneficial community involvement. It would combine well with a community festival, pioneer days celebration, living history museum, or other attraction relevant to the Old West theme.

A third possibility is an interview project. Each student should interview an older relative or neighbor who can tell stories of a family migration—the reasons for it, the difficulties and adventures, and the gains or losses. Like the other projects mentioned here, the interview project requires students to improve their communication skills and to use those skills in a rewarding way.

CHECKING UP (Short Answer) *Page 226*

1. Why doesn't Pa want Mary to travel with the family? Pa is reluctant to take Mary because he doesn't have enough food and money for his own family.

2. Why does the group stop at the cabin? The horse is too worn out to pull the wagon up the mountain roads any longer. The cabin provides shelter while Pa goes off to find food.

3. Where does Pa go when he leaves Mary and the children at the cabin? He goes to the town where his Uncle John lives or used to live. He expects to obtain food there.

4. Why does Mary refuse at first to give any of the mushroom to the children? She doesn't know whether it is edible or poisonous.

5. How do you know that Mary stays on with the family? In the final sentence of the story, the narrator reveals that Mary became his stepmother.

TALKING IT OVER *Page 226*

1. Writers often use details of setting to establish an overall *atmosphere* or *mood.* In the first part of this story, up to the point where the travelers come to the old, empty cabin, what mood does the setting create? The mood is somber, almost desperate, as the travelers struggle against hunger and other hardships.

2. Pa makes it clear that he doesn't want to take anyone else along on the trip. Why, then, does he allow Mary to join the family? She stands up to him, saying she will travel with any wagon that will take her, but she would rather go with a family and look after children. She says she "ain't going back." (Some students will read between the lines and say that Pa is a decent and kindly man in spite of his scowl.)

3. How does Mary save the children from starving? She feeds them a large mushroom that she found in the woods; she tests it on herself before giving it to the children.

4. How does Mary show that she is courageous and strong-willed? She chooses to go with Pa and his children instead of staying with people who have beaten her. She takes care of the children, roasts the porcupine, looks for the lost horse that was scared by a bear, and brings back the mushroom. She refuses to let the hungry children touch the mushroom until she is sure that it has not poisoned her. **How does she show that she can be gentle?** She confides in the boy after she eats the mushroom, giving him encouragement and telling him to go to bed. When she is sure the mushroom is safe, she feeds the children and tells them stories.

5. At the end of the story, what change occurs in the family's attitude toward Mary? They accept her, appreciate her, and love her. She becomes Pa's wife and the children's stepmother.

SETTING

Setting and Plot *Page 227*

Find at least five details in the story that give you a sense of what life was like on the frontier. The homesteaders' crops have rotted in the heavy rain. Pa needs venison to feed his family, but he never spots game. Mary roasts the porcupine and cries because of the smoke. The family has to take shelter in a musty old cabin. Pa cannot catch any fish in the creek. He becomes so bitter that he says, "There ain't anything good left in the world, or people to care if you live or die." A bear scares away the horse. The children cry because they are scared and hungry. Many other details could be cited.

UNDERSTANDING THE WORDS IN THE STORY (Matching Columns) *Page 228*

1. anxiety — f. restlessness
2. gaunt — g. thin
3. grim — j. severe
4. whimpered — a. cried softly
5. squalling — c. loud crying
6. scowled — e. frowned
7. savoring — i. enjoying
8. rummaged — h. searched thoroughly
9. sedately — d. calmly
10. gruffly — b. roughly

WRITING IT DOWN

A Sketch of Time and Place *Page 228*

The writing exercise will give students excellent practice in interviewing someone from another generation. Students may already be anxious to learn about their family history, or they may be acquainted with a neighbor who likes to relate stories of the past. One way in which to expand the exercise is to organize a tour of historic landmarks, or design a display of old photographs, maps, and artifacts from your own town. Students can visualize the changes that have occurred in their own area since the turn of the century.

THE WILD DUCK'S NEST

Michael McLaverty **Page 230**

INTRODUCING THE SELECTION

A place like Rathlin Island ought to be part of the experience of every boy and girl. A schoolmaster and writer like Michael McLaverty ought to be there as a guide for each young person. Like Colm in "The Wild Duck's Nest," the boy or girl would feel the excitement and wonder of nature wild and unprofaned.

Your students may want to find Rathlin Island on a detailed map of the British Isles. It lies in the North Channel north of the town of Ballycastle, Antrim County, Northern Ireland. Also note the city of Belfast, some fifty miles south, where the author Michael McLaverty was a secondary school headmaster for many years. Your class may want to search the school library for *National Geographic* articles and other reference sources on Irish life and literature.

After students have become acquainted with Ireland through books, films, and travelogues (or travel), they will understand why there is poetry in the everyday speech of the Irish. Irish-born playwright Bernard Shaw let an Irishman explain to an Englishman in *John Bull's Other Island:* "Your wits can't thicken in that soft moist air . . . . You've no such colors in the sky, no such lure in the distances, no such sadness in the evenings. Oh, the dreaming!"

One way to approach the reading of "The Wild Duck's Nest" is to ask students to open their journals or notebooks and to complete a sentence beginning, "I think _______ is the most beautiful place I have ever seen because _______." Have students read their sentences to the class. Their choices may vary widely from buildings and bridges to parks and landscapes and oceans. Let students share their feelings about these places.

Mention that in McLaverty's story, a young boy has strong feelings about his home island. Ask students to be aware as they read of how Colm responds to the attractions of his outdoor world. Challenge students to enter imaginatively into the story and to use their senses as keenly as Colm uses his.

PRESENTATION

After students have read "The Wild Duck's Nest," use the questions on the pages following the story to guide discussion. Encourage students to read aloud relevant passages of the story as they answer the questions. Let students closely examine several of McLaverty's sentences, paying close attention to their smooth structure, strong verbs, and lively imagery.

If you can spare time for creative writing, let each student develop a paragraph about the place he or she mentioned earlier. Suggest that students include their own actions and sensory impressions.

"The Wild Duck's Nest" might prompt some students to voice their concern for the environment. What can students and teachers do to improve their home community and the school grounds? What conservation measures require political action?

What careers should students consider if they want to protect the natural world and all living creatures, helping them to live in harmony (or at least in balance) with mankind?

Another spinoff of the story may be an interest in further reading of Irish authors. If students have written about their choice of beautiful places, they are sure to like "The Lake Isle of Innisfree" and "The Fiddler of Dooney" by William Butler Yeats.

CHECKING UP (Multiple-Choice) *Page 233*

1. The period of time covered by this story is
   a. a little more than a week
   (b.) approximately twenty-four hours
   c. one afternoon and one evening

2. Colm follows the bird in order to
   a. catch and tame it
   b. rob its nest
   (c.) discover its nesting place

3. Paddy is Colm's
   a. cousin
   b. older brother
   (c.) schoolmate

4. Colm's chief fear is that
   (a.) the bird will desert its nest
   b. Paddy will steal the duck's egg
   c. the rain will destroy the nest

5. Colm is relieved when
   a. the bird moves on the nest
   (b.) he sees a second egg in the nest
   c. the wild duck flies off toward the sea

TALKING IT OVER *Page 234*

1. **In the first part of the story, we get a sense that Colm lives in harmony with nature. Which details express his delight in the beauty and wonder of nature?** He watches the sunset and is reminded of a painting of the Transfiguration. When the wind rumbles in his ears, he shouts exultantly. He skims the lake with flat stones and listens to the echoes of his happy shouts. Many other details express Colm's harmony with nature.

2. **Colm is unusually sensitive to the natural world. Why, then, does he pursue the wild duck and lift its egg from the nest?** He wants to discover the location of the nest. Momentarily he feels that he owns the nest; he has found it.

3. **You have seen that in some stories the central conflict is internal. Although Colm comes into brief conflict with Paddy, the more important conflict in this story is the psychological conflict within Colm. Explain why he is torn by guilt.** Colm feels guilty and anxious because he fears that the wild duck will forsake the nest now that he has touched the egg.

4. **How is Colm's conflict resolved at the end of the story?** He discovers that the wild duck has not forsaken the nest; in fact, she has laid a second egg there.

5. **Do you think Colm will visit the nest again? Give reasons for your answer.** Students' answers will vary. Some will say that Colm will visit the nest again, at a respectful distance, because of his interest in the duck and her brood.

SETTING

Setting and Character *Page 234*

How does the setting reflect Colm's inner conflict on the following day? Find descriptive details that mirror his sadness and concern. The rain that dribbles down the school windowpanes fills his mind "with thoughts of the lake creased and chilled by wind: the nest sodden and black with wetness; and the egg cold as a cave stone" (page 232). Colm shivers and fidgets and can hardly wait to see the nest again.

UNDERSTANDING THE WORDS IN THE STORY (Multiple-Choice) *Page 235*

1. The members of the winning soccer team walked *jauntily* onto the bus.
   a. carefully
   b. boldly
   (c.) cheerfully

2. Zeke was *exultant* when the Muskrats won the championship.
   a. disappointed
   b. understanding
   (c.) joyful

3. The students walked *languidly* into the classroom that hot Friday in June.
   a. sadly
   b. quickly
   (c.) lazily

4. Not convinced that the trip was a good idea, Yetta boarded the bus *reluctantly.*
   (a.) unwillingly
   b. slowly
   c. nervously

5. Boots the cat crept *stealthily* toward the unguarded turkey roast.
   a. steadily
   b. slowly
   (c.) slyly
6. His mind elsewhere, Carlo nibbled *indifferently* at the food on his plate.
   a. hungrily
   (b.) without interest
   c. slowly
7. Percy *meandered* through the mall, trying to kill time.
   a. moved slowly
   (b.) wandered aimlessly
   c. walked quickly
8. The toddler *peered* around the corner before taking cookies from the table.
   (a.) looked searchingly
   b. turned carefully
   c. walked on tiptoe
9. To Buchi, the new school building seemed a *maze* of hallways leading nowhere.
   (a.) complicated network
   b. large collection
   c. pleasing arrangement
10. Chuck knew that his muscles *tautened* whenever Rodman went to the foul line.
   (a.) tightened
   b. relaxed
   c. departed

(Matching Columns) *Page 237*

1. clambered	**d.** climbed with difficulty
2. spattered	**g.** spotted
3. matted	**a.** thickly covered
4. forsake	**i.** desert
5. vague	**h.** indefinite
6. vexation	**j.** annoyance
7. wavered	**f.** became unsure
8. sodden	**b.** completely soaked
9. interminably	**e.** endlessly
10. transfixed	**c.** made motionless

WRITING IT DOWN

A Description *Page 237*

A variation on this exercise is to have students leave the classroom for a few minutes. Have them walk outside or sit quietly and observe as much as they can. After they return to the classroom, ask them to write down all the details they remember.

Sensory Images *Page 238*

This writing exercise continues to build on students' observational skills and attention to detail as they begin to flesh out a setting for a short story.

La Puerta

José Antonio Burciaga

Page 240

INTRODUCING THE SELECTION

Even though the chances of winning a national or state lottery are infinitesimal, many people succumb to the illusion that they, among millions of people, will be "chosen by fate." José Antonio Burciaga plays on these fantasies in "La Puerta," but with a new twist—the protagonist, Sinesio, actually wins the *Lotería Nacional* of Mexico. However, winning is not the instantaneous doorway to a beautiful future. Sinesio pays the price in frustration, humiliation, and anger in order to redeem his dream ticket worth one hundred million pesos.

Students may be interested to learn the history of lotteries. The word *lottery* comes from "lot," which was an object used to settle a dispute. Parties would "cast their lots" in the form of a bean, pebble, or other small object, in order to determine ownership of property, for example.

Lotteries are used as a basic form of taxation in the United States and in most countries, including those of Latin America. Although many people consider lotteries objectionable, lotteries can provide a means of raising money for beneficial purposes. New York State, for example, uses forty-five percent of all lottery income to fund educational programs and college scholarships. In Mexico, where "La Puerta" takes place, the lottery provides revenue for education and welfare funds. The Mexican lottery originated in 1770, when King Charles III of Spain established it by royal charter. The odds of winning in Mexico are actually much higher than they are in the United States. A person has a thirty-one percent chance of winning back at least the price of his ticket, a policy known as a "refund prize." Three times a year, there is a drawing for the grand prize, known as El Gordo (the Fat One). Brochures distributed by the young boys who hawked tickets on the streets of Mexico City used to read "Spend Little, Win Plenty!" This is a maxim common to lotteries around the world.

The basic principles of the lottery have not changed in hundreds of years. The premise is simple, requiring no specialized skill or knowledge, and the price of a ticket is relatively low. Alexander Hamilton, the first Secretary of the Treasury, pronounced a lottery successful if it appeared to present "few obstacles between hope and gratification." Opponents have condemned the system's simplicity because it attracts any fool willing to fritter away his or her money. Former President Reagan called lotteries "an undignified means for states to raise revenues." Most often, the victims of the lottery's impossibly high odds are those who need the money most. In Burciaga's story, Sinesio plays the lottery because he and his family need money desperately. His gambling is a constant source of tension between him and his wife.

PRESENTATION

This story is fairly straightforward and can be covered in a single class period. After a silent reading, proceed with the discussion questions and the literary feature on setting and atmosphere, which figure heavily in this story. Point out that a number of other stories in *Impact* are written by Hispanic or Latin American authors: "Three Wise Guys" (page 39), "The No-Guitar Blues" (page 54), "Gentleman of Río en Medio" (page 159), "The Circuit" (page 291), and "Just Lather, That's All" (page 325). How does each author impart the flavor of his or her heritage and locale to the story? How many use Spanish words in the text?

You might begin your discussion by asking students how a million dollars would change their lives. What problems would be solved by such a windfall? What problems could not be solved, such as the conflict between Sinesio and Faustina? You can discuss the morality of lotteries in general—if the funds from the lottery go to support education, does the end justify the means? Should advertising for lotteries be curbed, or at least the facts of the impossible odds be made plain to everyone?

Ask students why they think the story ends where it does. What if Burciaga had gone on to describe Sinesio's redemption of the ticket or his disappointment at arriving too late? What do students think happens directly after the story ends? By leaving the story with no closure, Burciaga calls our attention more to the condition of the hopeful poor in this Mexican community than to the simple plot twist of the winning ticket. The story ends on an ironic note rather than a triumphant one. Sinesio has seen his greatest dream fulfilled, only to be stymied at the last possible moment. Even though Sinesio and Faustina may soon be rich, their troubles are not over.

CHECKING UP (Short Answer) *Page 245*

1. When Sinesio returns from work, why is Faustina angry with him? She accuses him of throwing their money away by wasting it on lottery tickets.

2. What decision does Sinesio make after reading his brother's letter? He decides that he will go to the United States and try to find work there.

3. How does Sinesio learn that a lottery prize has gone unclaimed? On his last trip home from work, he overhears the news in a conversation between two young men on the bus.

4. What has Faustina done with the lottery ticket? She has attached it to the door to keep the rain from coming in.

5. How does Sinesio finally manage to take the ticket downtown? He is afraid to tear the ticket off the window pane, so he breaks the door off its hinges.

TALKING IT OVER *Page 245*

1. What details of the story's setting show that Sinesio and Faustina are poor even though they work very hard? The author describes the "two-room shack" where the couple lives, mentioning the "half tin, half wooden rooftop." He also refers to Sinesio, the story's leading character, as "dog-tired . . . from his job in a mattress sweat shop." Faustina, his wife, is busy ironing shirts for people who can afford such luxuries. **How is the stormy weather an important part of the story?** The stormy weather enhances the gloomy, desperate circumstances under which Sinesio and Faustina live. When the door begins to leak in the heavy rain, Faustina patches the hole with the lottery ticket. Sinesio must tear the door from its hinges and run through the driving rain to catch the bus.

2. What does the author's use of Spanish words and phrases contribute to the story? The use of Spanish adds an authentic flavor to the story, helping the characters and situation to become vivid.

3. Explain how Aurelio's letter prompts an *internal conflict* for Sinesio. Sinesio realizes that leaving for the United States, as Aurelio has done, would be economically advantageous, but he doesn't wish to be separated from his family.

4. Why do you think Burciaga used the title "La Puerta" for this story? The title gives the story a Spanish flavor. "La Puerta" is a central element in the story, both literally and symbolically. **What is the significance of a door for Sinesio and Faustina?** The door is a barrier between their ramshackle dwelling and the flood of water outside. It becomes significant in the story after Faustina pastes the lottery ticket over a leaky hole in the glass. The door becomes disposable when Sinesio tears it off its hinges, letting the rain blow into their home. Money has, quite literally, "opened the door" for the family, though not in the way we expect. The door can be interpreted as a metaphor for the doorway to a new world, riches, and prosperity. It might also be seen as symbolic of the breakdown in Sinesio and Faustina's relationship; their very home is being torn apart over a lottery ticket.

5. Why do you think the story ends where it does? Why didn't Burciaga tell us whether or not Sinesio succeeded in claiming his prize? Answers will vary. Some students may suggest that the focus of the story is on Sinesio's uphill struggle to achieve his dream, rather than on the dream's actual fulfillment. This emphasis would explain why the author stops short of portraying Sinesio claiming his prize. Encourage students to support their opinions.

SETTING

Setting and Mood *Page 245*

1. What mood is established by the setting of "La Puerta"? The setting establishes a mood of anxiety, depression, and restlessness. The residents of the *colonia* are so poor that survival is a daily struggle. They live in dilapidated surroundings and work at jobs that pay so little that they can barely make ends meet. Escape to the United States as illegal aliens offers one of the few hopes of breaking out of this cycle of misery.

2. How do the details about Sinesio's home and neighborhood contribute to the atmosphere of the story? The atmosphere is one of depression and desperation. The neighborhood roofs are made of tin, wood, and cardboard, and the children play in the rushing waters along the streets. Sinesio's home can barely withstand the elements. His family eats from a table covered with an oily green tablecloth. His wife reminds him that he cannot even afford a mattress from the factory where he works. **How does the weather affect the mood of the story?** The rain noisily beating against Sinesio and Faustina's roof is a constant reminder of their dreary surroundings. It may make Sinesio long for America, where hope lies. In the final scene, the weather rushes into the house after Sinesio tears the door free, leaving Faustina drenched and overwhelmed.

3. How does the stormy weather reflect the relationship between Sinesio and Faustina? The stormy weather reflects the constant conflict between Sinesio and his wife. Faustina resents Sinesio's spending money on lottery tickets, and he resents her disparaging his dreams.

UNDERSTANDING THE WORDS IN THE STORY (Jumbles)

Page 246

Jumble solutions are as follows:

1. abundance **2.** drudgery **3.** blurted
4. emphatic **5.** inevitable

WRITING IT DOWN

A Short Story *Page 247*

The writing exercise in this unit assists students in the writing of original short stories. Students may want to write a descriptive piece on setting before they proceed with the story map.

A Day's Wait

Ernest Hemingway

Page 249

INTRODUCING THE SELECTION

Ernest Hemingway's "A Day's Wait" may leave a reader initially amused at the naiveté of Schatz, who believes his temperature has risen fifty-eight degrees above normal. However, when we realize that the boy has spent the entire day waiting for his own death, we begin to feel compassion. In light of this understanding, the father's trip to hunt quail can be seen as an unwitting abandonment of the boy. By giving his father leave to go out, Schatz has made a generous sacrifice. He does not want to make his father watch him die, nor does he want his father to catch his "fatal" illness.

Hemingway's objective, reportorial style demands that the active, imaginative will of the reader reach beyond the mere surface events of the story. Insightful students will sense Schatz's private grief.

When you refer students to the author's biography on page 254 of *Impact,* you may ask volunteers to look up additional facts about Hemingway's life and influential career. Ask students to locate on a world map some of the places where Hemingway sought adventure and subject matter: Kansas City, Missouri, where he wrote for the Kansas City *Star* after leaving his hometown, Oak Park, Illinois; Italy, where he drove an ambulance during World War I; Paris, France, where he served as a *Toronto Star* correspondent and shared literary aspirations with such other Americans as Gertrude Stein, F. Scott Fitzgerald, and Ezra Pound; Africa, where he hunted for big game, as recounted in *The Green Hills of Africa*; Cuba, where he fished for marlin and gathered lore for *The Old Man and the Sea*; Spain, where he supported the Loyalists in the Spanish Civil War and found the inspiration to write *For Whom the Bell Tolls*; China, where he reported on the Japanese invasion; London, England, where he served as a foreign correspondent in World War II; and Ketchum, Idaho, where he spent the last year of his life.

Students will notice for themselves the clarity and vigor of Hemingway's style. The eminent English writer J. B. Priestley praises this style in *Literature and Western Man*:

> It has been the most richly rewarded style in modern literature. Its virtues are many and remarkable; it makes sense at once to the most casual reader, who enjoys it without knowing that a style is there; the cultivated reader can appreciate its true rhythms, its deliberate economy, its hard masculine accuracy of statement, its immense power of suggestion and evocation, all the more effective because its suggestion of laconic reporting tricks the reader, so to speak, into using his imagination. Most of us nowadays are suspicious readers, anxious not to waste sympathy and emotion, but if a narrator, describing happiness or terror or horror, is colder and curter than we think he ought to be, then we release sympathy and emotion. Though its rhythms and deliberately limited vocabulary are based on American speech (with at least a few helpful hints from *Huckleberry Finn*), this style of Hemingway's, arriving at its perfection in *A Farewell to Arms,* does not come out of action and the reporting of action, as a simple reader might imagine, but out of the art of literature and Hemingway's intense single-minded devotion to it over many years. This long-sustained effort, for which he deserves the highest praise, not only made him a writer, but probably saved him as a man from the results of some trauma, some open war wound in his inner life. But sometimes, reading his earlier work, aware of the tension, we feel as if the style were like some magical coat of mail, not keeping its wearer active in the battle but preserving him from the threatened collapse.

While thus acclaiming the hard-earned style, Priestley glimpsed beneath its armor "some trauma, some open war wound" in Hemingway's inner life. Priestley's words, penned not later than 1960, seem remarkably prescient. Hemingway suffered a nervous collapse, was given electroshock treatments at the Mayo Clinic in Rochester, Minnesota, and took his own life with a shotgun in his home in July, 1961.

Without dwelling on the morbid subject of Hemingway's suicide, you might tell students that the apparent hardness of objective writing does not mean that the writer himself is callous and unfeeling. Rather, the writer is trusting readers to respond with appropriate emotion and thought.

PRESENTATION

You should be able to cover "A Day's Wait" in a single class period. A silent reading is suitable for this story. To compensate for differences in reading speed, ask students who finish early to continue with the Checking Up questions. The literary feature on point of view (page 253) will prove helpful, since the misunderstanding in the story and our compassion for the boy hinge on the father's ignorance of his son's plight. Students may want to discuss the nature of misunderstandings and their role in both tragic and comic circumstances. Can they name television shows, books, and movies whose plots rely on miscommunication or misinterpretation?

You may want to design an assignment that asks students to compare Hemingway's spare and objective style with that of other authors in *Impact.* Jim Heynen, the author of "What Happened During the Ice Storm" (Page 265), uses an objective point of view that limits our entry into the minds and emotions of his characters. At the other end of the spectrum, Edgar Allan Poe's frenetic, mad, and unreliable narrator in "The Tell-Tale Heart" (Page 373) allows us few glimpses at any objective reality. You can explain to students how a story's form and function are interdependent. The form the story takes, including the author's style and point of view, will always depend on the story that must be told. In the best stories, we recognize the author's skill in creating the ideal form for the story he or she wants to tell. When writing their own stories, students should feel free to choose the point of view, narrative style, and tone according to the demands of the story.

CHECKING UP (Short Answer) *Page 252*

1. How does the father know that the boy is ill? The boy is shivering, his face is white, and his forehead feels hot.

2. What is the doctor's diagnosis of the boy's illness? The doctor's diagnosis is influenza.

3. How does the father pass the time as he sits in the boy's room? The father reads aloud to the boy.

4. What does the father do when he goes outside for a while? He takes the Irish setter for a walk and goes hunting for quail.

5. Why doesn't the boy let anyone else into the room? He does not want visitors to catch his disease. He believes that his illness is fatal.

TALKING IT OVER *Page 252*

1. Why does the boy assume he is going to die before the day is over? The boy thinks he is going to die because he has overheard the doctor say he has a temperature of one hundred and two degrees. In France, he heard boys say that a temperature of forty-four degrees is fatal. The boy does not realize that the French boys were talking about a measurement in centigrade. On a centigrade thermometer, a normal temperature is about thirty-seven, rather than almost ninety-nine degrees.

2. The story turns on a misunderstanding between the father and the boy. What does the boy mean when he tells the father ". . . you don't have to stay if it's going to bother you"? The boy assumes that his father knows he is going to die. He is generously releasing his father from the duty of remaining with him while he dies, because he knows that it would upset him.

3. How does the boy behave in the face of what he believes to be his own death? Until the end of the story, the boy behaves stoically, refusing to talk about his fear of imminent death. He also refuses to let anyone enter the room so that no one else will catch what he believes to be a fatal disease. **How does the father explain the boy's behavior?** The father assumes that the discomfort of the illness and fever is troubling the boy and that his son is "lightheaded" from the medicine.

4. How would you describe the relationship between the father and his son? The relationship seems close and affectionate. The father calls the boy "Schatz," a term of endearment. **How does each show concern for the other?** The father shows concern for the boy by staying with him and reading to him. The son tells his father, "You don't have to stay in here with me, Papa, if it bothers you."

5. How does the boy's behavior change when he realizes he is not going to die? The boy gradually releases the tight rein he has kept on his emotions, and he cries "very easily at little things that were of no importance." Hemingway suggests that people who face a crisis often hold back their emotions, at least for a while.

POINT OF VIEW

First-Person Point of View *Page 253*

1. The narrator in this story does not have all the facts. At what point in the story do you realize that his point of view is limited? Answers will vary. At certain points the narrator notices that Schatz seems preoccupied, strange, and light-headed. However, the narrator doesn't know the reason behind these symptoms. We realize that there are things about Schatz the narrator does not know; he cannot read the boy's mind. Comments such as "you don't have to stay if it's going to bother you" and "You mustn't get what I have" indicate that Schatz believes there is something more deeply wrong with him than the narrator can impart to us.

2. Imagine that the boy rather than the father is the narrator. How would the story be different? The misunderstanding on which the story turns would not function without the first-person viewpoint of the father, who does not know what the boy is thinking. In general, the use of the father's point of view increases our sympathy for the boy. The father's obvious affection for his son, as well as his incomplete understanding of the situation, evokes the reader's compassion for both him and the boy. This compassion might not be so keenly felt if the boy were telling the story himself. Students may suggest that if the boy were telling his own story he might seem more self-conscious and less stoical than in Hemingway's story. If he were recalling the story as an adult, he might be capable of light self-mockery, and could tell the story as an amusing anecdote. Students may also point out that certain details about the doctor's instructions would have to be omitted, as well as the quail-hunting episode.

UNDERSTANDING THE WORDS IN THE STORY (Analogy) *Page 253*

1. sorrowful : joyful :: detached : _______
   a. separate c. bored
   b. curious (d.) involved
2. removed : took away :: flushed : _______
   (a.) drove out c. pushed in
   b. moved away d. grew dim
3. bounding : leaping :: slithering : _______
   a. crawling c. hissing
   (b.) sliding d. sneaking
4. kin : relatives :: covey : _______
   a. place c. cave
   b. container (d.) group
5. shaking : trembling :: poised : _______
   a. falling (c.) balanced
   b. motioned d. confirmed

WRITING IT DOWN

A Letter *Page 254*

The writing assignment builds on the point-of-view exercise (page 253) by asking students to explore how the story might be altered if told from the boy's point of view. Students will have to decide what details to retain, invent, and alter in order to make the same events authentic from an entirely new standpoint. As a follow-up exercise, ask them to compare the tone of the piece with that of Hemingway's original story. Has the mood shifted?

ZLATEH THE GOAT

Isaac Bashevis Singer **Page 256**

INTRODUCING THE SELECTION

Much of the charm of "Zlateh the Goat" derives from the author's felicitous use of the omniscient point of view. We get to know not only the thoughts and feelings of Reuven's family, especially those of Aaron, but also the trusting and amiable nature of Zlateh herself. Furthermore, we hear the humorous and philosophical comments of the narrator, emphasizing points in the survival story like a good rabbi or minister.

Be sure that your students read the biography on page 264. Singer, a graduate of the Warsaw Rabbinical Seminary, emigrated from Poland before the outbreak of World War II. If your students have been pointing out places associated with authors and their stories on the world map, ask them to find Poland and New York City for Singer.

One way to introduce Singer's story is to ask students what animal, in their opinion, has proved most valuable to human beings. They will probably cite various animals from the honeybee to the whale and will include most of the common domestic animals.

You or someone else will mention goats as being remarkable all-purpose animals, producers of milk, cheese, meat, kid leather, and wool (even cashmere and angora from the breeds so named). Goats need much less grazing space than do cows, and they can be used to keep the grass clipped in a fenced yard. They can be trained to pull carts, and they make attractive pets, though they are a bit bumptious on occasion. What other animal is so versatile?

American colonists often brought their prized goats with them from the Old World. The Dutch, for example, kept goats in and around the settlement of New Amsterdam, later New York City. There used to be a stuffed goat in a drugstore near Columbia University. It bore the inscription "Harlem's Last Goat, 1907."

Such a discussion should prepare the way for Zlateh, the nanny goat owned by Reuven the furrier and his family, who live in a Polish peasant village. Is she too old to be useful? Ask students to find out what happens to faithful Zlateh.

PRESENTATION

After the reading of "Zlateh the Goat," take up the discussion questions, the vocabulary exercise, and selected writing assignments. Take time to enjoy experiences that your students can relate of other engaging animals.

You might share with students the following Associated Press story about animals that participated in a service at the Episcopal Cathedral of St. John the Divine. Students might write a story from the point of view of the owner of one of the animals in attendance.

> Throughout the time of worship in the magnificent, packed cathedral, an unlikely, intermittent sound arose from various places in the congregation—the barking of dogs.
>
> Sometimes, it was the rapid, thin yapping of a poodle, sometimes the deep, commanding thunder of a Great Dane or assorted other canine notes amid the hymns and prayers.
>
> Also, intermingled with the singing of robed choirs and orchestral melodies, there came recorded howls of wolves, lions growling, the calls and twittering of forest birds, the whistling of whales and dolphins.
>
> "All God's creatures, all of the Earth, show forth God's glory," said the Very Rev. James Park Morton, dean of New York's Episcopal Cathedral of St. John the Divine, in a service last Sunday marking the feast day of animal-loving St. Francis of Assisi.
>
> "The strength and mystery of animals, like the rain and forest, make us human," Morton said. "Without animals, our humanity is impoverished. God's glory is diminished. We would not be human without them."
>
> Then as the smoke of incense rose around the white-and-gold altar and dancers ringed it in a swirl of leaps and spins with colored banners waving, the great bronze front doors opened—and in strode the beasts.
>
> A grand, old elephant, with a string of flowers around his neck, lumbered at the head of the strange procession up the long central aisle the length of two football fields.
>
> Among the approximately 7,000 assembled worshippers moved a placid, swaying camel, a sorrel horse, a nervous brown llama, a donkey, multicolored goats, sheep, a turkey, duck, parrot, and boa constrictor.
>
> Out among the congregation, the sporadic barking still broke out from pets brought by their owners, while cats squirmed in people's arms or slept and kids sat big-eyed on parents' shoulders.
>
> Around the glowing altar, the animals formed a circle, standing there as blessings and prayers were spoken.
>
> "We give you thanks most gracious God, for the beauty of earth and sky and sea; for the richness of mountains, plains, and rivers; for the songs of birds and the loveliness of flowers, for the wonder of your animal kingdom."
>
> Momentarily, the jittery llama reared, turning his head about with pointed ears and anxious eyes, but a purple-robed handler calmed him as prayers and music continued and white-clad dancers fluttered in the aisles.
>
> The choir earlier sang the Canticle of the Sun, with phrasings taken from St. Francis, the twelfth-century friar who cherished wild life as well as people, preached to birds and made friends with "brother wolf."
>
> Amid the singing came recorded hums and cries of nature. Then the people recited that famed, selfless prayer of Francis:
>
> "Lord, make us instruments of your peace.... Grant that we may not so much seek to be consoled as to console; to be understood as to understand; to be loved as to love."

CHECKING UP (Short Answer) *Page 261*

1. What is Reuven's trade? He is a furrier.

2. Why does Reuven decide to sell Zlateh? The winter has been too mild so far for Reuven's business. He needs the money for his family's Hanukkah celebration. Also, Zlateh is old and gives little milk.

3. What does Aaron dream about during the storm? He dreams about warm weather ("green fields, trees covered with blossoms, clear brooks, and singing birds").

4. What decision does Aaron come to in the haystack? He decides he will never part with Zlateh.

5. How does the family celebrate Hanukkah? They eat pancakes, and the children play dreidel.

TALKING IT OVER *Page 261*

1. In what way are Reuven and his family dependent on nature for their livelihood? Reuven's fur business thrives in cold winter weather. If the weather is mild, he has little income.

2. Aaron and the goat almost perish in the snowstorm. How does the storm ironically turn out to be a godsend for the family? Now that the cold weather has arrived, the villagers again need Reuven's services as a furrier.

3. At one point in the story, Singer interprets Zlateh's thoughts: "We must accept all that God gives us." In what way does the story show that all the characters are in God's hands? They are dependent on the weather, on each other, and on fellow creatures like Zlateh. All are God's creations.

4. How are the bonds of the family strengthened by their hardships? After their financial troubles, anxiety about Aaron, and futile search for him, they are happy and thankful to be together for a beautiful Hanukkah celebration.

POINT OF VIEW

Third-Person Omniscient *Page 262*

Find three other passages in the story that demonstrate Singer's use of the omniscient point of view. Below are three passages that students may cite:

It was completely dark, and he did not know whether night had already come or whether it was the darkness of the storm. Thank God that in the hay it was not cold. (page 258)

When he patted her, she licked his hand and his face. Then she said, "Maaaa," and he knew it meant, I love you too. (page 260)

Aaron's family and their neighbors had searched for the boy and the goat but had found no trace of them during the storm. They feared they were lost. (page 260)

Students can, of course, choose other passages to demonstrate Singer's use of the omniscient point of view.

UNDERSTANDING THE WORDS IN THE STORY (Matching Columns) *Page 263*

1. necessaries	h. essential items
2. dense	d. thick
3. penetrated	j. got through
4. wonderment	f. surprise
5. astray	i. out of the right way
6. imp	a. devilish spirit
7. glazed	c. coated
8. chaos	g. disorder
9. exuded	b. gave off
10. wailed	e. cried

WRITING IT DOWN

Other Points of View *Page 263*

This writing assignment encourages students to experiment with several different points of view. They may find that filling out the chart will help them to clearly identify each character's point of view.

An Informative Paper *Page 264*

A student might illustrate his or her report on Hanukkah, the Feast of Dedication or Festival of Lights, with pictures or candles. Parallels with other religious holidays might interest many students.

What Happened During the Ice Storm

Jim Heynen

Page 265

INTRODUCING THE SELECTION

Jim Heynen's "What Happened During the Ice Storm" is one of the shortest pieces in *Impact*, but its power is undiminished by its brevity. Rather, the story leaves us with a sense of wonder and awe at the boys' flurry of retreat back to the house, the pheasants cloaked with the warmth of their jackets. That the pheasants might be doomed despite the boys' action makes the gesture seem a thing of fleeting beauty.

Many of Heynen's stories in *The One-Room Schoolhouse,* from which "What Happened During the Ice Storm" is taken, concern the small miracles of redemption that occur amidst the sweat and drudgery of farm life in Iowa. Often ribald and funny, these stories are rarely more than two pages in length. They are anecdotes, for the most part, but anecdotes that run deep. In the midst of frivolity, dirt, and even violence, the boys of these stories encounter the small wonders of existence. In "Bird Songs," a boy who shoots birds with his BB gun also delights in their songs. When he has shot a wren, he studies the bird's warm body within his hand to locate the mystery of its song. Like the boys in "What Happened During the Ice Storm," he begins with violent intentions but is struck, as if against his will, by fragile beauty and grace. Many of the stories are vignettes, or "prose pieces," of boys at play, daring each other to great heights of disgust and danger, and delighting in tricks played on the adults. Although writing about seemingly mundane subjects, Heynen grants these short pieces resonance and depth. The mundane somehow becomes sacred, even miraculous.

Students may be surprised that the piece ends so suddenly. You can tell them that this kind of brief fiction has been called "flash fiction" or "sudden fiction." Stories such as this can have a compressed, highly charged power. The elements of the "sudden" story may be similar to those in longer works, but they are more tightly wound. Like a coiled wire, they have a potential energy that the same wire, stretched to its utmost, would lack. Students may be curious about the forms a short story can take. Ask them to try defining a short story. You might refer them to the introduction to the second edition on page xi of *Impact,* which mentions Edgar Allan Poe's dictum that, from the first word of a story, every single element should contribute toward the overall effect. There should be nothing in a story that does not advance the action. Do students agree? "What Happened During the Ice Storm" should help teach them that there are few restrictions on what a story can be. As brief as Jim Heynen's story is, it is a complete piece. Students may want to try writing short-shorts of their own, although this is more difficult than it appears. Shorter does not necessarily mean easier—ask people to describe themselves in one sentence, for example, and notice how carefully they choose their words.

PRESENTATION

You may want to have your students read this short piece silently in class—they should finish at about the same time—and then observe their immediate reactions. Ask students to take careful note of the strong imagery, which compensates for the lack of an extended and complicated plot. In many ways, the story is like a photographic collage; we are left with a series of images: the ice hardening like glass on the trees; the boys, silent, breathing along with the ice-blinded pheasants; the pheasants enclosed and protected by the boys' coats. The story leaves us with a sense of deep winter silence.

Ask students to think about how the objective point of view enhances the story. An emotional narrator might spoil the quiet, evocative quality of the scene. We do not enter the boys' thoughts, and are allowed to witness them as an observer might. Another story in this unit, Ernest Hemingway's "A Day's Wait" (page 249), offers another example of the objective style. Perhaps because the story is told matter-of-factly, it helps us stop and notice moments of such grace in our own lives. Students who appreciate the beauty of the scene will impart their own emotions to the narrative. The author does not need to make a fuss and demand that we comprehend the rarity of the incident. He merely needs to tell us that it happened. You could liken this to someone describing a spaceship landing on earth. To tell us that the experience was incredible and unusual would be redundant. Point out to your students that this story is an excellent example of the general rule of fiction: "Show, don't tell."

CHECKING UP *Page 266*

1. What did the farmers do with their livestock during the ice storm? They moved the livestock into the barns.

2. Why were the pheasants helpless during the storm? They became helpless because their eyes froze shut.

3. Where did the boys find the pheasants? They found them huddling along a fence.

4. How did the boys save the pheasants? They took off their coats and covered the crouching pheasants to protect them from the icy rain.

TALKING IT OVER *Page 266*

1. The opening paragraph describes the effects of the ice storm. How did people react to the freezing rain at first? How does the story's atmosphere, or mood, change in the opening paragraph? At first, people exclaim at the beauty of the ice that glazes everything outdoors. The continuation of the storm, however, causes tree limbs to break and forces the farmers to move their livestock indoors. At the end of the first paragraph, the pathetic detail of the pheasants' eyes frozen shut emphasizes the storm's destructiveness, in contrast to its beauty.

2. *Imagery* is descriptive language that appeals to the senses. To what is the freezing rain compared in the story's opening? The freezing rain, as it hardens on the trees, is compared to glass. **How does the imagery in the third and fourth paragraphs draw a comparison between the boys and the pheasants?** Both the boys and the pheasants are portrayed as perfectly still, breathing out white puffs of steam. The boys, like the pheasants, are dripping with the freezing rain that hardens to ice on their coats. This image implies that they share some sort of common ground with the birds. Both boys and pheasants are frozen into immobility. **How does this imagery make you feel about the birds?** Answers will vary. The birds seem quite pathetic and helpless, and we feel sorry for them. They seem almost otherworldly and magical, glazed by a coating of ice.

3. How does the author build suspense in the second paragraph? He tells us that the boys, like the farmers, are looking for the pheasants, and we know that the farmers have clubbed the birds. When the boys come upon the pheasants, the author takes us step by step through each detail—the boys slide up close and the pheasants hide their heads. We see how vulnerable the birds are.

4. What is going through the boys' minds as they look at each other, "each expecting the other to do something"? Answers will vary. Most students will suggest that each boy is waiting for someone else to make the first move—either to capture or kill one of the pheasants. However, none of the boys seems ready to "pounce on a pheasant, or to yell Bang!"

5. What *did* happen during the ice storm? Answers will vary. Students may note that there is very little surface action in this story. However, something quite powerful happens. A group of boys set out to do harm but instead show sympathy and compassion toward helpless creatures. **Why do you think the author felt that the boys' actions were worth reporting?** In most circumstances, the boys would have followed their original intentions in order to "go along with the group" and follow the example of the farmers. Because one boy dares to remove his jacket to protect the birds, the others follow suit. The action is so unexpected and so noble that it is almost magical. Some students may refer to the author's comment on page 269, in which he tells how an incident of people killing blinded pheasants resonated in his memory for years. The author probably wanted to "rewrite" the incident as a scene of human kindness, not cruelty.

POINT OF VIEW

Objective Point of View *Page 267*

1. What do you think is gained by the objective point of view in this story? Do you think that the action requires direct commentary and interpretation, or are such conclusions better left to the individual reader? The objective point of view enables the reader to study the story without being forced to take sides. Jim Heynen apparently trusts the reader to draw certain conclusions about the boys' compassionate behavior without having to state these ideas explicitly.

2. The story has an unusual title. Whereas most story titles capture some key element of the story, the title "What Happened During the Ice Storm" is vague. Also, the characters are not described or named. Why are names not important in this story? How is the author's treatment of the title and the characters consistent with his use of the objective point of view? Both features of the story are consistent because they enhance the effect of objectivity. The language in the title deliberately avoids characterizing or interpreting the action, and the lack of proper names avoids any implication that the events can be narrowly localized or particularized as the actions of specific people. As a result, the story seems to touch on universal themes.

WRITING IT DOWN

A Newspaper Article *Page 268*

Students may find that writing an objective newspaper article is a difficult task, since objectivity requires the suppression of personal opinion. You might suggest that students try publishing their work in the school newspaper or other forum.

SPEAKING AND LISTENING

Discussing Objectivity *Page 268*

Students may want to come to a consensus on which art form they find most objective—writing, photography, or fine art. Can they find examples to illustrate their conclusions?

As a follow-up to this exercise, you might ask students to bring in news stories in which they can detect a particular opinion or political stance. Remind them that the choice to include or exclude certain quotations and specific details may be a reflection of the writer's or the newspaper's point of view. In addition, the photographs accompanying a newspaper or magazine article may be a clue to the opinion held by the writer or publisher.

THE PIECE OF YARN

Guy de Maupassant **Page 270**

INTRODUCING THE SELECTION

In "Of the Novel," Guy de Maupassant wrote the following statement:

> Life, moreover, is composed of the most dissimilar things, the most unforeseen, the most contradictory, the most incongruous; it is merciless, without sequence or connection, full of inexplicable, illogical, and contradictory catastrophes.

Maître Hauchecorne's cruel fate in "The Piece of Yarn" seems to be one of the "catastrophes" of which Maupassant writes. The villagers of Goderville seem to operate on the premise that a man is guilty until proven innocent; a chance misunderstanding marks a man a thief. Obsessed with clearing his name, he dies a broken man. The brutality of public opinion is presented with a darkly comic irony.

Maupassant's characters are often simple people whose lives become quite complex. In the short story "The Necklace," an ironic misunderstanding dooms a couple to a life of poverty and toil. Guy de Maupassant does not necessarily blame his characters for their destinies, although he does seem to mock them for their failure to handle crises. He takes an almost existential view of a world that is cold, capricious, and without mercy. There is little that his simple characters can do to defend themselves against "inexplicable, illogical, and contradictory catastrophes."

Direct students to the biography on page 279. Maupassant was a prolific writer who tried his hand at several genres, but was best known for his short stories. Initially a slow and meticulous writer, he later came to believe that his true voice would emerge whatever the speed of his work. His prose style is simple and clear.

PRESENTATION

Assign "The Piece of Yarn" to be read at home, or have students read it silently during class. Students who have no difficulty with the story can proceed ahead to the Checking Up questions and vocabulary exercise. Continue with the questions in Talking It Over when all the students have finished reading.

You might want to ask students if they can draw any parallels between justice in "The Piece of Yarn" and our modern system of justice. Although Maître Hauchecorne is not tried in a courtroom for the theft, the weight of public opinion condemns him. Do students believe that defendants today are truly considered "innocent until proven guilty"? What aspects of our judicial system do they consider fair? unfair? How might Maître Hauchecorne's case be handled in a United States courtroom today? You can suggest that students arrange a mock trial, casting people as villagers, witnesses, lawyers, plaintiff, defendant, judge, and jury. Using the same basic set of circumstances, students should come up with their own prosecution and defense.

Some students may have difficulty with the pronunciation of French names of places and people. If any students study French, ask them to try to pronounce these words for the rest of the class. As a cross-curricular option, you may want to collaborate with the language or social studies department to teach students about provincial France. You could organize brief lessons in geography, politics, history, cooking, and the arts, or perhaps have students design a classroom display. Ask students to locate France and Normandy on a map. Can they determine whether the towns Maupassant writes of are real or fictional?

CHECKING UP (Short Answer) *Page 277*

1. Where does this story take place? The story is set in rural Normandy, a region of northwestern France.

2. Why does Maître Hauchecorne pick up the piece of yarn? He is thrifty and frugal.

3. Who accuses Hauchecorne of stealing the pocketbook? Monsieur Malandain, the harness maker, accuses him.

4. Who makes the announcement about the missing pocketbook? The town crier makes the announcement.

5. What happens to Hauchecorne in the end? He weakens, sinks into delirium, and finally dies.

TALKING IT OVER *Page 277*

1. Why does Hauchecorne try to conceal the piece of yarn he picks up? He tries to conceal it because he sees Malandain watching him. He doesn't want his old enemy to see him doing such an embarrassing thing as saving a bit of string. **How is this action important later in the story?** The incident is important because it adds credibility to the theory that Hauchecorne is guilty of stealing the pocketbook.

2. What aspects of the villagers' character do the opening paragraphs of the story reveal? The opening paragraphs reveal the villagers' frugality: for example, we are told of their long drawn-out bargaining in the market and of the innkeeper's knack for making money. The story's opening section also reveals the peasants' suspicion of one another. This aspect of their character is shown when we are told that Hauchecorne doesn't want Malandain to know what he picks up, because he feels humiliated to be seen scrabbling in the dirt for a bit of yarn. Even the bargaining farmers are always in fear of being taken in, and they are always hoping to discover deception in others. **How do these details prepare us for their behavior later in the story?** These characteristics of frugality and suspicion prepare us for the neighbors' attitude toward Hauchecorne after he is cleared. They continue to believe that he is lying.

3. Guy de Maupassant was famous for his accurate observation of life. How does the description of the lunchtime scene at Jourdain's inn illustrate the author's careful attention to detail? Students should cite the two paragraphs beginning with the words, "At Jourdain's the large hall was filled with diners . . . " and "Next to the seated diners the immense fireplace . . . " (page 272). The details in the first paragraph give a vivid picture of the vehicles in the courtyard; the details in the second paragraph describe the food being roasted on spits.

4. Despite his efforts, Hauchecorne cannot convince the villagers of his innocence. Why does he fail to clear his name? Among the reasons students may cite are the following: Hauchecorne is known for petty behavior, as in his holding a long-standing grudge against Malandain; he is hot-tempered and stubborn, able to hurl insults at his accuser for an hour; others in the town are, like him, uninterested in a rational search for the truth, as shown by their unwillingness to listen to or believe his story; the villagers are basically suspicious and disposed to believe that everyone is a rogue; Hauchecorne protests so much that they assume he is guilty. At bottom, Hauchecorne knows that he really is "capable of doing what he has been accused of, and even boasting about it as a good trick."

5. *Situational irony* occurs when events turn out to be quite different from what we expect. What are some of the ironies that occur in this story? Maître Hauchecorne is attacked and officially interrogated for picking up an insignificant piece of yarn; it seems he might have been better off in the end had he actually stolen the money; although Hauchecorne has many faults, it is his innocence that finally brings about his downfall. **What do these ironies reveal about human nature?** Answers will vary. In general, students may suggest that the ironies show, in this context at least, that human nature is often irrational, cruel, ignorant, and unjust.

POINT OF VIEW

Third-Person Limited Point of View *Page 277*

Find several key passages in the story that offer insight into the motives for his [the old peasant's] actions and that explain his reactions to events. Among the passages students may cite are the following:

Maître Hauchecorne felt a bit humiliated at having been seen by his enemy scrabbling in the dirt for a bit of yarn. He quickly thrust his find under his smock, then into his trousers pocket; afterwards he pretended to search the ground for something he had lost . . . (page 271)

The old farmer, struck speechless, in a panic over being suspected and not understanding why, stared at the mayor. (page 273)

He got more and more annoyed, upset, feverish in his distress because no one believed him, not knowing what to do, and always telling his story. (page 274)

He went home, feeling humiliated and indignant, strangled with anger and mental confusion, especially crushed because, as a shrewd Norman, he knew himself capable of doing what he was accused of, and even boasting about it as a good trick. (page 276)

"Ha! With such an explanation, he must be lying!" they said behind his back. He sensed this, ate his heart out, and exhausted his strength in useless efforts. (page 276)

UNDERSTANDING THE WORDS IN THE STORY (Matching Columns) *Page 278*

1. stance	**g.** way of standing
2. laborious	**h.** involving hard work
3. hasten	**i.** to cause to hurry
4. swathed	**a.** wrapped
5. immense	**b.** huge
6. delectable	**j.** delicious
7. pungent	**d.** sharp; penetrating
8. baffled	**c.** perplexed; confused
9. receding	**f.** fading away
10. pompous	**e.** self-important

WRITING IT DOWN

An Advice Column *Page 278*

Students may enjoy taking a modern stance when writing an advice-column response to Maître Hauchecorne.

A Literary Analysis *Page 279*

This writing assignment will be challenging for certain students because it requires them to move away from personal response and into more formal, critical analysis. An additional challenge would be to have students develop their own topics and thesis statements for a critical paper.

The Lady, or the Tiger?

Frank R. Stockton **Page 280**

INTRODUCING THE SELECTION

Frank R. Stockton's "The Lady, or the Tiger?" was an immensely popular story when it first appeared in 1882; so much so, in fact, that Stockton later encountered difficulty publishing anything that wasn't up to its high standards. The story poses an ethical dilemma that, over one hundred years after its appearance, still causes great speculation. It will be a springboard for lively classroom discussion.

Modern authors rarely use the device of the self-conscious narrator. Can students name any other stories in which this style is used? One that may come to mind is O. Henry's "The Gift of the Magi" (page 403). The self-conscious narrator sometimes appears in old-fashioned children's books, and may address the audience with such remarks as "Dear reader." In most modern stories, the author stays behind the scenes and doesn't intrude to tell us what we should think. Sometimes an author will use the voice of an unseen character to tell the story. That character will be free, unlike the author, to make comments and value judgments. In other cases, the author employs a modern style known as **metafiction**. This is fiction in which the author self-consciously makes a point of the fact that he or she is writing fiction. The author might mock or refer to the conventions of fiction, or use an overblown metaphor and then call attention to it. T. Coraghessan Boyle, whose story "Top of the Food Chain" appears on page 314, has used the device of metafiction in his writing. Stockton's style, on the other hand, is of the old-fashioned variety. The device gives him the freedom to address the reader directly, effectively putting the ball in our court.

PRESENTATION

You may need to allow more than one class period for discussion. Guide students who have difficulty with the language and allow them more time to digest the selection.

After students have completed a silent reading, the Checking Up questions, and Talking It Over, you might return to the issues raised in the prereading question. Students may suggest sports such as boxing, football, and hockey, which rely on violent, rough activity to excite crowds. Do any students believe that these sports promote violence, or do they see them as harmless arenas in which to test physical strength and skill? Perhaps students might suggest that the sports culture satisfies a human desire for physical competition and mastery that might go unchecked if no arena were provided. Because we have tame, acceptable forms of combat, we have no need for gladiators and lions. Stockton's story suggests that when "entertainment" is presented in so acceptable a manner, people fail to question its inhuman aspects.

The king's "institution" is described as popular because the people thrive on extremes of sensationalism. Does this description of popular taste—especially that surrounding celebrity trials or weddings—have any application in the world around us today? Most students will readily point to contemporary parallels, including the media's treatment of celebrities and people's interest in the fortunes of the rich and famous. Encourage students to discuss specific examples.

CHECKING UP (True/False) *Page 286*

F 1. The king is stern and ill-tempered.

T 2. The arena is used to determine whether an accused person is guilty or innocent.

F 3. The people feel that the judgments of the arena are unfair.

F 4. The princess does not know which door holds the tiger.

T 5. The princess is jealous of the lady chosen for her lover.

TALKING IT OVER *Page 287*

1. What are some of the ironies of the king's system of justice? Irony is pervasive in the king's system. This is communicated through many verbal ironies: "a man of exuberant fancy" (page 280); "the minds of his subjects were refined and cultured" (page 280); "purposes far better adapted to widen and develop the mental energies of the people" (page 280); "This vast amphitheater . . . was an agent of poetic justice" (page 280); "the rich growth of his barbaric idealism" (page 281); "the king allowed no such subordinate arrangements to interfere with his great scheme of retribution and reward"(page 281); and "Its perfect fairness is obvious" (page 282). These phrases are all verbally ironic because on the surface they appear to praise the king and his system, while in reality they demonstrate the king's barbarity and indifference to justice.

2. Why is the institution of the arena so popular with the people? The people enjoy being surprised. They never know whether they are to witness a tiger devouring a victim or a merry wedding celebration. The people also believe that the king's system of justice is fair, and that being witness to it enriches and broadens their minds. Stockton is making a disheartening point about the part of human nature that thrives on sensationalism and barbarity, believing it to be socially acceptable, civilized, and culturally enriching.

3. What internal conflict is at the root of the princess's dilemma? The princess must choose between hatred and jealousy of her rival and the wish to save her lover from death.

4. What is the reaction of the audience as the young man enters the arena? They greet his appearance with a hum of admiration and anxiety.

5. How does the young man know that the princess has discovered the secret of the doors? He knows her nature well and is confident that she will have been successful in solving the mystery.

6. The author challenges you to guess the outcome of the story. From what you know of the princess, which door do you think she would point to: the one concealing the lady, or the one concealing the tiger? Give reasons to support your answer. Here are some facts that support each resolution:

The Lady: (1) The princess loves the young man; (2) The princess dreads the prospect of her lover being killed by the tiger; and (3) The princess may prefer to have her lover live, even though married to another.

The Tiger: (1) The princess hates the lady; (2) The princess is furious at the prospect of her lover marrying the lady; (3) The princess might rather see the young man dead than married to the lady; and (4) The princess is her father's daughter—semibarbaric, capricious, and cruel.

Students may come up with their own creative solutions. One possibility is that the princess, who has already circumvented her father's rules by learning the secret of the doors, would once again exercise her strong will by indicating the lady's door while plotting to have the lady somehow eliminated afterward! Another possibility is that the clever princess might bribe a guard to tranquilize the tiger with some ancient opiate. One way or another, the princess would try to outwit her father's scheme of justice.

POINT OF VIEW

Self-conscious Point of View *Page 287*

The narrator makes a direct comment on the king's system of justice when he says, "Its perfect fairness is obvious." How do you know that this statement is ironic? The statement is ironic because it is the opposite of the truth; the system is not fair at all. **Find other passages in the story that demonstrate the presence of a self-conscious narrator.** Answers will vary. Students may cite the following passages, among others:

As is usual in such cases, she was the apple of his eye . . . (page 282)

In after years such things became commonplace enough . . . (page 283)

Now, the point of the story is this: Did the tiger come out of the door, or did the lady? (page 285)

The more we reflect upon this question the harder it is to answer. (page 285)

The question of her decision is not one to be lightly considered, and it is not for me to presume to set myself up as the one person able to answer it. (page 286)

UNDERSTANDING THE WORDS IN THE STORY (Matching Columns) *Page 288*

1. florid	**d.** flowery; showy
2. genial	**i.** friendly; cheerful
3. valor	**g.** courage
4. decrees	**f.** official orders
5. incorruptible	**j.** unable to be bribed or tainted
6. emanated	**a.** came forth
7. doleful	**c.** sad; melancholy
8. dire	**h.** dreadful; terrible
9. subordinate	**e.** secondary
10. tribunal	**b.** court

(Multiple-Choice) *Page 288*

1. An *impartial* decision
- (**a.**) shows no favoritism
- **b.** is unfair
- **c.** is made quickly

2. Something *procured* is
- (**a.**) obtained
- **b.** well fed
- **c.** safe to eat

3. A scheme of *retribution*
- **a.** redistributes wealth
- **b.** asks questions
- (**c.**) punishes wrongdoing

4. A person with an *imperious* nature is
- (**a.**) arrogant
- **b.** heir to the throne
- **c.** soft-spoken

5. *Ardor* can be described as
- **a.** a love for trees
- **b.** burning resentment
- (**c.**) strong feeling

6. The *portals* of a building or structure are its
- **a.** windows
- (**b.**) doors
- **c.** roof lines

7. The *parapet* on which the princess's right arm lay was a
   a. cushion
   (b.) low railing
   c. desk

8. *Devious* paths are
   (a.) roundabout and winding
   b. long and exhausting
   c. clearly indicated and pleasant

9. *Reveries* are
   (a.) daydreams
   b. jealous rages
   c. wake-up calls

10. The *deliberation* that preceded the decision of the princess was marked by
   a. a hasty search for documents
   b. bitter arguments
   (c.) careful consideration

WRITING IT DOWN

Another Point of View *Page 289*

Students may have already had practice changing a story's point of view in earlier *Impact* writing assignments. They may want to try to rewrite several paragraphs of the story, each with a different point of view. Ask students to share their interpretations.

THE CIRCUIT

Francisco Jiménez

Page 291

INTRODUCING THE SELECTION

The "circuit" in the title of Francisco Jiménez's story refers to the pattern of his characters' lives. As migrant workers, they are forced to move continually from farm to farm, aligning their lives with the waxing and waning of each crop's harvest season. In accordance with its title, the story moves full circle, beginning and ending with the loss of yet another temporary home.

The narrator's sadness over moving is at first disheartening, but as his new life in Fresno takes shape our hopes for him grow. Unfortunately, at the end of the story, his progress at school and his budding friendship with Mr. Lema are cruelly ended. The story ends as he returns home to find his family's belongings neatly packed in boxes.

Panchito's life is exhausting, and he longs for stability. He is denied the chance to forge lasting relationships or to make significant progress in school. We might imagine that his education is disjointed, comprising bits and pieces of knowledge. As the child of migrant workers, he can do little to escape the endless "circuit."

The circumstances described in "The Circuit" are not exaggerated. California's migrant workers are paid low wages and they often have trouble finding work. Because they must follow the crop seasons, they rarely settle down and establish roots. Migrant families often suffer from malnutrition and poor medical care. The children are often needed in the fields as well and, like Panchito, sometimes work for twelve hours a day. As a result, they miss out on a complete education. Many schools have set up summer programs to further the education of migrant children.

Jiménez says that "The Circuit" is an autobiographical short story about his childhood experience in California's San Joaquin Valley. Like Panchito, he endured exhausting labor and endless upheavals as a child. He, too, found a childhood mentor in one of his teachers, who encouraged her students to write personal narratives. Jiménez wrote about what he knew best. Although he had difficulty completing his education, he eventually earned a Ph.D. from Columbia University.

PRESENTATION

Begin with the prereading question on page 291. After students have written about or discussed aspects of moving from one's home, proceed with a silent reading of the story. Follow your reading with Talking It Over.

The narrator's tone in this story is serious. We might surmise that Panchito has run the gamut of emotions during his previous moves—from excited and anticipatory, like his younger brothers and sisters, to fiercely angry and resentful. At this stage in his life, however, he regards his circumstances with sadness and resignation.

Although the story itself is sad, the life of its author is hopeful. Jiménez has shown how determination—and education—can help a person overcome poverty and hardship and, ultimately, achieve success. Students should be encouraged to write about their own personal histories.

CHECKING UP (True/False) *Page 296*

T 1. The story opens at the end of the strawberry season.

T 2. Panchito is unhappy about moving to Fresno.

F 3. Mamá is tired of her old, dented pot.

T 4. Roberto will go to school when the cotton season ends.

T 5. Panchito spends his lunch hours studying English.

TALKING IT OVER *Page 297*

1. What is the main external conflict that confronts the family in this story? The main conflict is the family's need to eke out a living through migrant labor. **How is this struggle related to Panchito's internal conflict?** The struggle is directly related to Panchito's unhappiness, because the family's constant need to move means that Panchito can never settle down and make friends like other children.

2. What details in the story suggest that the family members remain strong and united despite the hardships that they face? The parents in the story provide for their family through love and hard labor. The mother cooks regular meals in her favorite pot and everyone sits down to eat together at mealtime. Before they settle into Mr. Sullivan's barn, they try to make it habitable by sweeping and plugging up the holes.

3. Why is Panchito unable to face his brother on his first morning of school? He feels sorry for his brother, who must work through another crop-picking season before attending school.

4. How do you think Panchito feels at the end of the story, when he sees the packed boxes? Most students will say that Panchito feels disappointed and sad.

5. How is the story's plot structure reflected in its title? The story itself is structured as a "circuit." It begins and ends with the family packing up to move. Both the plot structure and the title suggest that the family is stuck in an endless cycle of hard work and poverty.

6. What do you think will happen to the narrator? Will he complete his education? Answers will vary. Panchito might complete his education, for he seems to like school and to flourish under the guidance of teachers like Mr. Lema. On the other hand, the story implies that Panchito faces serious obstacles, given his family's circumstances.

TONE

Recognizing Tone *Page 297*

1. Find details in the story that reveal the hardships faced by workers and their families. Answers will vary. The family must pack everything they own in boxes and move as the crop seasons change. They must sleep in an old, dirty garage. Panchito works in the fields in one-hundred degree heat. Just as Panchito develops a friendship with his teacher, it is time to leave.

2. Locate some of the passages in the story that convey Panchito's feelings of sadness and resignation. Answers will vary. Among the passages students may cite are the following:

"Suddenly I felt even more the weight of hours, days, weeks, and months of work. I sat down on a box. The thought of having to move to Fresno and knowing what was in store for me there brought tears to my eyes." (page 291)

"As we drove away, I felt a lump in my throat. I turned around and looked at our little shack for the last time." (page 293)

WRITING IT DOWN

An Analysis of Tone *Page 298*

The critical reading of newspaper articles will illustrate the ways in which a writer's attitude is present even where it is unexpected.

A Secret for Two

Quentin Reynolds **Page 300**

INTRODUCING THE SELECTION

This sentimental story of a milkman and his faithful horse will appeal to many students. As every high school teacher knows, there are certain teenagers who cherish horses of their own or daydream of owning one someday. These students will enjoy meeting Joseph, Pierre's big white horse, in "A Secret for Two," and will be ready to tell of the remarkable feats of other horses of their acquaintance. In a sense, the horseless carriage has never replaced the horse.

Excellent journalist that he was, Quentin Reynolds knew how to interest the public with his war correspondence and biographies of famous persons. As his biography on page 306 of *Impact* shows, this enterprising American reported stories from London, Paris, Italy, and the South Pacific during World War II. Like cartoonist Bill Mauldin and columnist Ernie Pyle, he chronicled the daily lives of soldiers—"the guys that wars can't be won without." Students might ask their grandparents the part that such journalists played in the war effort.

In "A Secret for Two," Reynolds uses an old French neighborhood in Montreal for his setting. Students who have studied the French language will enjoy helping classmates with the footnoted words. If you or your students have traveled to Montreal, share impressions of this beautiful and cosmopolitan city, the largest in Quebec and in all of Canada.

Although residents call Montreal "the second-largest French-speaking city in the world," they actually conduct most of the city's business affairs in English. Students might be interested in reporting on the dual public school system of Quebec—Roman Catholic schools with instruction in French, and Protestant schools with instruction in English.

You might ask students how they customarily receive their milk and other groceries. In most parts of our country, families depend on shopping trips to a supermarket. In fact, teenagers are the principal bag-boys and bag-girls of retail grocery stores. Mention that when their great-grandparents were young, families depended on milk wagons, grocery wagons, and ice wagons drawn by one or more horses. In those days children and young people often knew the names of the horses as well as of the deliverymen.

In "A Secret for Two" students will meet an old-time milk wagon driver named Pierre and a special horse named Joseph. What secret do the man and the horse share?

PRESENTATION

After oral or silent reading, continue with the discussion questions and the exercises.

As suggested in the first writing assignment on page 306, students might focus on the relationship between a person and an animal in a popular novel. Consult *Books for You* and other book lists from the National Council of Teachers of English for other fine animal stories.

Students might also like to report on scientific studies of animal communication. One celebrated study is Dr. Francine Patterson's use of five hundred signs with the gorilla Koko near San Francisco, California. See the article "Koko's Kitten" in *National Geographic,* January, 1985.

Students might report on animals trained to help people who are blind, deaf, or otherwise incapacitated. Such cooperation, whether in real life or in Reynolds' story, is impressive and heartwarming.

CHECKING UP (Short Answer) *Page 304*

1. What is Pierre Dupin's job? He works as a deliveryman for a milk company.

2. Why does Pierre boast about Joseph? Pierre boasts that he never touches the reins because the horse knows the route so well.

3. How does Pierre explain his use of the walking stick? He says that he is growing old and tired.

4. From what task does Jacques regularly excuse Pierre? He excuses him from making out the weekly bills and collecting the money.

5. How does Pierre die? Blind with cataracts, Pierre steps off the sidewalk and into the path of an oncoming truck.

TALKING IT OVER *Page 304*

1. What does the "secret" in the title of the story refer to? The secret is that Pierre Dupin is blind. **Why are the two friends able to keep this secret from others?** Joseph knows the route so well that Pierre doesn't need to guide him. Since Pierre has never learned to read, his customers and employers depend on oral communication. Pierre uses a walking stick and pulls his cap down over his eyes.

2. What details of setting and language in the story help to create a sense of place? Among the details that students may mention are the description of Prince Edward Street in Montreal, the account of Pierre's morning routine, the names of the families, and the use of French phrases.

3. What details in the story foreshadow Pierre's blindness? Pierre brags: "He knows just where to stop. Why, a blind man could handle my route with Joseph pulling the wagon" (page 301). When he grows old, Pierre uses a walking stick and pulls his cap down.

4. How do you know that the author has a warmhearted view of his characters? He describes them in a kindly fashion, and he has them say and do things that make them likable.

TONE

Sentimentalism *Page 304*

1. Note how Reynolds focuses on the relationship of Pierre and his horse. How does he develop the sense of a special bond between

man and animal? When Pierre first meets the horse, he strokes him, talks about the beautiful spirit shining out of his eyes, and decides to name him after St. Joseph. Later, he talks to Jacques and brags about the horse's abilities. He refuses to retire because he doesn't want to leave Joseph. The old man and the old horse seem to be at their best when they are working together.

2. Note the reactions of other characters in the story. How do their comments and actions create sympathy for Pierre and Joseph? The other drivers smile and say that Joseph seems to smile in response to Pierre's greetings. Jacques jokes with Pierre about the horse's abilities. The cooks sing out how much milk they need. Jacques excuses Pierre from making out bills and collecting money. The president readily agrees to Pierre's retirement and to the continuation of his salary as a pension. Such comments and actions show that other characters are fond of Pierre and Joseph.

3. Note the direct comments of the narrator. Find several examples that reveal his attitude toward the different characters. On page 301 the narrator says of the man and horse, "this splendid combination would stalk proudly down the street." On page 302 he says, "Jacques, who was a kind man, understood. There was something about Pierre and Joseph which made a man smile tenderly. It was as though each drew some hidden strength from the other." (Other direct comments could also be cited.)

4. How does the final episode in the story make you feel? Answers will vary. Some students may say they are glad that the man and horse could be such close friends and could even die at the same time. Some may feel sad that such a friendship had to end. A few may express surprise that Pierre had been blind for so many years.

UNDERSTANDING THE WORDS IN THE STORY (Completion) *Page 305*

1. When Pierre first saw the big white horse, he stroked the sheen of the horse's belly.
2. The horse was as familiar with the milk route as Pierre was.
3. After the wagon was loaded, the man and animal would stalk down the street.
4. At the stable, Pierre used to boast of his horse's ability.
5. When they returned, Joseph would be put in his stall.
6. The snow that had fallen during the night glistened like diamonds.
7. Jacques soothed Pierre with the news that Joseph was looking peaceful.
8. After he left the stable, Pierre began hobbling down the street.
9. Although the driver called a warning, Pierre apparently heard nothing.
10. The truck driver protested that the accident was unavoidable.

WRITING IT DOWN

A Book Report *Page 306*

This exercise should help students develop their critical reading and writing skills.

A Personal Account *Page 306*

Students may enjoy writing about an episode from their own experience. Remind them that their feelings toward the event should be conveyed through tone.

THE PRINCESS AND THE TIN BOX

James Thurber

Page 307

INTRODUCING THE SELECTION

It is unlikely that "The Princess and the Tin Box" will be students' first acquaintance with the inimitable humor of James Thurber. His name should bring smiles to their faces if they have read "The Secret Life of Walter Mitty," "The Unicorn in the Garden," or other Thurber favorites. They may want to bring in some of Thurber's satirical cartoons of huge, imperturbable dogs and perturbable men and women who resemble, as Dorothy Parker said, unbaked cookies.

You might ask a student volunteer to supplement the *Impact* biography on page 312 by looking up anecdotes from the life of Thurber.

When Thurber was six years old, he and his brothers were playing a game of William Tell in the backyard of their temporary home in Falls Church, Virginia. An arrow pierced Thurber's left eye. Eventually physicians decided to remove the eye, but by that time the sight in his right eye was also badly impaired.

Despite his handicap, the boy excelled in schoolwork in his hometown, Columbus, Ohio. In Sullivant Elementary School a tougher boy named Floyd became Thurber's bodyguard when he discovered that Thurber could spell "Duquesne." In East High School Thurber wrote his first published story, "The Third Bullet," which appeared in *X-Ray*, the school magazine. Although he could have become editor of the magazine, his mother asked that he not be appointed because she feared further damage to his eyesight. He did, however, become president of his senior class, graduated with honors, and continued his education at Ohio State University.

In 1918 Thurber trained as a code clerk for the State Department. Then he served in Washington and Paris, becoming quite proficient in breaking codes, according to his co-worker Stephen Vincent Benét. Years later he used his knowledge of cryptography in his book *The 13 Clocks*.

After World War I Thurber worked as a reporter for the Columbus *Evening Dispatch*. In 1924 he returned to Paris to try to write a novel. He did not write the novel, however, and, it is said, he did *not* meet Ernest Hemingway, Gertrude Stein, F. Scott Fitzgerald, John Dos Passos, William Faulkner, and other luminaries of the Lost Generation. Instead, he served as a Paris and Riviera correspondent for the *Chicago Tribune*.

In 1927 James Thurber began his thirty-year association with Harold Ross's newly founded magazine, *The New Yorker*. As an editor and contributor, Thurber became one of America's best-known humorists. He worked with such writers as E. B. White, Dorothy Parker, and Robert Benchley. Although they held him in high regard, they had to beware of his practical jokes. In *The Almanac of American Letters,* Randy F. Nelson reports as follows:

> . . . Thurber's most elaborate caper involved fellow writer E. B. White and a daring bank robbery in Ardsley, New York. Gangsters stole White's Buick and used it in the holdup, and the car was recovered only after a fierce shoot-out with police. Of course detectives wanted to interview White as a matter of routine, but Thurber got wind of events and went out of his way to make White nervous before the police arrived. The interview did not go well. White grew even more jittery, and so did the cops. By an incredible stroke of bad luck White had written the date of a dentist's appointment on a memorandum sheet in his office; and, as one would guess in such an instance, it was the exact date of the bank robbery. The devilish Thurber found the memo and before the police arrived scribbled *dertag* beside the date. Wary detectives actually questioned White a number of times, and on each occasion, Thurber would call into the office using the best and loudest gangster imitation emphasizing words like *caper, dough,* and *hideout.* Only after days of torment did White recover his shot-up car.

Your students, too, must be on guard. Thurber's humor may seem gentle and whimsical, but it has an undercurrent of sadness and irony. The writer once remarked that he would kick to death the next man who described him as "elfin."

PRESENTATION

In Thurber's story, the beautiful princess must choose from five suitors, all of royal birth. How can she possibly decide? What kind of husband does she desire? After the oral or silent reading, proceed with discussion questions and vocabulary exercises. The suggestion for writing, on page 312, is an especially enjoyable project. Students might even write this tale as a play script for class presentation.

CHECKING UP (True/False) *Page 309*

T 1. The princess's toys were all made of precious metals and gems.

F 2. All the suitors' gifts were placed on the princess's ivory bed.

T 3. The first of the princess's suitors brought an enormous golden apple.

T 4. The princess made her choice on the basis of what was most valuable.

F 5. The princess in this story believes that it is better to give than to receive.

TALKING IT OVER *Page 309*

1. In fairy tales the beautiful princess and the handsome prince fall in love, marry, and live happily ever after. What has replaced the importance of love in Thurber's story? The value of material things has replaced love.

2. Why does the princess choose the jewel box? What does this choice reveal about her values? As she says, it is a very large and expensive box that she can fill with all the gifts she expects to receive in the future.

3. Do you think Thurber admires the princess, or do you think he is poking fun at her? Support your opinion with evidence from the story. He is poking fun at her. She "squeals with delight" when she sees the small tin box. She uses language unsuitable for the occasion: "The way I figure it is this. . ." She plainly shows her vanity and greed.

4. How does this story show Thurber's keen understanding of human nature? Although people enjoy old-fashioned fairy tales, the same people, if given a choice, may take wealth and power over poverty and honor. People cannot survive on love alone.

TONE

Genial Satire *Page 310*

1. Note, for example, Thurber's account of the privileged childhood of the princess. Which details are particularly absurd? Toys made of precious metals and jewels are absurd. The rejected wooden blocks, china dolls, rubber dogs, and linen books would be much more suitable for a child. The "boxwood flute" of the blackbird could be enjoyed as well as the "lyre of gold" of the nightingale. Throwing pearls instead of rice at a wedding is extravagant and silly.

2. Note the princess's manner of speaking in Thurber's story. How is her speech *incongruous,* or inconsistent, with the traditional image of a storybook princess? Her speech does not have the elevated style and graciousness that one would expect of a princess receiving princely suitors. Instead, she speaks informally: "The way I figure it is this."

UNDERSTANDING THE WORDS IN THE STORY (Multiple-Choice) *Page 311*

1. The *hyacinth* is a
   a. small, furry animal
   b. precious gem
   (c.) plant with sweet-smelling flowers

2. The *lyre* is used to
   (a.) make music
   b. weave precious cloth
   c. house birds

3. An *ambassador* is
   (a.) a representative of one country to another
   b. an official who arranges royal weddings
   c. a servant in charge of palace expenses

4. An *ebony* table is made of
   a. precious jewels
   (b.) wood
   c. stone

5. One rides a *charger*
   a. at a carnival
   (b.) into battle
   c. to deliver mail

6. One rides *astride* when one sits
   (a.) with one leg on each side of a horse
   b. with both legs on one side of a saddle
   c. on a horse with no saddle

7. One is *disdainful* when feeling
   a. ill at ease in someone's presence
   b. talkative and friendly
   (c.) superior to someone or something

8. An example of *tawdry* jewelry is a
   a. string of cultured pearls
   (b.) rope of flashy glass beads
   c. diamond engagement ring

9. To be *glutted* is to
   a. have just enough
   b. experience hunger
   (c.) be filled beyond the point of satisfaction
10. One expects *revelry* during a
   (a.) feast
   b. concert
   c. test

WRITING IT DOWN

A Satirical Retelling *Page 312*

This writing exercise should cultivate the students' ability to write humorously. Other tales well suited to satirical rewriting are "Snow-White," "The Sleeping Beauty," and "Little Red Riding Hood."

Top of the Food Chain

T. Coraghessan Boyle

Page 314

INTRODUCING THE SELECTION

The events of T. Coraghessan Boyle's "Top of the Food Chain" are told as a dramatic monologue. The narrator, a scientific "expert" testifying before a Senate committee, describes an outrageous cause-and-effect sequence of events in an attempt to explain away a series of foolish blunders.

According to the testimony, a group of scientists appointed by the government decide to spray DDT over Borneo in an charitable effort to control the country's infestation of flies and mosquitoes. DDT, the narrator is quick to point out, was banned in the United States but *not* in the "developing world." In a torrent of verbiage upheld by flimsy logic, he goes on to explain how the DDT threw Borneo's ecosystem into chaos. One disaster led to another, culminating in the preposterous government solution to airdrop 14,000 cats into Borneo.

Boyle's satirical message is conveyed solely through the voice of his narrator, a ridiculous figure whom we might imagine reclining in an easy chair as he testifies before the Senate committee. Alarmingly unaware of the havoc he has wreaked, he behaves like a schoolboy caught in a childish prank. The narrator's offhand witticisms and glib responses before the Senate committee make light of scenes of absolute devastation. Lives are never at stake; each disaster is a mere irritation. The narrator even attributes reports of Bubonic plague to "hysteria."

The narrator's speech is peppered with incongruities; he projects his own modern context onto the lives of the villagers. For example: "the young mother so racked with the malarial shakes she can't even lift a Diet Coke to her lips" and "they love those [running] shorts, by the way, the shiny material and the tight machine-stitching. . . ." He trivializes the plight of the people who cannot sleep with the sound of rain drumming on their new tin roofs.

One reason for the satire's success is the narrator's consistency. Were he to give us glimpses of sensible, logical thought, the story would lose much of its humor. Boyle sets up a farfetched situation and maintains it. The story harks back to a satirical tradition that includes such works as Jonathan Swift's "A Modest Proposal."

Although the mood of the story is light and satirical, the tale does raise some troubling questions. Ask students whom Boyle intends as his target. He may be making an exaggerated point about bureaucratic agencies that, in their zeal to enlighten or help the "developing world," do more harm than good.

The narrator is a caricature, and we easily recognize the type: an overbearing and ill-informed person who imposes his ideals on others. Ask students to explain why a satirical tone is sometimes more effective than a serious one.

T. Coraghessan Boyle, whose biography appears on page 323, claims he never read a book before the age of eighteen. After idly hanging around for many years, as he describes it, he attended the Iowa Writers' Workshop in 1972 and began his literary career. Boyle has been widely hailed for his wickedly comic short stories and novels. Outlandish situations, exaggerated characters, and a mastery of language and metaphor typify his prose. *New York Times* writer and critic Lorrie Moore has written:

> Indeed, it is hard to think of writers to compare him with. In his sheer energy and mercilessness, his exuberantly jaundiced view, he resembles perhaps a middlebrow Donald Barthelme, or Don DeLillo crossed with Dr. Seuss, or Flannery O'Connor with a

> television and no church. The emotional complexity that could secure his characters at a safe distance from caricature confines him, slows him down. In his few stabs at poignancy or earnestness . . . he cannot shake the mean and theatrical habits of irony, the repudiating hiccup of sarcasm.

PRESENTATION

It may take you more than one class period to read and discuss "Top of the Food Chain." Students may find it helpful to consult a dictionary if they encounter unfamiliar terms.

Ask students to note Boyle's use of tone. The narrator relates incidents of absolute devastation in a casual, offhand way. An uninformed reader might take the narrator's statements at face value, but students should be able to detect a satirical edge to an author's prose. Ask students to locate places in the story where the author uses humor, exaggeration, and incongruity. The narrator's use of clichés, slang terms, and casual speech are even more humorous, given that he is testifying before a Senate committee.

You might suggest that students imagine the physical details that the dramatic monologue leaves out. How do they perceive the narrator's appearance and actions? Is he sifting through piles of scientific notes? What are the expressions on the Senators' faces? Visualizing the narrator's movements and expressions may help students imagine his tone of voice.

CHECKING UP (Short Answer) *Page 319*

1. Where do the events described by the speaker take place? The events take place on the island of Borneo.

2. Why, according to the speaker, was DDT used? DDT was used to control the mosquitoes and flies.

3. What happened to the caterpillars when the wasps were killed off? When the wasps died, the caterpillars proliferated and began destroying the thatched roofs of the people's huts.

4. Why did the cats begin to die? They ate the geckos that had been poisoned by contaminated flies.

5. What plan was devised to control the rats? The experts rounded up 14,000 cats and dropped them in by parachute.

TALKING IT OVER *Page 319*

1. Boyle plunges right into the story without identifying either the speaker or the setting. Who is the speaker? On what occasion is he reporting these events? The speaker appears to be a government-sponsored scientist. He is testifying at a Senate hearing about a project on the island of Borneo.

2. This story involves a cause-and-effect chain that threatens to spiral out of control. How did the seemingly simple act of spraying for the flies and mosquitoes turn out to have such far-reaching consequences? The use of DDT has the side effect of killing a type of small wasp that preys on caterpillars. As a result, the caterpillars proliferated and ate the palm leaves used to thatch the roofs of the people's huts. This caused the roofs to cave in. Meanwhile, the use of DDT to kill flies led to the poisoning of large numbers of geckos, who had gorged themselves on the dead flies. When the cats devoured the geckos, they too were poisoned and started to die off. This led to a rapid increase in the rat population, as well as human illness and crop damage. Finally, bubonic plague broke out. The workers then rounded up 14,000 cats and dropped them by parachute into Borneo.

3. What is the climax of the story? The climax of the story is the narrator's description of airlifting 14,000 cats: "and you should have seen them, gentlemen, the little parachutes and harnesses . . . 14,000 of them, cats in every color of the rainbow . . . all of them twirling down out of the sky like great big oversized snowflakes . . ."

4. The term "food chain" refers to the earth's cycle of food and energy. The chain begins with inorganic substances (like water and certain minerals), continues with food producers such as trees and plants, and then culminates in two levels of "consumers." Primary consumers (such as rabbits and squirrels) eat plants, grass, seeds, and nuts. Secondary consumers (such as hawks and foxes) eat smaller animals. Human beings are considered to be at the "top of the food chain." Why is the title of the story ironic? The story shows that although human beings are the earth's dominant species, they are not always the wisest. Also, the narrator's mention of the way toxins accumulate and move up the food chain suggests that humans will eventually suffer the same consequences as the other creatures.

5. How would you describe the attitude of the speaker toward his job and the people he is supposed to be helping? The speaker's attitude is condescending and arrogant. For example, he continually shirks responsibility for the disaster by claiming that no one could have foreseen the consequences of various decisions. He is scornful of environmental matters, referring sarcastically to the EPA and implying that environmental impact statements are a nuisance. He refers frequently to the indigenous people's primitive customs; he is disdainful of their culture; he repeats his disgust for the rainy weather and the other inconveniences of life in Borneo; and he is ignorant of the people's language.

6. A *dramatic monologue* is a narrative in which a single character speaks to one or more listeners whose replies are not given. Why do you think Boyle chose to write his story as a monologue? Answers will vary. The monologue is more effective than a dialogue in this story because it emphasizes the speaker's superficiality, ignorance, self-absorption, and eagerness to escape accountability for his decisions. Also, it adds immediacy to the narrative.

TONE

Forceful Satire *Page 320*

1. What is ironic about the speaker's statement, "It was like all nature had turned against us"? The statement is the opposite of the truth; with all their interference, the workers had, in effect, turned against nature.

2. How does the author use exaggeration in the story's climax? The description of 14,000 cats being parachuted onto the rat-infested island throws a spotlight of absurdity on the ill-fated decisions of the scientists. **How does the speaker use understatement, or deliberate restraint, when he describes the collapse of the thatched palm-leaf roofs?** He minimizes the headman's sense of horror and loss by focusing on the man's running shorts and by referring to the man's serious complaint as a "diatribe." He then dismisses the calamity by saying "But who was to make the connection between three passes with the crop duster and all those staved-in roofs?" **when he refers to the fate of the plague victims?** Rather than emphasize the outbreak of bubonic plague and the resulting deaths, he tries to minimize the tragedy by saying that they tracked down all the reports and made sure that the people got antibiotics. He then says casually, ". . . but still we lost a few." Furthermore, he attributes the nonstop reports of people "turning black, swelling up and bursting" to hysteria.

3. Find other examples of jargon in the story. Other examples that students may cite include the phrases "environmental impact statements," "went to the air," and "ground sweeps." **List other examples of cliché in the story.** Students may cite the following: "can't get enough of them," "nothing's perfect," "an error of commission rather than omission," "you name it, they've got it," "to make a long story short," "things really went down the tube," and "to every cloud a silver lining."

UNDERSTANDING THE WORDS IN THE STORY (Multiple-Choice) *Page 321*

1. Something that has *compounded* a problem has
   a. eliminated it
   (b.) made it worse
   c. caused it

2. A *contingent* is
   (a.) part of a larger group
   b. always well informed
   c. usually stingy

3. The *eradication* of pests refers to their
   (a.) elimination
   b. breeding
   c. multiplying

4. A *diatribe* is a long speech of
   a. praise
   (b.) criticism
   c. explanation

5. The *magnitude* of a problem refers to its
   (a.) extent
   b. location
   c. causes

6. The *efficacy* of a plan refers to its
   a. logic
   b. economy
   (c.) effectiveness

7. Your *nemesis* always seems to
   (a.) get the better of you
   b. ignore you
   c. help you

8. When the rats were *scuttling* all over the narrator's trailer, they were
   (a.) scurrying
   b. creeping
   c. falling

9. *Adverse* conditions are
   a. unexpected
   (b.) unfavorable or harmful
   c. well recognized
10. An action performed *inadvertently* is
   a. inexcusable
   b. irrational
   (c.) unintentional

WRITING IT DOWN

Dialogue *Page 322*

This exercise will give students practice in critical reading and in writing dialogue.

Another Tone *Page 322*

This assignment will build students' skills in using tone in their writing.

A Research Report *Page 323*

This exercise will tie current events to the students' writing and build up practice in using tone.

SPEAKING AND LISTENING

Preparing an Oral Interpretation *Page 323*

Reading the story aloud will give the students practice in oral interpretation.

JUST LATHER, THAT'S ALL

Hernando Téllez **Page 325**

INTRODUCING THE SELECTION

In "Just Lather, That's All," we see a man facing an agonizing decision. Through carefully chosen, intimate details, Téllez reveals the barber's inner conflict. We see in his every action a poised hesitation; as he draws the razor over Torres' neck, he is torn between his professional pride and his loyalty to the rebel cause. Should he uphold the honor of his profession, or should he take the life of a man who is responsible for the death of many of his comrades? He weighs both sides of the issue, visualizing himself both hailed as a hero and condemned as a murderer. Ultimately, he bases his decision to save Torres on an issue larger than his own personal gain or safety. He wants the killing to stop, and he doesn't want to make the sacrifice of becoming a murderer.

The story's ironic truth is kept from both the narrator and the reader until the final moment. The revelation that Captain Torres has known the barber to be a rebel all along and has simply been baiting him takes most readers by surprise. We might go back and reread the story in an entirely new light, this time understanding that Torres, as well as the barber, could have struck at any moment.

PRESENTATION

You can assign "Just Lather, That's All" for a silent reading. Students who finish early may proceed quietly with Checking Up and the vocabulary exercise. When all the students are finished, continue with Talking It Over.

You may want to discuss Captain Torres's surprising comment to the barber: "But killing isn't easy. You can take my word for it." Some students may suggest that his failure to kill the barber redeems him. Has he regained a measure of morality by stating that killing is not easy? Will he now curb his punishment of the rebels? Other students may suggest that the statement does not compensate for Torres's crimes. From the barber's reports, we know that Torres is cruel and inhumane. Students may point out that his facility for killing despite his admission makes him appear even worse. Does his final statement to the barber seem hollow in light of his past actions?

You might encourage students to imagine what takes place after Captain Torres leaves the barber shop. Will the barber flee? Will Torres allow the barber to live, knowing that he is an important link for the rebels? Imagining the outcome of the incident may help resolve the debate over Torres's morality.

CHECKING UP (True/False) *Page 329*

T 1. The captain has been searching for rebel troops.

T 2. The barber takes pride in his work.

T 3. The barber is an informer for the rebels.

F 4. The barber has killed many of Torres's men.

F 5. Torres does not know that the barber is a rebel.

TALKING IT OVER *Page 329*

1. We learn from the narrator's opening comments that the customer's presence is making him nervous. When does it become clear that the two characters are on opposite sides of a political struggle? It becomes clear when the narrator says, "He probably thought I was in sympathy with his party."

2. Why does the barber feel it would be wrong to let Torres go? Why, on the other hand, does he believe it would be wrong to take the captain's life? The barber thinks that it would be wrong to let Torres go because the captain is planning to execute more rebels that evening. On the other hand, his profession obliges him to shave this beard as he would that of any other customer. Also, he thinks that killing Torres when the captain is powerless would be cowardly. **In what way can the decision he makes affect the course of his own life?** If he murders the captain, he would be forced to flee, yet the rebels would consider him a hero. If he lets Torres go, he would be betraying the rebel cause.

3. What, in the end, is the barber's reason for sparing Torres? He does not want to make the sacrifice of becoming a murderer.

4. Near the end of the story, the narrator makes the surprising suggestion that there is a fine line between a reputation as a hero and a reputation as a murderer. Do you agree or disagree with this opinion? Can you give some examples from real life to support your view? Answers will vary. Some students will argue that the fine line between the two reputations is confined to the barber's specific predicament. Other students may counter that instances from real life support the barber's opinion. These students may, for example, cite the historical fact that revolutionaries opposing colonialism have been variously described as "terrorists" or "patriots," depending on people's different points of view and on the outcome of their struggles.

TONE

Irony *Page 330*

1. Find passages in the story that illustrate this ironic situation. Examples are the passages that begin: "I would be obliged to shave that beard like any other one, carefully, gently, like that of any customer, taking pains to see that no single pore emitted a drop of blood." "There, surely, the razor had to be handled masterfully, since the hair, although softer, grew into little swirls."

2. What is ironic about the barber's claim that he is a revolutionary and not a murderer? Revolutionaries are known for their willingness to effect radical change by any means, including murder.

3. How is this dramatic irony turned around, or ironically reversed, in the last paragraph of the story? The dramatic irony is reversed at the end of the story when it is revealed that Captain Torres knew the barber's identity all along.

UNDERSTANDING THE WORDS IN THE STORY (Matching Columns) *Page 331*

1. caress	d. gentle touch
2. feigned	g. pretended
3. faction	i. dissenting group
4. obliged	j. compelled; forced
5. emitted	a. gave forth; discharged
6. conscientious	h. careful; responsible
7. excursion	b. short trip
8. rejuvenated	e. made youthful again
9. glistening	f. shining; sparkling
10. ineradicable	c. permanent; irremovable

WRITING IT DOWN

An Opinion *Page 331*

This assignment provides an opportunity for critical thinking.

A Defense *Page 331*

This writing exercise should help students develop skills in analyzing a story and in writing persuasively.

SPEAKING AND LISTENING *Page 332*

Discussing a Comment

The questions about Captain Torres's comment should inspire lively debate among the students.

The Emperor's New Clothes

Hans Christian Andersen

Page 333

INTRODUCING THE SELECTION

You might ask students if they have previously read "The Emperor's New Clothes" and the other Andersen tales mentioned in the *Impact* biography on page 340. Some students may have also read "The Snow Queen," "The Little Fir Tree," and "The Constant Tin Soldier."

Since these stories are often referred to as *fairy tales,* you will need to define the term. Fairy tales are imaginative narratives of adventures with fantastic forces and beings (fairies, elves, goblins, monsters, trolls, and the like). They are told and retold to generations of children and are enjoyed by young and old alike. The swindlers in "The Emperor's New Clothes" are human beings, yet they meddle in the Emperor's affairs as fantastically as any troll or goblin.

Many popular fairy tales have folk origins that have been lost to antiquity. The tales have been gathered, retold in countless variations, and augmented with newer tales. Among the famous writers who have rewritten or invented these tales are Hans Christian Andersen, the brothers Grimm, and Charles Perrault.

Hans Christian Andersen was born in Odense, Denmark, and would not have gained enough education to become a writer without the generous assistance of Jonas Collin, a director of the Royal Theatre in Copenhagen. Andersen's plays and novels, as well as his letters and diaries, are known principally in Denmark; his tales, however, have been translated into most of the world's languages and appear in new editions year after year.

Although Andersen never married, he did fall in love with the singer Jenny Lind, known all over the world as "the Swedish nightingale." Andersen's personal correspondence reveals him as an observant, high-strung, and determined man who valued his other writings more than his fairy tales. It is interesting to note that one of the failings of this gifted storyteller was extreme vanity—the trait that causes the Emperor's downfall in Andersen's most famous tale.

Vanity can crop up anywhere. A story is told of a modern man who seemed impervious to flattery until a clever acquaintance remarked, "My friend, you are the only man I know who is immune to flattery."

PRESENTATION

You might ask your students why small children like to hear the same stories again and again and again. There are many possible answers, one being that children are memorizing the story and enjoying the expectation of what the characters will do next.

Ask why high school students are sometimes given stories to read that they may have read years ago. There are again many possible answers, but one explanation is that older students consider the stories from a more mature viewpoint, seeing themes and values that they may have missed when they were younger. Perhaps students can cite examples such as *Gulliver's Travels, Robinson Crusoe, The Adventures of Huckleberry Finn,* or classical myths. Sometimes students view a television version or read a simplified retelling of a work, then discover it later in its original form. High school students can double their appreciation of a familiar story with their deeper insight and wider experience.

After students have read "The Emperor's New Clothes," use the text questions to guide discussion of story happenings and theme.

CHECKING UP (True/False) *Page 337*

T **1.** The swindlers in this story take advantage of the Emperor's vanity.

F **2.** The swindlers claim that their fabric is invisible to anyone who is dishonest or cowardly.

F **3.** The old Chamberlain pretends to admire the fabric because he wishes to trap the swindlers.

T **4.** The only honest person in the story is a little child.

T 5. At the end of the story, the people of the town admit that the Emperor hasn't got any clothes on.

TALKING IT OVER *Page 338*

1. **What does the Emperor's obsession with fine clothes reveal about his character?** He is vain and foolish.

2. **Why are the swindlers able to dupe the Emperor, the Chamberlain, the courtiers, and the people watching the procession?** The people all believe what the swindlers have told them. They think that if they admitted they couldn't see any clothes on the Emperor, they would be labeling themselves as stupid and unfit for their positions.

3. **How does the child's innocence expose the folly and deceitfulness of the other people in the story?** The child gasps, "but he hasn't got any clothes on!" The other people know that the little child must be telling the truth because he has no motive for pretense.

4. **At the end of the story, the Emperor realizes that he has been tricked. Why does he decide, nevertheless, to go through with the procession?** He feels that there is no other course of action open to him. He must salvage whatever dignity he can.

5. **The swindlers claim that people who cannot see the cloth are stupid or unfit for their posts. How do the events of the story show, ironically, that this judgment is true?** In not telling the truth, the people are indeed showing themselves to be stupid and unfit for their jobs.

THEME

Understanding Theme *Page 338*

How would you state the theme, or central idea, of "The Emperor's New Clothes"? Answers will vary. One possible statement of the theme is as follows: Vanity can cause people to be deceived or act foolishly.

UNDERSTANDING THE WORDS IN THE STORY (Completion) *Page 339*

1. The old Chamberlain told the two swindlers that their work was exquisite.
2. The Emperor finally went in person to see what the two wily swindlers had woven.
3. They asked if the Emperor would deign to examine the cloth.
4. The Emperor nodded and said that the fabric had his imperial approval.
5. The Emperor's entire suite looked at the empty looms and said that the material was wonderful.
6. The courtiers praised the splendor of the regal robes.
7. The Emperor looked at himself in the mirror, pretending to admire his attire.
8. The courtiers could not be induced to admit that they could not see the cloth.
9. The people watching the procession would not acknowledge that they could not see the Emperor's new clothes.
10. Finally, it began to dawn upon the Emperor that he had been swindled.

WRITING IT DOWN

Ideas for a Theme *Page 340*

Encourage students to think of some sayings and proverbs in addition to those in the book. Their notes on plot, character, and setting can be used later in planning the structure of a short story.

A NINCOMPOOP

Anton Chekhov

Page 342

INTRODUCING THE SELECTION

Refer students to Chekhov's biography on page 347 of *Impact*. Chekhov wrote comic sketches for humorous journals to support his parents and sisters while he studied medicine in Moscow. He graduated from the University of Moscow and practiced medicine even after he was well established as a writer.

Western readers recognize Chekhov's social sympathies more easily than his keen sense of humor.

The characters in his short stories are often the victims of society. In "Heartache," an old cabbie can find no one who will listen to his sorrow over the loss of his son—no one but his horse. In "A Doctor's Visit," fifteen hundred factory workers "labor without rest in unhealthy surroundings . . . and only occasionally sober up from the nightmare of their lives by getting drunk." In "A Nincompoop," the governess does not seem to recognize the absurdity of saying *"Merci"* when she has been cheated of most of her wages. If we smile a little at the absurdities of Chekhov's stories, we feel their pathos more deeply.

Elements of ironic humor appear in many of Chekhov's most serious works. He insisted that his mature dramas, such as *The Three Sisters* and *The Cherry Orchard,* were comedies, not tragedies, and he wanted them played with the lightest touch.

A Russian critic once congratulated Chekhov on "being able to lead a hundred lives, while having paid only for one." The intended compliment is an understatement, for Chekhov's fascinating characters live and breathe in more than six hundred short stories as well as in his ten plays. However, in working so hard to support his family, Chekhov did indeed pay for one life, ruining his health and dying at the age of forty-four.

Frank O'Connor, eminent Irish American short-story writer and critic, wrote an essay on "The Slave's Son," concluding thus:

> I feel sure that "The Bishop," written the year before he died, is, like Mozart's final "Requiem," a celebration of his own death. The bishop, a poor boy who has been raised to eminence in the Church, struggles through his duties, though each night he collapses in pain as Chekhov himself was collapsing. He thinks back upon his youth, and everything that recurs to him is transfigured, and yet he remains a lonely man, as lonely as the old cab driver whose son had died or the man who has had to get rid of his horse and dog. He mother has come to visit him, along with his nieces, but his mother still calls him "Your Grace," putting the immense barriers of society between him and the only human contact he can hope for. I can't help wondering whether Chekhov's mother did not once upset him by addressing him as "Doctor." It is only just before he died that the false personality *she* has built up for herself because of her distinguished son collapses, and she calls him again by the intimate names she had called him when he was still only a little boy who could not button his own trousers. It is the final affirmation of Chekhov's faith in life—lonely and sad, immeasurably sad, but beautiful beyond the power of the greatest artist to tell.

PRESENTATION

Write the word *nincompoop* on the chalkboard and ask a student to define it. This synonym for *fool* or *simpleton* will probably be no surprise to students, who enjoy collecting such epithets. Interestingly, the origin of *nincompoop* is unknown.

You might also write the Russian names on the chalkboard so that students can practice saying them. Explain that Julia Vassilyevna is a governess hired by the narrator to teach and care for his daughter Vanya and his son Kolya. Considering the importance of her daily work with the children, would students expect Julia Vassilyevna to be entitled to a good salary? Students should try to find out who is the nincompoop in Chekhov's story. You might ask a girl to read Julia's lines and a boy to read all other lines.

After the reading of "A Nincompoop," continue with the discussion questions and exercises. Discuss the life of Chekhov, the range of his writing, and his influence on other writers. Why do other writers as well as general readers admire stories like "A Nincompoop"?

Your students may benefit from further consideration of "A Nincompoop." Do they think that a meek person can learn to be more assertive in his or her own behalf? When is self-assertiveness essential or desirable? What suggestions do students have for friends who are meek like Julia Vassilyevna? What can be done about a person who tries to trample on the rights of others?

CHECKING UP (True/False) *Page 344*

T **1.** The person telling the story is Julia Vassilyevna's employer.

F **2.** The narrator wishes to cheat the girl.

F **3.** Julia Vassilyevna works as a maid.

T **4.** Julia Vassilyevna is used to being cheated.

F **5.** At the end of the story, the girl decides to leave her job.

TALKING IT OVER *Page 344*

1. Why is the narrator "overcome with anger" at the girl's passive acceptance of the eleven rubles? He is robbing her of her rightful pay, yet she is thanking him for a pittance.

2. The speaker says he wants to teach the girl "a cruel lesson." What is the lesson he wishes her to learn? He wants her to learn to protest when she is unfairly treated. He wants her to be brave enough to stand up for her rights.

3. In your opinion, does Julia Vassilyevna learn the lesson? Give reasons for your answer. Answers will differ. It might be argued that the girl does not learn the lesson. She simply agrees with the speaker that it is possible to be a nincompoop.

4. Do you think that the speaker learns another lesson from this episode? Explain your answer. His last words, "How easy it is to crush the weak in this world," suggest that he has learned what it means to be alone and unprotected among ruthless people.

5. Do the lessons in this story have any application in today's world? Support your answer with some examples from your own experience or from your reading. Answers will vary. Most students will agree that the story's lessons are equally valid in today's world. Encourage students to discuss news reports or personal experiences from such areas as labor relations, international politics, or everyday life. Some may cite examples of powerless people who have been victimized by unfair systems or bureaucracies. Others may point to people who have fought for their rights and met with success.

EXPLICIT THEME *Page 345*

Cite some specific passages in the story that help to create sympathy for Julia Vassilyevna. Here are three examples:

Subtract nine Sundays . . . you know you didn't work with Kolya on Sundays, you only took walks. And three holidays . . . "

Julia Vassilyevna flushed a deep red and picked at the flounce of her dress, but—not a word. (Page 342)

"Only once was I given any money," she said in a trembling voice, "and that was by your wife. Three rubles, nothing more."

"Really? You see now, and I didn't make a note of it! Take three from fourteen . . . leaves eleven." (Page 343)

"But you know I've cheated you—robbed you! I have actually stolen from you! *Why* this *'merci'*?"

"In my other places they didn't give me anything at all." (Page 343)

UNDERSTANDING THE WORDS IN THE STORY (Matching Columns) *Page 345*

1. governess — h. instructor
2. ceremony — j. formal act
3. flushed — a. turned red
4. flounce — g. ruffle
5. heirloom — d. precious possession
6. heedlessness — i. carelessness
7. spineless — e. cowardly
8. protest — b. object to
9. nincompoop — f. fool
10. expression — c. look

WRITING IT DOWN

A Story Map *Page 345*

Students can use their notes from the writing exercise on page 340 to make story maps. This assignment should help them improve their creative writing skills.

AMBUSH

Tim O'Brien

Page 348

INTRODUCING THE SELECTION

Tim O'Brien's "Ambush" reads much like nonfiction. The narrative is presented so seamlessly and in such a straightforward voice that it seems it must have happened "exactly that way." Students may be surprised to learn that although O'Brien did serve in Vietnam, he does not have a daughter named Kathleen.

"Ambush" is taken from *The Things They Carried,* a collection of short stories. Many of these stories are interrelated; characters and motifs reappear throughout the book, and the result is a collage of incidents. All are linked in theme to the Vietnam War, which provided fertile ground for O'Brien's writing. Some of the stories occur in the midst of the war, whereas others take place after the war's end. In the collection's first story, the men in the unit carry their loves and hopes to war, as well as weapons, first aid supplies, mementos, letters—all neatly parceled into pounds and ounces. In "Ambush," as well as in other stories by O'Brien, we see what the young soldiers carry out—haunting memories of violence.

Tim O'Brien has said that he despised the Vietnam War but accepted his draft induction to win love and approval from friends and relatives. Despite his opposition to the war, he distinguished himself in battle and earned a Purple Heart. When he returned to the United States, he felt compelled to hide what he considered the shameful secrets of his wartime experience. Like the narrator of "Ambush," he had done things he regretted terribly—things he feels a nine-year-old child is not ready to hear. The narrator pretends, for the moment, that the girl is a grown-up, freeing him to tell the truth. We can interpret the action of writing, both for the fictional narrator and O'Brien himself, as catharsis. The secrets of the war are finally given voice.

The critic Pico Iyer writes of O'Brien's work:

> O'Brien's clean, incantatory prose always hovers on the edge of dream, and his specialty is that twilight zone of chimeras and fears and fantasies where nobody knows what is true and what is not. In Vietnam, of course, he locates the ultimate "spirit world," an eerie land of shadows where kids shot at phantoms, unable to tell friend from enemy, uncertain what they were fighting for.

O'Brien's portrayal of the Vietnam War, which is still a source of controversy, is one that appears in many books, television programs, and movies. The conflict began when North Vietnam, supported by other Communist forces, mounted an attack on South Vietnam. The North Vietnamese troops and the Viet Cong, guerrilla fighters from South Vietnam, waged war against the South Vietnamese army, which received assistance from the United States. Although the United States never officially declared war on North Vietnam, it began sending troops to Southeast Asia in 1965, increasing their number until 1969, when over 543,000 troops had been engaged. The United States became involved in the dispute because many believed that the civil war in Vietnam would be a significant threat to world peace.

Although many young men were eager to fight for their country, they weren't always certain of what they were fighting for. Grandiose visions of war were often crushed by brutal realities. Many dissenters in the United States criticized the war severely. In 1973, after approximately 57,000 United States soldiers had died—not including those wounded or missing in action—a cease-fire treaty was signed. Both North Vietnam and South Vietnam violated the agreement and continued to fight, however, until South Vietnam surrendered to the Communist forces in 1975.

PRESENTATION

"Ambush" is a suitable story to read and discuss in one class period. You may want to devote additional time to discussion of the Vietnam War and the issues it raises. You might choose to read the story aloud and then proceed with the discussion questions in Talking It Over.

Undoubtedly, many students will have heard and read a number of war stories by this time, many of them tragic and discouraging. They should recall other stories of war in *Impact*, among them "The Sniper" (page 213) and "War" (page 70). Encourage them to compare the various treatments of war in this anthology.

Ask students to further their knowledge of the Vietnam War through research. They may be interested in reading other stories and novels by Tim O'Brien, listed in the biography on page 353 of *Impact*. "Field Trip" might be a good story to compare with "Ambush"— it also involves the character Kathleen and her reactions to her father's history.

CHECKING UP (Multiple-Choice) *Page 350*

1. The narrator recounts the episode to
   a. protest the war
   b. show how brave he was
   (c.) explain why he keeps writing war stories
2. The episode takes place on a
   a. sunny day
   b. windy night
   (c.) foggy morning
3. As the young man moved up the trail, the narrator felt
   a. courageous
   (b.) terrified
   c. angry

4. After the grenade landed, the narrator
   (a.) wanted to warn the young man
   b. wanted to run away
   c. felt great relief

5. Kiowa told the narrator that
   a. they had been in peril
   b. his act was courageous
   (c.) he had done the right thing

TALKING IT OVER *Page 357*

1. At the beginning of the story, the narrator does not want to answer his daughter's question. Why does he hope that she will ask him the same question again when she is older? He wants to tell her about his experiences as a soldier when she is better able to understand them.

2. What kind of atmosphere, or mood, does the story's setting help create? The setting—a hot, foggy, mosquito-ridden night at an ambush area—helps create a tense, ominous atmosphere.

3. Just as the grenade was about to land, the narrator realized that he had made a mistake. How does he explain his action? He says that his action was entirely automatic and that he wanted to make the young man go away. **What internal conflict did he face after the incident occurred?** He struggles with the guilt of having taken a life. **How did his fellow soldier, Kiowa, try to justify the action?** Kiowa asked him to imagine what would have happened if the situation had been reversed.

4. The story's title refers to the narrator's "ambush" of his unsuspecting enemy. How does the story's ending suggest that, long after the episode, the young man would, in a sense, "ambush" the narrator? Long after the war, the recurring image of the young enemy soldier coming out of the morning fog haunts the narrator. In this sense, the roles are reversed, because the memory of the young soldier "ambushes" the narrator when he least expects it—when he is reading a newspaper, for example, or sitting alone in a room.

THEME

Implied Theme *Page 351*

Why does the narrator keep writing war stories? Writing about his war experiences may help the writer come to terms with his feelings about the horror of killing other human beings.

WRITING IT DOWN

A Comparison *Page 352*

Comparing the treatment of war in "The Sniper" and "Ambush" will necessitate a thoughtful review of the stories.

SPEAKING AND LISTENING

Comparing Two Works *Page 352*

In addition to improving their speaking and listening skills, students will see how a similar theme is treated in a different genre.

A GAME OF CATCH

Richard Wilbur **Page 355**

INTRODUCING THE SELECTION

If "A Game of Catch" appeared anonymously, one might suspect the writer of being a poet as well as a short-story writer. His images of the boys playing catch are sharp and clear, and he interprets perfectly the poetry of motion. Moreover, he understands the friendships and rivalries of twelve- and thirteen-year-old boys. Richard Wilbur is a Pulitzer Prize-winning poet, as indicated in his biography on page 362 of *Impact.*

American teenagers, with their firsthand experience of similar games of catch, should have no difficulty visualizing the action of Wilbur's story. They are bound to appreciate his psychological insight and the humor and pathos he brings to his characterizations of Monk, Glennie, and Scho.

You might wish to discuss the effort and concentration of great athletes. Some students may bring up the fact that many sports figures make competition look easy. Others may mention ways in which athletes cooperate with their teammates.

Mention that two of the boys in Wilbur's story seem to be well on their way to competence in sports. A third boy seems less adept. Suggest that students, as they read, be alert for more than one kind of game the boys play.

PRESENTATION

You may want to read "A Game of Catch" aloud in class and then proceed to a discussion based on the questions following the story, the two vocabulary exercises, and the writing assignment.

CHECKING UP

(Putting Events in Order) *Page 359*

Scho stands on the lawn watching Monk and Glennie play catch.

Glennie asks Scho if he has his glove.

Monk throws a bumpy grounder to Scho.

Scho throws a ball that strikes the trunk of the apple tree and bounces onto the sidewalk in front of the firehouse.

Scho pulls himself up into the apple tree.

Scho begins singing in an exaggerated way.

Monk and Glennie stop the game and sit down under the apple tree.

Monk begins to climb the apple tree.

Scho falls from the tree and lands on his back.

Monk and Glennie kneel beside Scho, asking how he is.

TALKING IT OVER *Page 359*

1. **The game of catch between Monk and Glennie is described as a kind of "dance in the sun." What features of dancing does the narrator have in mind?** The features of dancing are graceful movements, smooth patterns, and coordinated rhythms.

2. **What problem does Scho's presence introduce?** Scho wants to be included in the game, but he doesn't have his glove, and he isn't as good a player. **Why do you suppose Monk and Glennie ease Scho out of the game?** They are much better players and can have a better time without his bumbling.

3. **Some people react to rejection by withdrawing or showing anger. How does Scho get even with the other boys?** He hangs around and teases and torments them. **What makes his "game" effective?** He makes such a pest of himself that the others can no longer concentrate on their game and enjoy it.

4. **At the end of the story, is the conflict between Scho and the other boys resolved? Or does it take another form?** It is not really resolved. It takes another form. After Scho falls from the tree, the other boys show concern and anxiety, but Scho manages to recover his breath enough to taunt them further. As they leave, he croaks after them "in triumph and misery, 'I want you to do whatever you're going to do for the whole rest of your life.' "

5. **Why do children's games often end in conflicts or broken friendships?** Conflicts arise when children do not accept each other regardless of varying levels of skill.Their pride and their hurt feelings are expressed through hostile action. **What insight does this story offer into the relationships and motivations of young people?** Young people are motivated by the need to excel in what they do and to establish relationships with others. They may be able to avoid childish conflicts by helping each other to develop certain kinds of expertise and by being generous in their appreciation of what others do. (Students will have additional ideas.)

THEME

Theme and Conflict *Page 360*

How would you state the theme of "A Game of Catch"? Answers will vary. One possible statement of the theme is as follows: People need the companionship and respect of their peers.

UNDERSTANDING THE WORDS IN THE STORY (Multiple-Choice) *Page 360*

1. When Monk would *lob* the ball, he would
   (a.) throw it in a high, arching curve
   b. bounce it along the ground
   c. throw it overhand
2. When Glennie would *burn* the ball, he would
   a. catch the ball on the fly
   (b.) throw it very hard
   c. pitch the ball in a curve
3. A *negligent* movement is
   a. unskillful
   (b.) careless
   c. dangerous
4. The boys are *entranced,* or
   a. competing with one another
   b. enclosed on all sides
   (c.) filled with delight
5. Glennie notices Scho *dawdling,* or
   a. smiling
   (b.) idling
   c. moving restlessly

6. The *brake* is
   (a.) an area covered with bushes
   b. a recess from the game
   c. a wall around the firehouse
7. When Scho spoke *tentatively,* he sounded
   a. stubborn
   (b.) uncertain
   c. angry
8. Scho's voice was *mocking,* because he was
   (a.) making fun of the boys
   b. laughing
   c. talking loudly
9. When Scho's voice was *exuberant,* it was
   (a.) gleeful
   b. annoying
   c. hushed
10. Something *clenched* is
   a. opened wide
   b. gathered closely
   (c.) shut tightly

(Matching Columns) *Page 361*

1. resume	i. begin again
2. serene	j. calm; peaceful
3. indolently	f. lazily
4. supple	g. bending easily
5. jouncing	a. bouncing
6. absorbed	c. completely involved in
7. abstractedly	h. absent-mindedly
8. persisted	e. continued stubbornly
9. intense	b. serious; earnest
10. scrambling	d. climbing hastily

WRITING IT DOWN

Another Point of View *Page 362*

The story will be quite different when told in the first person by one of the boys. You might ask students to review the exercise on page 253.

THE RETURN

Ngugi wa Thiong'o

Page 363

INTRODUCING THE SELECTION

The backdrop of "The Return" is Kenya at the time of the Mau Mau rebellion. The Mau Mau were Kikuyu (or Gikuyu) people of central Kenya who, in the 1940s, attempted to overthrow British rule in Kenya. The movement was led by the Kenya African Union and its president, Jomo Kenyatta. In 1952, the Mau Mau launched a campaign of terrorist attacks and the British government responded by jailing thousands of rebels in detention camps. Widespread fighting broke out. By the time the fighting ended in 1956, about 11,000 rebels and 2,000 African loyalists had been killed. Kenya did not achieve independence from Great Britain until 1963.

In Ngugi's story, Kamau is one of the Kikuyu rebels. When he returns home after spending five years in detention camps, he finds that much of what he had loved and longed for during those years did not wait for his return.

Ngugi rejected Christianity in the 1960s because of its link to colonialism. At that time he renewed his commitment to Kikuyu culture by choosing to write only in the Kikuyu language. Ngugi was instrumental in influencing the University of Nairobi to transform its English department into the Department of African Languages and Literature.

PRESENTATION

"The Return" may be read at home and discussed in class the following day. You might want to emphasize the symbolism in the story, because this element is the key to understanding the theme of the narrative.

Kamau's bundle symbolizes the burden of his bitter past, a past he clings to. He hurries to the river to take his life, but when the bundle falls into the river and floats swiftly away, he is suddenly released from his burden. He then accepts the changes that have taken place in his absence.

Early in the story, Kamau is closely identified with the river; he feels a kinship with it. You might point out the element of personification here—Kamau wonders if the river will recognize him. The river may be understood as a symbol of Kamau's life or, possibly, the continuity of life itself.

CHECKING UP (True/False) *Page 368*

F 1. Kamau is returning home after five years of military service.

F 2. The river that Kamau played in as a child has dried up.

F 3. The village women give Kamau a hero's welcome.

T 4. Kamau's mother and father were told that Kamau was dead.

F 5. Kamau throws his bundle into the river.

TALKING IT OVER *Page 369*

1. Kamau quickens his step as he approaches the river. Why is the Honia river so important to him? In his youth the river meant everything to Kamau. It reminds him of his past and represents the continuity of his life.

2. Why does Kamau receive a cold reception from the villagers? They have heard that he is dead, and his sudden reappearance frightens and confuses them. Also, they may be uncomfortable since they know that Kamau's wife has left. **What was your reaction to their treatment of him?** Reactions may include surprise, curiosity, or even suspicion. At this point, some students may begin to realize that something is about to go wrong.

3. Like Kamau, many men were swept away by the colonial forces and taken to detention camps. What did they talk about constantly? They talked of their homes and families.

4. What are Kamau's hopes for the future? Kamau anticipates being reunited with his wife, Muthoni, finding a job in Nairobi, paying the remainder of the bride price to Muthoni's parents, and starting a family.

5. What reasons do Kamau's parents give for allowing Muthoni to leave? They had been led by Karanja to believe that Kamau was dead. Since they have no security—the political upheaval has left them without land and food—they let Muthoni go with Karanja.

6. Kamau returns to the river with thoughts of taking his life, but he does not. Why does watching his little bundle float down the river cause him to change his mind? Kamau associates the bundle with the bitter years of his detention. When it floats away, he feels released from the burden of his past.

THEME AND SYMBOL *Page 369*

1. Reread the passage in which Kamau decides that he will not share the details of his suffering with his brothers and sisters. How does this passage show that he is burdened by the events of his recent past? He looks forward to seeing his brothers and sisters, but he fears their questions about his years in detention. He decides not to unburden himself on them; he will not let go of his suffering.

2. At the end of the story, what is symbolic about Kamau's little bundle floating swiftly down the river? How does this episode become a "turning point" for Kamau? The bundle symbolizes "the bitterness and hardships of the years spent in detention camps." When it floats away, it is as if Kamau is being released from those terrible years. The episode is a "turning point" because Kamau decides not to take his life. He realizes that the past is behind him and that he is powerless to change it. Just as the river keeps flowing, so must his life go on.

3. What might the river symbolize? The river might symbolize Kamau's life, or the continuity of life itself.

UNDERSTANDING THE WORDS IN THE STORY (Matching Columns) *Page 370*

1. animosity	**g.** hostility; hatred
2. exhilaration	**h.** joyfulness
3. desisted	**f.** stopped
4. nostalgia	**i.** longing for the past
5. detainee	**d.** political prisoner
6. flout	**a.** mock; make fun of
7. discernible	**j.** able to be seen
8. dwelled	**e.** resided; lived at
9. incessant	**c.** continuous; unending
10. dispersed	**b.** scattered

WRITING IT DOWN

A Story *Page 370*

The students should feel free to be creative and to experiment with plot, tone, and point of view.

THE TELL-TALE HEART

Edgar Allan Poe

Page 373

INTRODUCING THE SELECTION

Your students have by now completed many short stories in *Impact* and have analyzed plot, character, setting, point of view, tone, and theme. All of these components contribute to the total effect of a story upon the reader. This unit emphasizing total effect begins appropriately with "The Tell-Tale Heart," in which the narrator's voice rises steadily in nervous agitation, culminating in the revelation of his crime. His final mad confession is the climax of this tale of utter horror.

Readers are both attracted and repelled by the story. Can we in any way identify with this madman who schemes so cunningly and suffers such terrifying consequences? How does Poe mesmerize us? The American poet Richard Wilbur has commented, "Poe's mind may have been a strange one; yet all minds are alike in their general structure; therefore, we can understand him, and I think he will have something to say to us as long as there is civil war in the palaces of men's minds."

Refer students to the text biography of the author on page 383. Since each new class rediscovers Poe, you may be inundated with reports on his life and works.

Poe published "The Tell-Tale Heart" in a magazine in 1843 while he was living with his wife and mother-in-law in Philadelphia. Their house at 530 North Seventh Street is now a museum operated by the National Park Service. In the same year he won a hundred-dollar prize from the Philadelphia *Dollar Newspaper* for "The Gold-Bug," a pioneering detective story. The prize was a small fortune to the Poes, who were nearly always in straitened circumstances despite the range and brilliance of the author's works.

Ironically, first editions of Poe's writings are extremely valuable now. Ask your students to look for a poorly printed pamphlet titled *Tamerlane* by "A Bostonian." This first publication of Poe's writing in 1827 by an eighteen-year-old printer named Calvin F. S. Thomas initially sold (if at all) for pennies, but now might fetch over five hundred thousand dollars on the collectors' market. The stock question among collectors of old books is "Do you have a *Tamerlane* in your attic?"

PRESENTATION

After some discussion of students' acquaintance with Poe through previous reading of his stories and poems, you might ask the meaning of *tell-tale:* "informing or talebearing." How can a heart inform us? Ask each student to place the fingertips of one hand on the wrist of his or her opposite arm near the thumb and feel the pulse. What does that strong, steady beat tell us? When does it vary its speed and rhythm?

If some of your students have read the story previously, do not let them say much about it until the whole class has read the story. Although silent reading will suffice, you may prefer an oral reading—your own or one from among the excellent recordings available.

The questions and exercises following "The Tell-Tale Heart" should clarify students' understanding of the vocabulary and story elements.

You might want to follow the discussion with a class period of poetry reading. Ask students to bring in their favorite poems by Poe and other poets to share with the class.

CHECKING UP (Multiple-Choice) *Page 378*

1. The narrator claims that his keenest sense is his sense of
- **a.** smell
- **b.** touch
- **(c.)** hearing

2. The narrator admits to being
- **a.** mad
- **(b.)** nervous
- **c.** depressed

3. His object in killing the old man is
- **a.** to possess his gold
- **b.** to revenge an insult
- **(c.)** to get rid of an obsession

4. The narrator is most pleased by his own
   (a.) cleverness
   b. strength
   c. courage
5. The sight of the old man's eye arouses the narrator's
   a. fear
   (b.) fury
   c. curiosity
6. Before he kills the old man, the narrator is aware of
   a. The ticking of a clock
   b. the sound of a drum
   (c.) the beating of a human heart
7. The narrator hides the body in
   (a.) the old man's room
   b. the parlor
   c. the bathroom
8. A neighbor reports hearing a
   (a.) loud shriek
   b. drumbeat
   c. ringing noise
9. When the police first arrive, the narrator feels
   a. vaguely uneasy
   b. very angry
   (c.) completely confident
10. The narrator suspects the police of
   a. brutality
   b. cunning
   (c.) hypocrisy

TALKING IT OVER *Page 379*

1. At the opening of the story, the narrator is trying to convince someone of his sanity. What examples does he use to demonstrate that he is in his right mind? To whom do you think he is speaking? He argues that if he were mad he would not have such sharp senses; he says he can hear all things in heaven and earth and many things in hell. He also argues that he could not be mad and still have proceeded so cautiously with his plan. Answers to the last question will vary.

2. What is the narrator's motive for killing the old man? Even though he says he loves the old man, he wants to get rid of the old man's "vulture" eye. **Why does he wait until the eighth night to commit the murder?** He waits until the old man's "evil eye" is open because it is the eye he hates, not the man.

3. Poe uses the first-person point of view in this story. At what points in the tale did your interpretations of the action differ from those of the narrator? The narrator's hatred of the old man's clouded eye is insane. His actions in visiting the old man's bedchamber night after night are not wise, as the narrator supposes, but a sign of insanity. His cruel stalking and slaying of the helpless old man are the actions of a psychopathic killer. The dismembering of the corpse is unspeakable. The narrator is a complete fool to invite the policemen to sit and visit in the murdered man's room. The loud beating of the heart is the narrator's hallucination, and his final outcry gives voice to madness and horror.

4. Point out several instances of *dramatic irony,* when you were aware of things that the narrator did not notice. The proof of sanity claimed by the narrator is actually proof of his insanity. The beating of the old man's heart could not possibly be loud enough to wake the neighbors, as the narrator fears. The narrator believes the murdered man's eye will trouble him no more, but the reader knows that the narrator has brought worse troubles upon himself. The narrator's "perfect triumph" as he seats himself above the corpse is a delusion. The policemen do not hear the sound of the beating heart which the narrator hears in his own diseased mind, and his wild accusation that they are dissembling is his own undoing.

5. What causes the narrator to lose control at the end of the story? He imagines that he hears the murdered man's heart beating louder and louder. He believes the policemen hear it too, and are mocking him.

TOTAL EFFECT *Page 380*

1. How would you describe the total effect of "The Tell-Tale Heart"? The total effect is one of horror. **List some words that contribute to this effect.** Some of the words are: "mad," "haunted," "mortal terror," "hellish tattoo," "uncontrollable terror," "dismembered," "corpse," "cunningly," "hideous."

2. What image does the narrator use to describe the old man's eye? He uses the image of a vulture's eye. **How does it contribute to the effect of the story?** The image is morbid, usually associated with death and decay.

3. What instances does the narrator give of his sensitivity to sound? In addition to hearing all things in heaven and earth and many things in hell, he claims he heard the beating of the old man's heart both before and after the murder. **How do these instances reveal that he is insane?** Most people do not hear such sounds; he is hallucinating.

UNDERSTANDING THE WORDS IN THE STORY (Multiple-Choice) *Page 380*

1. The narrator claims that his sense of hearing is *acute.*
   a. serious
   (b.) sharp
   c. painful
2. Once the idea of murder was *conceived,* he was haunted by it.
   (a.) imagined
   b. declared
   c. confided
3. He opened the door and *thrust* his head into the room.
   a. slipped
   (b.) poked
   c. crammed
4. He was *vexed* by the Evil Eye.
   a. delayed
   (b.) irritated
   c. enchanted
5. Only a *profound* person could have suspected his plan.
   a. suspicious
   (b.) highly intelligent
   c. sane
6. The old man *stifled* a groan.
   (a.) smothered
   b. grumbled
   c. uttered
7. The narrator often felt his soul filled with *awe.*
   a. grief and pain
   b. rage and jealousy
   (c.) wonder and fear
8. Dreadful sounds would *well up* from his soul at midnight.
   a. come
   b. fall
   (c.) rise
9. He was *distracted* by terrors.
   (a.) confused
   b. entertained
   c. frightened
10. The victim tried to imagine that all his fears were *causeless.*
    a. unnecessary
    (b.) unfounded
    c. silly

(Matching Columns) *Page 382*

1. stalked — i. approached secretly
2. enveloped — f. covered or surrounded
3. mournful — a. showing grief
4. resolved — j. determined
5. refrained — d. held back
6. precaution — e. care taken beforehand
7. dismembered — b. cut into pieces
8. deposited — g. set down
9. cunningly — h. cleverly
10. wary — c. very careful

(Completion) *Page 382*

1. At first the narrator spoke fluently while the police sat and listened.
2. The police made a search of the premises.
3. A neighbor had lodged a complaint with the police.
4. The narrator believed that the police knew the truth and were making a mockery of his feelings.
5. He grated a chair against the floor.
6. The remains of the victim reposed under the planks.
7. He was unable to endure the agony any longer.
8. He spoke with a heightened voice.
9. He could not bear their false, hypocritical smiles.
10. Anything would be more tolerable than their pretense.

WRITING IT DOWN

An Account *Page 383*

Writing an eyewitness account may increase the students' involvement with the story. Imaginative students might imitate the official language of the detective writing the report of the crime.

SPEAKING AND LISTENING

Discussing an Answer *Page 383*

Students should enjoy this assignment, which allows them to speculate about the narrator.

Comparing Narrators

This exercise will help the students develop skills in critical reading and interpretation.

AUGUST HEAT

William Fryer Harvey

Page 385

INTRODUCING THE SELECTION

In William Fryer Harvey's "August Heat" the total effect is one of bone-chilling horror. Harvey entices the reader with his first sentence and skillfully weaves a web from which there is no escape. His innocent narrator stops his storytelling just short of the violence that is sure to come. The lead-in on page 385 should be sufficient introduction to "August Heat."

Students will probably prefer to read this story silently at their own speed. The discussion questions and exercises should elicit good response.

PRESENTATION

Ask your students if they sometimes choose mystery stories and horror stories to read or to watch on television. What are their favorites? Why are reruns of old shows such as *The Twilight Zone* and *Alfred Hitchcock Presents* still popular decades after their original release?

Use the Speaking and Listening activities to guide a discussion of "August Heat" and "The Tell-Tale Heart." The narrators and the settings are quite different. The violence in "August Heat" is unstated, whereas Poe's narrator describes the murder and his pains to hide the evidence. Which story do they find more suspenseful and horrifying, and why? How does the tone of voice alter the atmosphere of the story? Some students may suggest that "August Heat" has a supernatural feel, whereas "The Tell-Tale Heart," despite its raving, unreliable narrator, is more realistic. Yet the fact that Harvey's story is told by a calm, coherent narrator may make the story more plausible, and therefore more frightening.

CHECKING UP

(Putting Events in Order) *Page 390*

Withencroft draws a sketch of a criminal.

Withencroft goes for a walk.

A boy asks Withencroft the time.

Withencroft hears the noise of hammer blows.

Atkinson greets Withencroft with a smile.

Withencroft sees the inscription on the monument.

Atkinson invites Withencroft to supper.

Mrs. Atkinson shows Withencroft an illustrated Bible.

Atkinson waters his flowers.

Atkinson sharpens his chisel.

TALKING IT OVER

Page 391

1. This story takes place during the *dog days*, the hot, uncomfortable part of summer between mid-July and September. People in ancient times reckoned this period from the rising of Sirius, the Dog Star. During this time, supposedly, dogs were especially apt to go mad. What is the connection between this belief and the events of the story? The extreme heat causes Withencroft and Atkinson to do things they would not ordinarily do. The odd coincidences of the drawing and the inscription on the monument are indications that something is very wrong. One or both of the characters may be driven to madness.

2. The narrator says that a "sudden impulse" makes him enter the yard. What evidence is there that the characters have no control over what is taking place? Although they have never met, they have recorded each other's likeness and name.

3. What rational explanations do the two men offer for the strange coincidences of the story? They assume they have met somewhere before or have seen each other's names. **Why are these explanations rejected?** They have never been in the same place or had any kind of connection.

4. Judging from clues in the last part of the story, what do you think will be the final outcome? Atkinson will use the chisel he is sharpening to kill Withencroft.

5. The background of this story is ordinary and familiar. There are references to the asphalt pavement, streetcars, the front yard and garden of a house. Why does this naturalistic setting make the events of the story more terrifying? It suggests that bizarre and horrible events can take place in the most ordinary setting and can happen to anyone.

TOTAL EFFECT *Page 391*

1. The narrator tells the story in a completely serious and naturalistic manner. How does the narrator convince us that the events he records are true? He appears to be an ordinary man with a prosaic life. He seems as mystified as we are by the odd coincidences that occur.

2. How does the setting make the action believable? It is to be expected that an artist would sketch at home and that a monument mason would work in his yard. Everything is realistic except the strange coincidences.

UNDERSTANDING THE WORDS IN THE STORY (Multiple-Choice) *Page 392*

1. The *outset* of something is its
   (a.) beginning
   b. middle
   c. end
2. An *oppressively* hot day is
   a. rainy
   (b.) unbearable
   c. pleasant
3. An *intent* gaze is
   (a.) earnest
   b. curious
   c. angry
4. *Stumpy* fingers are
   (a.) thick
   b. graceful
   c. bony
5. An *utter* surprise is
   (a.) total
   b. expected
   c. imaginative
6. To *sustain* something is to give it
   a. attention
   (b.) support
   c. understanding
7. A *recollection* is a
   (a.) memory
   b. fund
   c. book
8. Something that is *palpable* is experienced by the
   (a.) senses
   b. mind
   c. unconscious
9. When one is *roused,* one
   a. sleeps
   b. dreams
   (c.) stirs
10. To be lost in *reverie* is to
   a. forget
   b. travel
   (c.) daydream

(Matching Columns) *Page 393*

1. inscription	d. writing on a surface
2. intrusion	g. uninvited entry
3. flaw	j. defect
4. uncanny	c. weird; mysterious
5. plausible	h. seemingly true
6. coincidence	i. chance occurrence
7. prosperous	b. well-off
8. improbable	a. not likely
9. eaves	e. edges of a roof
10. stifling	f. smothering

WRITING IT DOWN

A Plan *Page 393*

This exercise will appeal to the students' imaginations.

Speaking and Listening *Page 393*

Comparing the literary techniques of two authors will increase the students' appreciation of the stories. They should also enjoy judging the level of suspense in each story.

LUCK

Mark Twain

Page 394

INTRODUCING THE SELECTION

Students may be familiar with Twain's "The Celebrated Jumping Frog of Calaveras County," his most famous tall tale. Or they may know some popular American tall-tale heroes: Paul Bunyan, Pecos Bill, Davy Crockett, and the like. Ask students if they have ever told a tall tale. Why do people like to exaggerate? Why do we enjoy reading tall tales?

The events in "Luck" are based on the career of a real person, Garnet Joseph Wolseley. One of the good friends of the Clemens family was their pastor, Joseph H. Twichell. Twain took long walks with him and used him as a source of rich anecdotes and comments on human nature. Twain says:

> In 1890 I had published in *Harper's Monthly* a sketch called "Luck," the particulars of which had been furnished to Twichell by a visiting English army chaplain. The next year, in Rome, an English gentleman introduced himself to me on the street and said, "Do you know who the chief figure in that 'Luck' sketch is?" "No," I said, "I don't." "Well," he said, "it is Lord Wolseley—and don't you go to England if you value your scalp." In Venice another English gentleman said the same to me. These gentlemen said, "Of course Wolseley is not to blame for the stupendous luck that has chased him up ever since he came shining out of Sandhurst in that most unexpected and victorious way, but he will recognize himself in that sketch, and so will everybody else, and if you venture into England he will destroy you."
>
> In 1900, in London, I went to the Fourth of July banquet, arriving after eleven o'clock at night at a time when the place was emptying itself. Choate was presiding. An English admiral was speaking and some two or three hundred men were still present. I was to speak and I moved along down behind the chairs, which had been occupied by guests, toward Choate. These chairs were now empty. When I had reached within three chairs of Choate, a handsome man put out his hand and said, "Stop. Sit down here. I want to get acquainted with you. I am Lord Wolseley." I was falling but he caught me and I explained that I was often taken that way. We sat and chatted together and had a very good time . . .

The facts of Wolseley's life may be read in the *Encyclopaedia Britannica* or in any history of Britain. "Entering the army as a second lieutenant in 1852," says the *Britannica,* "he reasoned that the surest way to advancement was to try to get killed every time he had the opportunity." Undeniably Wolseley did have amazing luck in fifty years of combat throughout the world, but he also had foresight and brilliance. He is credited with many dazzling accomplishments including the modernization of the British army. If Twain's story of meeting Wolseley is true, then the famous commander must also be credited with grace and humor.

PRESENTATION

The humor of this story lends itself to oral presentation. You might ask students to practice reading the speeches aloud, using appropriate inflections to convey the tone of each narrator.

After students have read "Luck," guide discussion with the text questions, and continue with the vocabulary exercises and your choice of the suggestions for writing.

CHECKING UP (True/False) *Page 398*

T **1.** At the opening of the story, the Reverend is attending a banquet to honor a former pupil.

F **2.** Scoresby passed his examinations at the military academy by cheating.

T **3.** Scoresby took first prize in mathematics.

T **4.** Scoresby's stunning military victories were actually blunders.

F **5.** During the Crimean War, Scoresby put the entire English army to flight.

TALKING IT OVER *Page 399*

1. The story has two narrators. What impression do you form of the first narrator? The first narrator is an admiring guest at a banquet in honor of Scoresby. **What is his attitude toward Lord Arthur Scoresby?** He is a somewhat naive man who is thrilled to look on the renowned military hero in person.

2. How does Twain convince you that his second narrator, the Reverend, is someone who can be

trusted to tell the truth? The first narrator says that he knows the Reverend as a man of strict veracity and as a good judge of other men.

3. What are the Reverend's motives for helping Scoresby? He feels pity for Scoresby because Scoresby knows so little. He wants to ease Scoresby's fall by teaching him some of the test material.

4. Why do you suppose that only the Reverend is aware of Scoresby's "secret"? The Reverend stays closer to him than anyone else and protects him as much as possible. Scoresby's blunders look like well-planned strategy to most people.

5. What is the point of Twain's satire in this story? Twain is poking fun at the adulation often accorded military heroes. He wants to show that luck is sometimes a factor in military success.

TOTAL EFFECT *Page 399*

1. Twain achieves his effects through a combination of exaggeration and comic deflation. Find examples of language in the first paragraph that glorify the figure of Lord Arthur Scoresby. The narrator refers to Scoresby as "Lieutenant-General Lord Arthur Scoresby, Y.C., K.C.B., etc., etc., etc." He states that Scoresby's "name shot suddenly to the zenith . . . to remain forever celebrated." He says that he looks with adulation at that "demigod" who is sweetly unconscious of his "greatness." **Why do you suppose Twain emphasizes the narrator's reverence for this man?** Twain exaggerates the hero worship so that the deflation of the hero will be more dramatic.

2. How does the Reverend's tale deflate this image of Scoresby? The tale makes Scoresby look like an "absolute fool" whose successes have resulted from blunders and incredible luck.

3. Which events in the Reverend's tale are improbable or comically absurd? It is improbable that a little cramming would result in Scoresby's passing the examinations "with flying colors." It is comically absurd that the Reverend would buy a cornetcy to "protect the country against" Scoresby. It is also absurd that Scoresby's blunders always look like "inspirations of genius" and that one such blunder results in the rout of the Russian army.

4. Some readers think that Twain's satire is aimed at debunking a military hero. Other readers think that Twain is expressing a cynical attitude toward life. What is your opinion of Twain's intention? Give evidence from the story to support your opinion. Twain's intention may be to show that people are wrong to make idols and demigods of military men who have achieved renown. Their success may be at least partly a matter of luck. Primarily, Twain intends to amuse us with his humor and exaggeration.

UNDERSTANDING THE WORDS IN THE STORY (Completion) *Page 400*

1. At high noon the sun is said to be at its zenith.
2. Character can be read in a person's countenance.
3. An idea is beginning to glimmer in your eyes.
4. A person who stands out in a crowd is conspicuous.
5. A demigod seems to be superhuman.
6. Scoresby had enjoyed an illustrious career.
7. Tears began welling in the eyes of the audience.
8. Despite the gravity of his expression, Scoresby was a fool.
9. Scoresby was renowned for his military victories.
10. The Reverend had a singular look on his face.

(Matching Columns) *Page 400*

1. veracity	g. truthfulness
2. preliminary	e. coming before
3. guileless	i. innocent
4. veritable	a. authentic
5. compassion	h. pity or sympathy
6. arouse	c. awaken or excite
7. stock	b. commonly used
8. superficial	j. on the surface
9. resolve	d. determine
10. conceive	f. understand; imagine

(Multiple-Choice) *Page 400*

1. The Reverend found, to his *consternation,* that Scoresby had passed his examinations.
   a. pleasure
   b. amusement
   (c.) dismay
2. Scoresby received an *ovation.*
   a. prize
   b. reward
   (c.) expression of approval

3. The Reverend found the outcome of the examinations *preposterous.*
   (a.) ridiculous
   b. frightening
   c. prejudiced
4. Scoresby was given *prodigious* responsibilities.
   a. unusual
   (b.) huge
   c. professional
5. Scoresby achieved a *sublimity* denied to other men of greater talent.
   (a.) supreme honor
   b. command
   c. reputation
6. The Reverend gave up a life of *repose.*
   (a.) calmness
   b. simplicity
   c. idleness
7. The Reverend was in a constant state of *apprehension.*
   a. controlled anger
   (b.) worried expectation
   c. intense fascination
8. The Russians did not expect a regiment to come *browsing* around.
   a. spying
   b. charging
   (c.) looking casually
9. Scoresby was responsible for the *rout* of the Russian army.
   a. blunder
   (b.) disastrous defeat
   c. loss
10. Scoresby was blessed with *phenomenal* luck.
   (a.) extraordinary
   b. absolute
   c. repeated

WRITING IT DOWN

Notes on Literature and History *Page 402*

Students will learn that garbled orders caused the Light Brigade to sweep down into "the jaws of death" in a valley near the Black Sea port of Balaklava instead of attacking isolated Russian forces on the heights. Students might say that in Twain's tale Scoresby misinterpreted orders yet fared better than Lord Cardigan's Light Brigade.

A Comparison *Page 402*

Probably the most quoted stanza of Tennyson's "The Charge of the Light Brigade" is this one:

"Forward, the Light Brigade!"
Was there a man dismay'd?
Not tho' the soldier knew
  Someone had blunder'd;
Theirs not to make reply,
Theirs not to reason why,
Theirs but to do and die;
Into the valley of Death
  Rode the six hundred.

Students will probably recognize that Twain pokes fun at Scoresby's charge in the wrong direction and his surprising victory. Students will also recognize the serious and admiring attitude of Tennyson toward the brave men who obeyed the orders that they knew were in error. Some students may prefer Tennyson's tribute to fighting men over Twain's humor at the same men's expense.

THE GIFT OF THE MAGI

O. Henry

Page 403

INTRODUCING THE SELECTION

Most of O. Henry's stories were written in the first decade of the twentieth century. "The Gift of the Magi" appeared in the collection *The Four Million,* which was published in 1906. The world has changed so much since then that your students might be distracted by the low prices, the quaint expressions, and the way Della and Jim live. Yet these ingredients are part of the story's enduring charm.

Refer students to the brief biography on page 412 of *Impact.* As a resident of New York City from 1902 until his death in 1910, O. Henry romanticized the lives of ordinary people in popular stories now regarded as social documents. Readers enjoyed his style, his humor, and his surprise endings. Caution students who have already read "The Gift of the Magi" not to give away its plot.

Tell students that the narrator, who seems to be O. Henry himself, comments on the characters from time to time like a kindly uncle who likes using big words. Remind students to use footnotes and glossary as well as context clues.

You might ask students if anyone of their acquaintance has very long hair—falling in beautiful waves to the waist. Perhaps they have family albums with photographs showing the crowning glory of their great-great-grandmothers. If women of that era did not have abundant hair of their own, they wore falls and switches of real or artificial hair to create elaborate and beautiful styles. Tell students that if they are perceptive readers, they will discover other characteristics of the period.

PRESENTATION

You might mention to students that "The Gift of the Magi" is one of America's best-loved stories to read at Christmas time or any time of year.

You might like to read this story aloud to students, or give it as a special assignment for one or more students in the class to rehearse and present.

In addition to using the discussion questions and vocabulary exercises, you will want to consider the suggestion for analytical writing.

CHECKING UP

(Short Answer) *Page 408*

1. When does the action of the story take place? The action takes place on Christmas Eve.

2. What is Della's proudest possession? Her proudest possession is her lovely long hair.

3. What does Della buy for Jim? She buys him a platinum fob chain for his watch.

4. What has happened to Jim's watch? He has sold it.

5. What is Jim's gift to Della? The gift is a set of tortoise-shell combs.

TALKING IT OVER *Page 408*

1. Which details in the story tell you that the events take place early in the twentieth century? A furnished apartment would cost much more than eight dollars a week now. Other details belonging to the period of the story are the powder rag, the pier glass, Jim's gold watch, the old-fashioned curling irons (not like electric curling irons now in use), Coney Island chorus girls, and tortoise-shell combs. Colloquial expressions in the dialogue such as "you had me going awhile" also point to an earlier era.

2. This story is famous for its ironic plot. How do the actions of the characters bring about unexpected results? Della sells her hair to buy Jim a watch chain, and Jim sells his watch to buy combs for Della's hair. **Are these actions consistent with the nature of the characters?** Their actions are entirely consistent with the generous love they feel for each other.

3. What is the *tone* of the story? The tone is warmly humorous, ge˙ial, and ironic. **Is O. Henry's attitude toward his characters sympathetic? mocking? amused? or something else?** His attitude is sympathetic, gently mocking, and amused, but is also kind, affectionate, sentimental, philosophical, indulgent, optimistic, and spiritual. Students may describe it in other ways.

4. Locate the statement in this story that best expresses its theme. "Of all who give and receive gifts, such as they are wisest."

5. Explain the title of the story. What is the "gift" associated with the Magi? The Magi were the three Wise Men from the East who brought gifts of gold, frankincense, and myrrh and paid homage to the baby Jesus. The greater gift associated with the Magi, however, is the gift of unselfish love. According to the Bible, God's gift of his Son to the world was revealed to the Magi. **What has this gift to do with Jim and Della?** Jim and Della love each other so unselfishly that they have sold their favorite possessions to buy Christmas presents. Such love, O. Henry says, is the wisest and best gift of all.

TOTAL EFFECT *Page 409*

1. How does the title of the story reveal O. Henry's purpose? By naming the story "The Gift of the Magi," O. Henry leaves no doubt that the self-sacrifice involved in Jim and Della's gift giving is an admirable quality.

2. The Magi were wise men who brought three gifts to Bethlehem. Why does O. Henry's title refer to a single gift? O. Henry shows that the single most important gift is love—especially the generous, unselfish, wholehearted love that is the spirit of Christmas and of all the best in human relationships.

UNDERSTANDING THE WORDS IN THE STORY (Matching Columns) *Page 410*

1. reflection	**i.** serious thought
2. vestibule	**e.** entranceway
3. prosperity	**a.** wealth and success
4. unassuming	**j.** modest
5. sterling	**b.** excellent
6. agile	**d.** quick
7. longitudinal	**f.** running lengthwise
8. depreciate	**g.** belittle or lessen
9. faltered	**c.** hesitated
10. ransacking	**h.** searching

(Completion) *Page 410*

1. Something that is evident or clear is said to be patent.
2. An object used to decorate or ornament something is an adornment.
3. A chaste style is restrained and simple.
4. A narrative or history is known as a chronicle.
5. Something of little significance is inconsequential.
6. Impulsive people tend to act without prudence.
7. An ardent love is intense in feeling.
8. That which calls for hard work is laborious.
9. To be subjected to scrutiny is to be examined carefully.
10. A mammoth undertaking is very big.

WRITING IT DOWN

A Comparison/Contrast Essay *Page 411*

This assignment will help strengthen the students' skill in formal writing.

HALF A DAY

Naguib Mahfouz **Page 413**

INTRODUCTION

Many critics consider Naguib Mahfouz to be Egypt's finest writer. Although he has been writing since the 1930s and has published more than forty novels, his work was largely unknown in English-speaking countries until October, 1988, when he became the first Arab writer to receive the Nobel Prize for literature.

Mahfouz popularized the novel and short story genres among the Arab peoples, for whom poetry has been the dominant literary form for generations. Mahfouz writes about life on the streets of Egypt's cities, where the poor live in distressing conditions. His prose works have been compared in spirit and tone with those of Charles Dickens and other nineteenth-century writers of social realism.

PRESENTATION

You may want to assign "Half a Day" to be read at home and discussed in class the following day. Take note of the students' reactions to the story; most will probably find it puzzling. You might ask if they feel that the author is merely playing a trick, or if he seems to be conveying a message about life.

It may be helpful to review the literary form of allegory, a tale in which characters, events, and settings represent abstract qualities or ideas. Recognizing the allegorical nature of "Half a Day" is the key to interpreting the story's meaning. "The Colomber," which appears on page 28 of *Impact*, is another story that may be interpreted as an allegory.

Mahfouz has compressed the events of a lifetime into one day. The narrator's school day encompasses the spectrum of life's joys, sorrows, problems, and lessons. Why is a school day an appropriate metaphor for life? The end of the narrator's day depicts the struggle of the elderly—vexation with change and with the brevity of life. How often have students heard an older person say, "It seems like only yesterday . . . "?

CHECKING UP (True/False) *Page 416*

F 1. The narrator is eager to begin school.

T 2. The narrator's father encourages the boy to smile and be a good example.

T 3. The narrator finds school surprisingly varied and interesting.

T 4. The narrator tries to return home on his own.

F 5. The narrator is delighted by the changes he encounters.

TALKING IT OVER *Page 416*

1. What is the narrator's attitude toward his first day at school? The narrator is skeptical; he does not understand why he must leave the intimacy of his home. He is also apprehensive—he clings to his father's hand and feels that he is a stranger when confronted with the other boys and girls.

2. According to his father, why is the narrator being sent to school? The narrator's father tells him that school is "the factory that makes useful men out of boys."

3. What lessons about life does the narrator learn at "school"? The narrator learns about love and friendship, rivalry and hatred, struggle and perseverance, and about achieving success and happiness.

4. What is the significance of the narrator's encounter with the middle-aged man? Answers will vary. The narrator's realization that he knows the man suggests that he might be encountering a peer or schoolmate. **What does this meeting suggest about the passage of time?** The meeting suggests that a span of time has passed and that the narrator himself is now middle-aged. The man addresses the narrator as if he were an adult, not a child.

5. As the narrator walks home from school, he notices changes in the landscape. What kind of changes have taken place? The narrator is surprised and confused by the hordes of humanity and the masses of vehicles in what he thought was a familiar neighborhood. Mounds of refuse have replaced the fields that bordered the streets, high buildings have been constructed, and the air is full of disturbing noises.

TOTAL EFFECT *Page 417*

1. What has happened to the narrator, in a sense, over the course of the story? The narrator has aged. **What does the "half a day" represent?** The "half a day" represents the passage of a lifetime.

2. What is the significance of the father's statement, "Today you truly begin life"? The statement appears to go beyond instruction on how to behave at school; the father appears to be giving his son advice on how to live his life.

3. The narrator describes his lessons and other school experiences in three paragraphs, beginning with the words, "We submitted to the facts" (page 414). What details in this passage hint that the narrator is really talking about more than his first day at school and that his words apply to life as a whole? The narrator describes more than could take place in just a few hours. Some details include the reference to a "path" being revealed, as well as the lessons he learns about hatred and fighting, about perseverance, and about taking advantage of opportunities. These are all lessons about life.

4. What do you think is the *theme*, or underlying message, of this story? Explain your answer. Answers will vary. One possibility is that life begins, in a sense, when one leaves home and becomes involved with the world outside. Another is that a lifetime passes by with astonishing quickness.

UNDERSTANDING THE WORDS IN THE STORY (Matching Columns) *Page 417*

1. unmarred	h. unspoiled
2. exceedingly	f. very; extremely
3. grim	g. stern; harsh
4. beneficial	j. helpful
5. contentment	i. satisfaction
6. presumed	d. assumed
7. rivalries	b. disputes; competition
8. exertion	e. great effort
9. perseverance	a. determination; endurance
10. hastened	c. hurried

WRITING IT DOWN *Page 418*

A Literary Analysis

Careful analysis will increase students' understanding and appreciation of literature. This assignment offers practice in formal writing.

Index of Authors and Titles